Sweetwater

Sinners

The Sequel to Holy Hustler

D1522927

P. L. Wilson is the pen name for Pat Tucker

Also by P. L. Wilson

Holy Hustler

Also by Pat Tucker

Daddy By Default

Proceed With Caution

Led Astray

Infidelity

The Hook Up

Try Me (Writing as Rikki Dixon)

(Anthologies and Novellas)

Summer Breeze:
The Night I Fell in Love

Around the Way Girls-3:
Armed and Dangerous

Caramel Flava:
Closet Freak

Sweetwater Sinners

The Sequel to Holy Hustler

P. L. WILSON

Rekcut Publishing
A Division of The Legacy Group

Sweetwater
Sinners

The Sequel to Holy Hustler

P. L. WILSON

Rekcut Publishing is a division of
The Legacy Group

ISBN 10: 0-9723850-0-2
ISBN 13: 978-0-9723850-0-8

Library of Congress Control Number: 2010920232

First Printing: June 2010

Printed in the United States of America

10 9 8 7 6 5 4 3 2 1

*This is a work of fiction. Any references or similarities to actual events, real
people, living, or dead, or to real locals are intended to give the novel a sense
of reality. Any similarity in other names, characters, places, and incidents is
entirely coincidental.*

Dedication

*For the loyal readers who email, asking when the sequel is coming
. . . Thank You!*

Support Black Authors
—We tell y**OUR** stories

sylkkep@yahoo.com
(I answer all reader emails)
—*P. L. Wilson*

Also visit: www.maddaddies.com
And share *your* drama!

Chapter 1

"**H**allelujah, Pastor! Hallelujah!" Voices rang out inside the massive sanctuary, bouncing off its vaulted ceilings and custom designed pews.

"I said: Ain't nobody gonna love ya like the Lord . . . and that's the only kind of love you need. You see . . . he's a good and mighty God, uh-huh!" Pastor Goodlove threw his head back and pumped his fist into the air to give his booming words even more life.

"Amen, Pastor . . . preach, preach!" Parishioners responded zealously.

"Oh, I saaaid . . . my God is a mighty, mighty God!"

Pastor Goodlove shook his hips, bent his legs at the knees and moved his body like a man possessed. With his arms flailing, he hopped on one leg. Despite his size, Pastor Goodlove moved like a trained dancer. Members and visitors alike had come week after week for his spirit filled sermons. And he rarely disappointed. He had a way of bringing God's word to life like no other.

One of the church mothers, Mama Sadie, who only months earlier had tried to have Pastor removed from the helm of his very own church, screamed before throwing her petite body to the floor. She wailed as her body bounced up and down like a fish out of water. Most of Sweetwater PG's members were accustomed to Mama Sadie's visits from the Holy Ghost near the end of Pastor Goodlove's weekly sermon, but to visitors, often, it was quite a sight to see.

"Aaamen, Pastor! Amen," she cried, clutching her silk scarf between her frail fingers.

"Is anybody in here?" Pastor Goodlove used one hand to cup his ear. He leaned toward his congregation. "I said: Heeeello, somebody!"

They roared back at him.

"Preach, Pastor. Preach!"

He sprinted from one end of the pulpit to the other, "I saaaid: I know a really, mighty God," he hollered. Pastor Goodlove hobbled and shuffled a few feet toward the front pew.

"He's a mighty, mighty, good God," he sang and broke into a sanctified dance. The organ player started up again.

Parishioners stomped and danced right along with Pastor Goodlove. Cardboard fans flapped, heads bounced and hands clapped.

"You don't know real love until you're loved by my God." He pointed at his chest. "I said: Heeello, somebody!" Pastor Goodlove screamed, this time much louder than before.

Mama Sadie began panting as she tried to catch her breath. The rest of the holy rollers were by her side as usual. Some were marking her forehead with blessed oil, others prayed over her, and yet another stood guard, making sure onlookers didn't come too close.

Sweetwater PG's holy rollers were a group of church mothers who were self-appointed, morality judges. They determined which behavior God might deem worthy, which needed his immediate scrutiny, and they made sure very little passed without their close inspection.

It had been an incredibly turbulent year at Sweetwater Powerhouse of God, one of Houston's largest mega churches. But Pastor Goodlove had simply told his congregation theirs had been a magnificent journey through the storm. He himself had made it through a very public sexual harassment scandal of a homosexual nature. After months of leading the evening news and being front-page headlines in the Houston Chronicle, the young man and a few others accusers quietly settled their lawsuits against Pastor Ethan Ezekiel Goodlove III. None of them had been heard from since.

Since then, Pastor Goodlove's eldest of three sons, was caught cheating on his wife, Michelle. She was later diagnosed with HIV. Pastor's middle son, Reginald, had embezzled money from the church and all but vanished. And the youngest son, Barry, was being stalked by a deranged woman who was determined to stop his impending high society wedding.

It had been a very trying year for Sweetwater PG indeed, but more than a year later, things were finally getting back on track and moving forward.

Just as Pastor broke into his famous strut, wrapping up yet another tantalizing sermon, the band and choir started up with a fierce roar.

Pastor Goodlove was a six-foot–five, thick, and solid man. His skin was the color of cocoa, and shimmered beneath a thin film of sweat. Pastor had worked himself into a frenzy and

P. L. WILSON

his clothes were saturated by the end of his sermon. But his parishioners had grown accustomed to his weekly performance and expected nothing less from their leader.

Before Pastor Goodlove brought his sermon to a complete close, the five-thousand-plus members of Sweetwater PG dug deep into their pockets, purses, and wallets. They knew it was time to give and they gave cheerfully, freely, and abundantly.

The entire band was in full throttle now. Pastor danced up and down the aisle. His moves were electrifying as he switched between hopping on one leg and pumping his fists as he strutted to the beat. The energy in the church was exhilarating and unparalleled. It was like electricity sizzled in the air during Pastor Goodlove's Sunday morning messages. People often came to be rejuvenated for the entire week ahead.

Once he turned and sprinted back up to the pulpit, Pastor Goodlove released a gut-wrenching scream, threw his head back again and pumped his fists into the air once again.

"I uh, saaaid . . ." Suddenly Pastor Goodlove grabbed and clutched toward his chest, his eyes grew wide, and he collapsed, tumbling down to the floor with a loud thud.

After a few seconds of uncharacteristic silence from the pulpit, the music finally paused. Pastor's young and vivacious wife, Theola, let out a piercing scream that brought the holy celebration to a screeching halt. Within minutes, the church was in a chaotic uproar. People started pushing and rushing toward the front, trying to see exactly what was going on. Others were screaming and some instantly fell to their knees to pray.

"OHMYGOD! Somebody please dial 9-1-1!" Theola screamed as she struggled to bend down over her husband's body. But her skintight pencil skirt made it near impossible. Once she was finally on the ground, she kept putting her ear to his chest, and then his lips in an attempt to determine whether he was still breathing.

She didn't dare shed a tear, but Theola was afraid. She figured there was no sense in messing up her makeup, so she turned toward the crowd and yelled, "Is there a doctor in here?" She put her ear back to his chest. "OHMYGOD! Dadd—ah, I mean, Pastor needs help!

Chapter 2

"Michelle Goodlove, under the plea agreement you entered with the Harris County District Attorney's Office you are prepared to enter a guilty plea, correct?" the judge asked.

Michelle's hazel eyes pooled with warm tears. Her slim five-foot-eight frame trembled as she stood next to her attorney. Michelle wrung her dry hands and tightly clutched the satin handkerchief her mother had given her before they entered the courtroom. It was supposed to bring her luck. It hadn't worked. The D.A. didn't drop the charges like she'd hoped, but at least she wouldn't have to go before a jury.

Michelle didn't want to face a jury trial for attempting to poison her husband, Deacon Damien Goodlove. It had been a year since the police came into the church and pulled her out, kicking and screaming. Her attorney had delayed the case for as long as he could, and they finally agreed to a plea bargain. But still, Michelle wasn't the least bit sorry. She felt that Damien deserved exactly what he had received.

She discovered he had given her HIV after running around with any short skirt he could find. Then, she lost her job and was virtually blacklisted. The arsenic she laced his food and drinks with had been her way of getting revenge, but he survived. And it didn't take long for the investigation into his attempted murder to lead directly to her.

Michelle turned to her right and saw a sea of support when she looked at her mother, Vernice, and a couple of her girlfriends. Michelle's daughters, Terry and Dana, stood between her grandmother and grandfather. They were all silent as the judge spoke to Michelle. Her father, Al, nodded in her direction and offered a weak smile.

"Mrs. Goodlove?" The judge waited.

"Yes, Your Honor?" She turned to face the judge. A frown creased her forehead, and her stomach quivered with a mixture of fear and disgust. There was no reason for her to even be here. It was Damien who had done wrong and forced her hand. She didn't deserve this! Hadn't she lost enough? Her job, her reputation, life as she knew it—it was all enough to make her angry every time she thought about it. She swallowed hard and tried to calm herself by counting to ten in her head.

"Need I repeat myself?" The judge peered over the reading glasses that sat on the very tip of his long, narrow, pimpled nose. His spongy face reminded Michelle of cottage cheese as he looked down at her. She saw no mercy in his dark beady eyes.

"No. No, Your Honor. The answer is yes. Yes, I'm prepared to enter a guilty plea." Michelle looked at her attorney then back at the judge.

"Okay then. As part of your guilty plea, you swear that no one has coerced you into entering this plea. You are pleading guilty by your own will, and you were not promised any-thing in return for your guilty plea. You also understand that under the sentencing guidelines, I can sentence you to anything from probation to one hundred and twenty days in jail, cor-rect?"

Michelle felt herself getting more heated as the judge spoke. He stared as he waited on her answer.

"Yes, Your Honor." Michelle narrowed her eyes, her nostrils flaring.

The judge flipped several pages in a folder, which lay opened on his desk.

"Okay . . . let's see. Michelle Goodlove, you have been found guilty of the offense of criminal assault. As a first time offender, you are hereby sentenced to two years of probation. As part of the plea agreement, you will serve fifteen-hundred hours of community service. And you will pay a fine of five-thousand dollars." The judge looked at the prosecutor. "Mr. Brown, you wanted to add something?"

"Yes, Your Honor. Mrs. Goodlove's attorney, Mr. Stew-art, and I have agreed that Mrs. Goodlove will do her commu-nity service at the Jester State Prison in Fort Bend County," the prosecutor replied.

Tears that filled Michelle's eyes suddenly came gushing down her cheeks. She could no longer control them or herself. She leaned over to her attorney.

"You said no jail time," she whispered through gritted teeth. She was on fire.

"This isn't jail time," he whispered back as he glanced at the judge and offered up a weak smile.

The judge looked up. "Mrs. Goodlove, is there a prob-lem?" He asked with a warning look on his face.

Michelle swallowed hard, her small nostrils flared even harder as she looked at her attorney then back at the judge. She balled her fists at her sides, and she could feel herself burning up. She was pissed, and thought for a second about backing out of the deal. Maybe she should fight this thing, take it to a jury, see if she could get sympathy from those who may have walked in her shoes.

"Mr. Stewart," the judge began. "Please advise your client to speak when she's spoken to. I asked if there is a problem!"

Chris Stewart, who towered over Michelle, looked down at his client, although she was standing. He spoke to Michelle without uttering a word. But Michelle's mind had already wandered off. A hot wave of humiliation washed over her. Here she was, a college educated, middleclass woman, with the proper pedigree. While she blamed her estranged husband Damien for the mess she was in, she had paid good money for this attorney who had come highly recommended. He almost guaranteed that Michelle would never step foot inside a jail. Now what kind of shit were they trying to *pull?* She should've known they'd find a way to disgrace her, despite the promise, and not to mention the price tag she had paid for this rent a cop of a lawyer.

"No problem," Michelle mumbled as she shoved the thoughts from her mind.

She glared at her attorney and took a step from him. She turned her nose up in disgust as she listened to the judge ramble on about what would happen if she violated her probation.

Regardless of the judge's threats, all Michelle could think about was how the hell would she, of all people, survive behind prison walls. She couldn't help but think she should've killed the bastard since she was going to jail anyway.

Chapter 3

The cold grip of fear hugged his heart, and he wanted desperately to cry. But Damien Goodlove couldn't remember the last time he had actually shed a tear. But standing there, watching his father's comatose body was enough to make him weak. The Gee-man, he and his brother's nickname for Pastor, had fallen to the floor and slipped into a coma. As Damien gazed down at his father's still body with tubes connecting it to a machine, he sniffled a few times. As a matter of fact, fresh tears were already pooled at the corner of his eyes, but still, he fought the urge. He had to be strong. The more Damien thought about it, the more the situation scared him. And it was as if he was facing this all alone. Barry was caught up in drama with his fiancé. And how convenient that Reginald still had not been heard from. Damien wished he could get his hands on Reginald himself. He wanted his middle brother to come clean and come back home.

Despite his own world of problems, Damien just had never given much thought to being without the old man.

Looking at the tubes connected to his father, he started to think that life was too short to stay caught up in drama and misery. He had been through so much over the past year—caught cheating with Jazzlyn, not living up his duties as a deacon, and fighting with his estranged wife, Michelle.

But he was going to change, he had to. At that very moment, he decided he'd stop fighting with Michelle and grant her the divorce she had been wanting. He avoided signing the papers just to get on her nerves, but it was time to let her go.

Damien rose from the chair, stretched his lean, muscular body, and looked around the room. It was like a hospital gift shop in there. Flowers, cards, balloons and banners were draped all over the place. Damien knew he didn't have much time left with his father because constant streams of visitors waited for their turn.

The visitation program was a compromise between the hospital staff and Theola. She wanted no one but immediate family to have access to him, but some of the church mothers and assistant pastors came to Damien, and with his help, they were able to overrule Theola.

Damien knew his stepmother, if you could call her that, didn't want to be sitting in a hospital room, watching over her husband's lifeless body for hours on end. So, he came up with the agreement, which called for the assistant pastors to take turns and allow members to visit with Pastor Goodlove for up to ten minutes each. That would free Theola up to do God knows what, but it was best for everyone involved, Damien decided.

As he walked out of the hospital, Damien used his cell phone to call the divorce lawyer his father had paid for. This was Damien's third time calling since he decided to give Michelle the divorce, but each time he was told his lawyer was unavailable.

"Mr. Goodlove, Mr. Bodsworth is still in court. I'll give him your messages when he checks in," the receptionist said.

As he waited for his car from the parking attendant, he plucked a copy of the Houston Defender Newspaper from the metal newsstand and scanned the front page. Of all the interesting headlines, it was a story in the right corner that caught his attention.

"Class Action lawsuit to be settled," Damien read aloud. "Wait a fucking minute," he spat, wrinkling his nose as he read. His eyes couldn't move fast enough across the words. "Five local people are to share thirty-five million dollars after settling a lawsuit in which they were wrongly diagnosed last year with HIV, the virus that causes AIDS."

Damien's heart nearly stopped beating. He shook his head. *This could not be happening*, he thought. He reread the article, and shook his head again.

"It just can't be," he said. He rushed back inside the hospital and grabbed a copy of the Houston Chronicle. The story wasn't on the front page there, but he found it in the paper's City and State section, and once again, his mind began to spin.

Behind the wheel of his SUV now, his mind couldn't help but go over his last few conversations with Michelle. Could this be the reason she had suddenly started hassling him about the divorce again? Damien felt the need to call someone. He needed proof before he drove himself nuts for nothing.

By the time he arrived at the church's office, he couldn't help feeling like Michelle may have been one of the patients he had read about in both newspapers. He himself had continuously tested negative after she tearfully accused him of infecting her with the virus that causes the deadly disease.

Since then, Damien had tried to change his ways. He had even tried to convince Michelle to take him back so that they could once again be a family. But she had insisted it was over.

She said she wanted a divorce, and for months, they had fought like crazy over material things. But despite all of that, he had been willing to give it another try. And Damien thought she was, too, after she stopped bugging him about signing the divorce papers. Thinking back now, he did find it odd that after a while, those fights stopped even though they hadn't resolved a thing. Then, just a few months ago, she started back up with the demands for divorce. And this time, she was near ruthless, even saying she didn't want anything. She just wanted out.

Damien smiled at the thought of finally figuring out why she was once again suddenly so desperate to make their separation legal and permanent. She was coming into some money and didn't want to share. And to think, he was about to call his lawyer and sign the damn divorce papers. For the first time since he tried to reach his lawyer, he was glad Sam had been too busy to take his calls.

Damien looked upward and said, "Thank you, God, for showing me that article."

His right hand started itching. He knew that meant he was coming into some money soon. *God is good,* he thought as he marveled at how he had come so close to making a multi-million dollar mistake.

Chapter 4

Theola Goodlove was more sexually frustrated than she had ever benn in her life. Even when her husband was up and well, his libido was no match for her insatiable sexual appetite. And now that he was hospitalized, she hated to think about what she might have to do. She had already grown bored with the array of toys she used on a regular basis. Trying to clear her mind, rolled over in the massive bed and pulled the down comforter over her head. She was not ready to get up, and she was definitely not looking forward to another day in that friggin' hospital. Despite the fact that she rose before the alarm clock sounded, she didn't feel much like going to church either.

It had been exactly one week to the day since her husband collapsed while wrapping up his sermon. And since then, she had never felt so much scrutiny. It was as if she was being tugged in every direction. Sweetwater's holy rollers kept sending lists of substitute pastors they wanted to see in charge. Her daughter in-law, Michelle Goodlove, had all but vanished, or at least was doing her own thing. And that meant there was no one there to supervise the ladies' auxiliary. In addition, Barry, Pastor's youngest son, was no longer working with the youth program. The congregation didn't know if he was still planning to marry his fiancé. Theola didn't think going forth with the wedding was a bad idea, but she could only hope no one expected she would step in to help with that fiasco since Pastor was down. She felt like everything was falling apart and feared she was bound to lose what little of her mind she had left. That's when an idea struck her.

She bolted upright in bed and reached for the phone that sat on her nightstand. Beneath it, she found the brochure that was mixed into her mail. Theola had no idea why she hadn't thought of it before. Of course she needed to go somewhere and clear her mind. Of course she needed to be surrounded by people who didn't judge her every move.

By the time Theola strutted into Sweetwater PG, she looked like brand new money. She sported a pair of spiked heeled sandals and fishnet stockings under a tight-fitting wrap dress that hugged her like it was sewn directly onto her curvy frame.

One of the guest pastors was in the pulpit, boring the congregation to death, but she didn't care. For appearances sake, she just needed to show her face long enough to at least appear appropriate. A few heads turned and noses tilted upward the moment she breezed in and took her rightful spot in the front pew.

When the man finished discussing a scripture, the parishioners rose and prepared for offering. Theola looked around the sanctuary searching desperately for Michelle, but she didn't see her daughter-in-law. Considering they were about the same age, she often chuckled at the thought.

Before service wrapped up, Theola rushed out of the building and into a waiting car. "I need to go to Bush Airport," she barked without as much as a greeting to the driver.

Hours later, the Soca music, which consists of a Caribbean beat with sprouts of fast-paced tempo and base booming throughout. The music pounded through multiple large speakers as sweaty bodies gyrated on the wooden dance floor. Everyone tried to fight for position in front of the large industrial-sized fans. Waitresses dressed in bikinis and flip flops moved around the room, offering up tropical drinks to all of the party goers. Despite how thick the crowds were on the dance floor, the temperature in the club without walls stayed cool and comfortable. The industrial fans blew a chilled breeze right off the aqua blue Mopan River on the coast of beautiful breezy Belize.

While the dance floor was a wide open space with several bars and a few tables and chairs, there were three offices toward the back of the massive room. Pleasure Paradise was known as the club without walls, but it was also known for the ten air conditioned private cabanas built along the river front.

The club's owner, Brian Broussard, was known throughout the Caribbean as the Pleasure Master. His little club-slash-resort located in the western section of Belize remained booked for months in advance.

He even had some VIP guests who spent their entire vacation right there on the club grounds. When one such VIP client called to make sure he'd be able to make room for a wealthy American woman who was in need of discreet attention, Brian had pulled out all the stops.

A private car had met Theola at the small airport and brought her to her personal cabana. Two hours after she had arrived that evening, Brian personally paid a visit to her room.

"If there is anything at all we can do for you, you just ring," he had said. "I hope your accommodations are up to your standards."

On her way in, Theola wasn't sure if she had picked the right spot. There was so much greenery on the drive from the airport, she wondered what the resort would look like. Many of the houses were tattered and beaten down, and some of the roads weren't even paved. The resort was located eight miles outside Belize City limits. On the drive there, she started to feel better about choosing the country. The resort itself was all she could've wanted. She had noticed a couple of the cabana companions she wanted to summon to her room, but told herself she'd get to that later. As Brian rose to leave, there was a gentle knock on the door.

"Come," Brian said before Theola could answer.

"Oh, Ms. Theola, this is Stone Pier. He's here exclusively for your pleasure," Brian said humbly, just before he smiled and eased out of the room.

Theola's eyebrows lifted as she looked up at the firm chocolate tower standing in front of her. He stood as if he was on display. Stone Pier's body was a mass of chiseled muscled perfection. He cut in all of the right places, wearing skin-tight swim trunks.

The trunk's snugness provided proof that he was working with a nice package. In addition to the trunks, he wore leather sandals and carried a duffle bag. The sight of his perfect nipples temporarily held her hypnotized. They looked like erect hunks of chocolate. Were they calling out to her?

"Would you like a massage?" his deep baritone asked, allowing her to momentarily shake the naughty thoughts from her head. "I understand your three-hour flight wasn't so pleasant," he offered with a confidential whisper.

The sound of his voice, deep and dreamy was enough to make her cream instantly. Theola crossed and uncrossed her legs, hoping the friction would offer some relief. She couldn't remember the last time her body had reacted to a man like this. Sur, she knew marrying a much older man meant she wouldn't be swinging from chandeliers. She wouldn't want to endanger his health, but she had thought that little blue pill might help their sex life. It hadn't. She crossed her legs again, this time more seductively than before.

"Ah, a massage sounds nice," Theola managed, already feeling her own nipples stiffen.

Stone Pier dropped his bag and extended his hand for her to take. When their skin touched, she swore a bolt of electricity shot through her veins. When his extra-soft lips grazed her hand, she wondered what else those lips could do.

"There's a massage table on the patio," he informed her.

Theola stood, allowed her hand to go limp in his, and decided she'd be willing to follow him straight through the gates of hell if he'd asked.

"Ah-hem," he motioned toward her before she made another step.

"What's wrong?" Theola asked.

"No clothes," he insisted, wrinkling his narrow nose. "The massage . . . it's just better that way."

"Oh, of course, you're right." Theola looked down at the wrap dress she was wearing, then pulled a string and the dress fell open.

Stone Pier walked over to his bag and removed a couple of small bottles and followed her out to the patio. Theola stepped out of her thong and matching bra when they arrived at the sectioned-off patio. The ivory-covered walls provided some privacy. But she couldn't care less if anyone had a glimpse of what was about to happen.

Beneath a blanket of stars above their heads, and with a cool island breeze blowing, Theola felt like she was in heaven as she climbed her naked body onto the table.

When Stone Pier's strong calloused hands touched her silken skin, all of her problems seemed to be a world away. She closed her eyes and allowed the oil and his hands to mix in a magical combination.

Before she knew what was happening, she turned over and pulled him closer. She could no longer resist, and the sweet agony was driving her mad.

He had already climbed atop the table to really work out the kinks trapped in her muscled flesh. She could feel his rock hard erection arched against her thigh.

Without hesitation, his mouth cupped hers. He sucked at her bottom lip then her tongue. Theola decided it would be best if she kept her eyes open so she could see this beautiful man at work. She felt drowsy with passion.

"You taste like the most exotic passion fruit," he said pulling back from her.

"You taste even better," she offered.

Theola lay still as he started kissing his way down the length of her lean body. From her neck, to the deep valley between her breasts, he licked her ribcage and bit at her stomach then lingered at her navel.

"Oh, yes," Theola cooed.

"Your skin is so soft," he said. "You smell good."

He moved until he was on his knees and between her parted thighs. In the darkness that blanketed them, Stone Pier eased his hands between Theola's thighs and slipped his thick fingers into the depth of her nectar. He massaged and jammed his fingers, working her flesh like he knew exactly what he was searching for.

"Ooooh God!" she shrilled wide-eyed, moving her hips rocking, and bucking into his hand.

He glanced up upon hearing the moan that escaped her lips. "What's your pleasure?" his slightly accented voice asked.

"I want you," Theola admitted. "I want you badly." Theola wasn't the least bit shy. She eased down to confirm that his package wasn't deceiving. From the moment she first saw it, she felt it had been screaming out to be touched.

When Stone Pier moved and re-adjusted himself between her thighs, she felt the thin layer of perspiration against his skin and knew he was ready.

"You'll let me make you feel good then?" Stone Pier asked in that husky voice that made her even hotter.

She eased back, pulled her legs over her arms allowing them to spread and touch her ears. She wanted and needed him to put out the fire that burned deep inside her.

When he dipped his head between her thighs and sucked her swollen button, her legs began to tremble. Theola gnawed at her bottom lip when she felt tiny shock waves rush through her body after the first eruption. And she wanted more.

Stone Pier looked up, her wetness still glistening on his face as he smiled at her. He guided her hand to his steel-like erection and stood back as she guided it to its target. He clutched her hips, holding her still and steady. Theola buckled at the sensation, arched her back, released a cry and wiggled against his movement.

Theola hadn't been there a good four hours yet, and already she was enjoying herself.

Chapter 5

Michelle was devastated by the time her parents swung their car into the driveway. How could she have possibly gone from floating on cloud nine to the depths of depression in a matter of hours? Before her court appearance, they had enjoyed a hefty meal at Houston's famous Breakfast Klub, and she was all giddy with excitement at the thought of finally getting through to that soon-to-be ex-husband of hers. But things turned for the worse in a matter of hours.

She had heard about what happened to the G-man, and she had hoped that would soften Damien enough so that he might want to sign the divorce papers. Michelle had less than sixty days to get him to grant her a divorce. She had no idea how she could convince him that there was no chance of a reconciliation, but she was determined to do so at any cost.

Her father glanced at her through the rearview mirror.

"You getting out?" he asked.

"I just want to sit here for a moment." She sulked. Michelle noticed the way her mother glanced at her father, but she chose to ignore it. She reached over to release her daughter's seatbelt and looked up at her father. "I just need a moment," she whispered, fighting back tears.

Upon hearing that, Michelle's mother sprang from the car and took her granddaughters inside. Her father sat there saying nothing.

"I can't believe I'm going to jail," she mumbled after a few more minutes of silence.

"You're not going to jail, Chelle. You'll be *working* at a jail. There's a difference," he reminded her.

She snickered. "Working?"

"It's all in how you look at it. You will be there for eight hours a day, for about 13 weeks. But the truth is, at the end of the day, you get to go home. If you were in jail, you'd be there 24-7, and that's the truth of the matter," he explained.

Michelle looked at the lines that had creased in her father's forehead. She noticed the patches of gray that covered most of his low-cut afro and wondered how her life got so out of control. She had done all of the right things. She married into one of the most prestigious religious families in all of Houston. Sweetwater PG and Pastor Goodlove were rivaled only by Pastor Blackwell and his empire.

Despite her newfound wealth, her life still sat in shambles.

"You've got so much going for you. I don't want you sitting up dwelling on that community service. You've gotta go and get it done. We'll be right by your side to support you as always," her father stressed.

Her father was right. She did have quite a bit going for herself. At the top of the list was the six-point-eight million dollars she was due to receive in less than ninety days. That reminded Michelle: She had even less time to convince that loser of a husband of hers to sign those fucking papers.

"Daddy, you're so correct. I'm about to be a millionaire soon. And when I get my money, I'm taking us all on an extravagant vacation. I'm also buying a brand new house for you and mom," she cheered.

"Ain't no need for all of that. We just want you and our grandbabies to be happy. We'd like to see your family back together again the way God intended, but if that's not possible, we just want you and Damien to be happy."

Michelle moved to get out of the car. She knew deep inside she had no desire to get back with her poor excuse of a husband. Theirs had been an embarrassing union for her. Throughout the years, rumors floated around the church about him cheating on her. But when she witnessed him running around with the church slut, then found his secret stash of used women's underwear, and saw his pictures of women wearing her own damn lingerie, she had finally had enough.

But when a doctor told her she had been infected with HIV, and she knew she had remained faithful to Damien, well that's when she wanted him dead. Michelle knew taking him away from their daughters would've been a big mistake, but still she was mortified. She had thought her life was over until that fateful phone call.

It was an attorney who made the initial contact.

"My name is Lonny Banks, and I was wondering if you are the same Michelle Goodlove recently diagnosed with HIV, the virus . . ."

"I know what HIV is, and how the hell did you get my name and number anyway?" Michelle had snapped. She was angry, and the thought that someone else knew about her status pissed her off even more. Wasn't it enough that she had received the death sentence through no fault of her own?

"Ma'am, I'm just trying to—"

"I know what you're just trying to do, and I'm not interested," she hissed. He had called at a bad time for her. She had been contemplating suicide, distraught over the idea of dying because of her worthless husband.

"Ma'am!" Lonny snapped back at her.

Something made her calm down and listen to what the lawyer was trying to say.

"I'm Attorney Lonny Banks, and what I'm trying to tell you is that you may be eligible for compensation. I was hoping we'd be able to meet so that we can talk about this in greater detail."

"Compensation?" Michelle was confused.

"There are five of you. And, Mrs. Goodlove, we're talking a significant amount of money here," Lonny had informed her.

Walking into the house behind her father, she chuckled at how nasty she had been to Lonny. Little did she know, he was about to change her life. Since then, her life hadn't been the same. She'd become near obsessed with getting Damien to sign the divorce papers, but he steadfastly refused.

By the time it was all over, she found out that she had been misdiagnosed in a scandal that rocked the Harris County Health Department and made news worldwide. It wasn't until after all of the headlines and evening news reports that she considered she may have been one of five people who had turned their lives upside down after having been given a false death sentence. But it was a phone call requesting she show up for an informational meeting that confirmed her suspicion.

Once the press obtained the victims' names through a Freedom of Information Act, she braced herself for the onslaught of vultures she expected to contact her.

But it was one of the other victims who told her Attorney Lonny Banks was handling a class-action lawsuit, which was settled quickly and quietly.

Michelle looked at her daughters sitting at the table and again told herself just how truly lucky she was. One of the other five people, a woman in her fifties had committed suicide after she received her false diagnosis. Her heirs are set to receive her portion of the thirty-five million dollar settlement. But by the grace of God, Michelle was still here, healthy as ever, and looking forward to a new life—well, once she finished her prison sentence, she thought.

Chapter 6

Damien waltzed into Sam Bodsworth's office like it was Bodsworth, not Michelle who owed him money, and he was there to collect. He was a man with a new lease on life, or at least that's how he felt. It had been nearly twenty-four hours since he'd read the newspaper articles. He had even cut several out to personally bring them to his attorney. But he really didn't need Bodsworth's confirmation—he knew for certain he was right about his assumptions.

Damien had stepped off the elevator on the fifteenth floor and walked down the long, carpeted hallway to the large oak desk beneath Bodsworth's name and title. A young woman sat wearing a headset and a sleek black business suit. She rose the moment she saw Damien headed in her direction.

"Yes, he has your messages," she said into the mouthpiece. She held a slender manicured finger up to pursed lips in order to quiet Damien before he could even speak. Damien's eyes immediately took in her high cheekbones and her bronze-colored skin as it glistened like it had been sprinkled with a dazzling ray of sunshine.

"I assure you he has, ma'am," the woman said into the phone, placing her hands on her hips.

Damien watched her green eyes darting as if her mind was working overtime. She was pretty, but too thin for his taste, he decided. He looked at her neutral French manicured nail polish and told himself that was even more of a reason she wasn't his type. From the tight bun her hair was pulled into, to the boring nail color and tiny pink lips, he wished there was something more enticing to keep him busy.

The moment she ended the call, Damien began. "I need to see Sam right away."

"Mr. Goodlove?"

"That's me," Damien announced proudly.

"Do you have an appointment?"

Damien shot her a look that apparently worked because she looked down at the switchboard and said, "I'll let him know you're here."

Moments later, Damien nearly skipped into Sam's office. "I know why she's started leaning on me to sign those damn papers again," he announced before his attorney could completely place his phone back into the cradle.

Sam Bodsworth was a big white man who still had the body of the former college football lineman he used to be. He had short, curly blond hair and a large gut to go with his massive frame. Damien wasn't sure where the G-man knew Sam from, but they had been good friends and Sam had assured Damien he was making the right choice by allowing him to handle his case.

"Let me guess: You found out about the settlement?" Sam smiled.

"You knew?" Damien was astonished. "Why didn't you say something?"

"I caught wind of it, but it took a couple of days to confirm she was, in fact, due to receive compensation. Details of the settlement were sealed, so I had to use a little you know . . ." Sam pumped his massive arm and smiled at Damien.

"Yeah, you had to work your jelly is what you're telling me." Damien eased back in the wing chair and giggled. "So, Sam, how much money are we talking here, and how much of it is mine?"

"By my calculations, she's due to receive a little more than six-point-eight mill." Sam ended his sentence with a little whistle.

"Whhhaaaat?" Damien smiled. "That's close to seven million dollars."

"Real close," Sam agreed. "And as for your other question, half of it is yours, buddy. Texas is a community property state, my man." Sam rubbed his hands together and grinned wide.

Damien leaned forward. "So, are you trying to tell me that I'm a multi-millionaire?"

"I ain't trying to tell you a damn thing." Sam leaned in, hovering over his desk. "That's a fact my, good man. That is simply a fact."

Damien had suspected as much, but to have someone of authority confirm it as the gospel made him want to jump up on Sam's desk and get downright jiggy.

"But hold off on the celebration there, pal." Sam leaned back in his leather chair.

It would take more than that little warning to crash the party Damien was feeling deep inside. He shook his head in confusion and stopped smiling long enough to give Sam his full attention.

"What I'm saying is this: That wife of yours is a smart one. She ain't just gonna hand over that cash without a real dogfight is all I'm trying to say." Sam wagged a finger. "And I've gotta warn you. It could get real dirty. I've seen some of these things drag out for years at times. Now I'm not saying that's what's gonna happen here, but I just don't want you running out and buying that twenty-six-foot yacht just yet."

"I hear you, but years?" Damien shrugged, frowning at the news.

"That's worst-case scenario. All I'm saying is, she's already tried to hide the fact that she was coming into the money. That tells me, when it comes to trying to keep you away from her millions, she's probably capable of doing a whole helluva' lot more."

Chapter 7

On her last day in her newfound paradise, Theola decided she needed to make plans to return as quickly as possible. Sure she had to make an appearance at church, but the truth was, from two p.m. Sunday to seven p.m. Saturday, no one cared about her whereabouts. She had to leave Belize at four because that was the last flight back to Houston, but she was already making plans to return.

Stone Pier had been more than attentive during her stay, and she hardly wanted to leave his side. And she knew he didn't want her to leave. He had simply outdone himself the night before.

It was their last night together. He had bathed her in hot scented water with floating rose petals as she sipped icy cold champagne. When he was done carefully washing every nook and cranny of her body, he used fluffy towels to dry her.

Once dried, he used scented oils to give her yet another full body massage. When he was through with that, he eased down and kissed the middle of her back.

"Oh, God," Theola moaned. She'd never felt so relaxed, nor had she ever had a man be so attentive. And although she knew it was his job, she really appreciated his attention to detail and strong work ethic.

As his once tender kisses turned into wet licks up and down her back, she felt her juices flowing uncontrollably. By now, her clit was throbbing, and she needed release.

"You can turn now," he instructed, easing away with distant eyes.

When she did, he slid his hands between her legs and inserted three fingers as deep as they could go. His mouth cupped hers.

Theola closed her eyes to savor the warmth and sweetness of his mouth. She moved her hips as she glazed his hand with her wetness.

He moved his fingers around as if he was searching for her G-spot instinctively, and Theola moaned like she'd never known pleasure like this before.

Her nipples were stiff like rock-hard berries when he took one between his lips and suckled it like the flavor got better with each stroke. Suddenly, he picked her up and carried her over to a nearby table, laying her flat on her back before she could ask what was he was about to do next.

Stone Pier stood and spread her legs as far as they could go then he used his fingers to trace up and down the length of her body as she lay still. Fingers from the other hand eased in and out of her until she could hear the swooshing sounds she helped create. She'd never experienced something so simple yet so tantalizing. His touch made her body quiver uncontrollably.

Soon, with his head dipping down, he flicked his tongue and connected with his target. He worked on her until she moaned like crazy.

"Take me," Theola cried.

And Stone Pier was rough, yet tender.

"Oh God, Ssstooone Peeeier," she cried. "Right there, baby . . . right there," Theola wondered if heaven was truly the best place to be.

Once his wicked assault on her clit resulted in back-to-back orgasms, he backed up and looked as if he was inspecting the work he'd done. Theola dug her hands into his back as she flinched with every powerful flick of his tongue. She wanted him something terrible. Theola moaned. The sound was low and desperate, but it fueled his passion.

And she didn't have to wait for long. Stone Pier thrust his steel-like rod, pushing it in, moving his hips up then pulling it out until he heard her release a squeal. Then, he'd repeat the motion again. Her back arched, her eyes grew wide, and her breath was caught in her throat.

"You like? You like?" he'd ask with little emotion in his voice.

"Oh, damn. Oh, yessss, yesss. Ssssssss, I . . . oh, oh . . ." and again she'd explode like there was no end to the pleasure she was experiencing.

He'd wait a few seconds until the trembling in her walls subsided then he tilted his hips to one side and hammered away until she begged for mercy. They spent the entire night repeating one pleasurable act after another until the sun began to peek through the slits in the wooden blinds that covered the windows.

Now, as she sat with her bags at her feet waiting for the car to take her to the airport, she hoped he understood she'd be back as quickly as she could.

But his spirit seemed to have left, because all morning, he seemed distant and for that, she was sorry. But she also knew she had to keep appearances up for the church folk. They were probably talking about her like a dog, as usual, and she knew the holy rollers would stay on her case.

"You'll come back to me when you return?" Stone Pier asked somberly.

"I'd like to take you home with me," she joked. "Yes, and I'll be back in one week, I promise."

When the phone rang, she knew their time was up. Theola slipped him the thick envelope as she rushed out to meet the car. Her heart ached so badly, she couldn't stand to watch as Stone Pier loaded her luggage into the trunk.

Four hours after kissing Stone Pier goodbye and heading out to the airport, her plane touched down in Houston, and she dragged herself through customs, then finally baggage claim to meet her driver.

She looked around and felt sick, like life as she knew it there was no longer worth living. While she was away, she'd experienced a kind of freedom she didn't know existed, and she longed for that feeling again.

As the driver pulled up to Blueridge's circular driveway, she shuddered at the thought of having to go into that massive house all alone. At that moment, Theola regretted not having at least one close girlfriend she could call upon to share her experience in paradise. She pulled herself up the stairs then opened the enormous doors and felt even worse knowing she'd be in the massive house all alone.

"Will you need anything else this evening?" the driver asked as he set her luggage down.

"I'll call if I do," she said, then turned to survey the foyer. The mail was neatly stacked on a side table, and she dreaded even thinking about all that had been neglected while she was away. Oh how she wished she could go back instantly.

Theola sighed and rolled her eyes. She looked toward her husband's study then for the first time in a while thought about him being in the hospital.

"Shit!" she hissed at the realization that she hadn't been to see her husband in nearly a week.

She was certain tongues had already started wagging about that, too, so she told herself to get ready for more drama once she strolled through the doors at Sweetwater in the morning. More sexually satisfied than she'd ever been in her life, but exhausted from jet lag and the emotions of leaving the best thing she'd found since sliced bread, she wanted nothing more than sleep.

"Mary!" she yelled from the stairs' second landing. "Mary!" she yelled again at the top of her lungs. Soon, an elderly woman came careening around the corner on the first floor.

"Oh, Missues Goodlove, you're home. I had no idea where you'd gone or when you were coming back. Church members have been calling as have your stepsons. Everyone's been worried sick," the woman informed her.

Theola rolled her eyes dramatically then held up a finger to silence Mary's rambling.

"I've just returned from a very long and exhausting business trip. I do not want to be disturbed no matter what until it's time for church in the morning," she instructed.

She noticed the roll of Mary's eyes when she said "business trip," but truthfully, Theola couldn't care less. She had other things on her mind—something that had been haunting her since she left Belize. How long had it been since she had gotten it that good? The way he touched her, the way she squeezed and nestled him like she never wanted to let him go—it was all too much, but still not enough. She needed more. If she was lucky, she thought, once she fell asleep, images of Stone Pier slamming into her would finally vanish from her mind.

Chapter 8

Michelle was vexed and there was absolutely nothing she could do about it. She thought having her father escort her to the Texas Department of Criminal Justice's Chester Unit in Richmond, a Houston suburb, would help subside her anger, but it hadn't. Not one bit. As a matter of fact, asking her father to come along so she could check in for her court-mandated community service was probably the worst thing she could've done.

The whole trip there, he spent time telling her how she could take this bad situation and make it good. Michelle failed to see how anything good could come from her having to do time, but she didn't feel like engaging her father because nothing he or anyone could say would make her believe that. She steadfastly decided she did not deserve this treatment because to her, the punishment did not fit the crime.

Once they pulled into the parking lot on Harlem Road in far Fort Bend County, Michelle told herself this was it. Her father pulled into a parking space then turned to her.

"I want you to know that your mother and I are behind you one hundred and ten percent. You made a mistake, but that mistake, or even this, does not define you," he said.

Michelle knew he meant well, but she was not in the mood. She faked a smile then pulled on the handle to open the door. She turned back and said, "Thanks, Dad. They said this check-in should take about two hours then I start serving time . . . um, I mean, start my service on Monday."

Her father hit a switch and his driver's seat easily reclined. "I'll be right here waiting for you," he said.

Michelle's eyes grew wide when she looked at him again. "You mean you're just gonna sit here and wait?"

"Yup. I'll be right here waiting for you. If you need anything you just yell, and I'll scale that bobbed wire fence if I have to," he said jokingly.

She smirked, and then reached over to peck his cheek before getting out of the car. "Thanks, Daddy," she said then took weary steps to the walkway that led to a gate. She built up her courage with each step she took toward this new and terrifying chapter in her life. Her stomach quivered with dread once she arrived at the gate.

A guard met her there. He was a small middle-aged white man whose uniform nearly swallowed him up.

"My name is Michelle Goodlove. I'm here to check myself in," she said somberly.

"For?" the guard asked unenthusiastically.

"Community service," she snarled.

At first the guard didn't say a word or move. It seemed as if an eternity passed before he pulled a clipboard from somewhere she couldn't see then looked down at it.

"Oh, I see you here, Michelle Goodlove," he repeated, reading from his list.

He grabbed a radio from his waist, hit a button then spoke into it. Michelle was furious. She couldn't believe she was here, much less having to get special clearance before being admitted—to jail. Suddenly the gate slid open and Michelle stepped in.

Thirty minutes after her paperwork was filled out, she was once again photographed and fingerprinted, and then an ID badge was created. She sat in a room with four other women and two men, including the person in charge of their group.

Michelle sat numb after the group leader encouraged them to go around the room and share a bit about themselves and why they were there. When it was her turn, a frown creased her forehead. This wasn't some kind of sorority meeting, she thought.

"I'm Michelle and I'm here because of a plea agreement for poisoning my soon-to-be ex-husband," she admitted. She rolled her eyes after a few snickers floated around the room. "I'm sorry that bastard didn't die," she mumbled.

The group leader's eyebrows elevated, but he didn't say anything about her comment. He was a massive man with greasy stringy dirty blond hair who looked like he had been on the losing end of one too many fights. His acne scarred face looked like he wore a permanent frown. And his pimpled nose had a noticeable curve as if it had been broken in one too many places. He looked down at a piece of paper then began.

"You are here because you've committed some type of crime, and you were able to get by with probation. I don't care whether you meet your commitment or not. As a matter of fact, I know you don't want to be here. But I can tell you if you don't show up, a bench warrant will be issued for your arrest, and you could be brought up on charges for violating your probation. Does anyone have any questions?" he asked. He looked around the group. When no one raised a hand, he looked back at his paper.

"You are not here to socialize or fraternize with inmates. If you're looking for a date, this ain't the place. You want to mingle with these guys, get ready to go to jail. It is illegal for you to carry on a relationship with an inmate confined to the Texas Department of Criminal Justice. You've been warned. Especially you women," he snickered. "These guys have every sob story you'll ever want to hear. They will target you, compliment you, they will do whatever they can to get you to break the rules because their lives are miserable, and you know what they say, misery loves company. If he's handsome, irresistible, and you must have him because your pathetic lives just don't lead you to anyone in the free world, wait until you've finished serving your sentence!" he snapped. Once again he looked around then asked, "Do you have any questions?"

When no one said a word, he looked up from his paper again and said, "Well, if no one has questions, you know the rules. You've been warned. There are two lists near the door. Check it for your name and number, and it will indicate which department you're working with. You know how many hours you're expected to be here, so do what you're supposed to do, and you'll be fine," he warned.

Before leaving, Michelle stopped by the list to see she'd be working with the Chester Ministry Services.

"Great!" she scoffed and frowned before leaving the room.

Michelle didn't want to talk about this when she returned to the car, but had a feeling her father would want to do nothing but talk. She and the other probationers followed each other out of the gate. Her father popped up the moment she arrived at the car door.

"Hey, how'd it go?" he asked the moment she opened the door and got in.

Michelle shoved thoughts of suicide from her mind and again faked a smile for her father's sake.

"I'll be fine, Daddy," she assured.

"Oh, I know you will, baby girl. I know you will, without a doubt." He cranked up the car and they pulled onto the road that led to her parent's house. "God don't give us more than we can handle."

Michelle was so glad when he turned up the radio. She leaned her head back on the headrest and closed her eyes. Immediately, she began thinking about what would be a definite cure-all to her problems. Instantly, visions of her soon-to-be ex-husband being struck by a bus finally brought a hint of the all-elusive smile to her lips.

Oh, the joy she thought as images of his funeral danced through her mind. She despised him in ways she never knew possible. She vowed at that moment to be there the day he finally got what was coming to him. As they drove home, Michelle had no way of knowing then just how much that mission would drive and change her life.

Chapter 9

D amien had been dreaming about church this Saturday morning. His eyes snapped opened, and he struggled to remember where he was. The bedroom definitely wasn't his. He looked to the left then quickly to the right when nothing was recognizable. His eyes took in the red and white decorations from dainty curtains to frilly table covers and the humungous fake flowers that seemed to bloom in every corner of the room. Damien knew for sure he had never been in this room before.

He nearly jumped when he realized the lump of a naked body lying next to him. He couldn't tell what she looked like because he was looking at the back of her head. Wild curls spread all over the pillow, her head, and bare wide back. He stirred and that made her turn to face him.

"You were a real tiger last night," she said, as an intense smile curved her full lips. But the stench from her morning breath lingered in the air long after she spoke her last words.

When he tried to raise his head, it began to throb and he had no choice but to ease back onto the large fluffy pillow. Red roses were plastered all over the pillows and sheets as well. Damien squeezed his eyes shut and tried to remember just how he had wound up in this red and white room. Then, it all started coming back to him.

He and one of the deacons from Sweetwater PG met up for drinks at Fox Sports Bar and Grill in the Galleria area the Friday night before. Damien had no idea Patrick had turned into a chubby chaser. He only admitted to his fetish when the two large women came and joined them at the table.

"I'm Charlotte Hunter, and this is Samantha Green," the cute one said.

Her friend wasn't as cute, but she wasn't bad looking, Damien thought. He'd never been interested in big girls before, but he figured there was nothing wrong with a little company.

"I didn't know this is the friend you were talking about, Patrick," Charlotte said, looking at Damien in a seductive manner.

"Yup, this is him, but you better watch out. Ol' Dee ain't nothing nice on the ladies," Patrick had joked.

As the night wore on, they laughed, drank and enjoyed their time together. So much so, that when it was time to call it a night, Charlotte said she didn't want to go home alone, and she was eyeballing Damien like he was a piece of the best USDA prime steak.

"You don't have to," Damien informed her, slurring as he spoke.

Ten minutes after they arrived at her apartment, Charlotte and Damien were rolling around on the floor and tearing at each other's clothes. She was thrilled to be enveloped in his strong embrace. She knew his reaction to her was probably alcohol induced, but she didn't care. She was just thrilled to finally have a shot at him.

"You like back door action?" Charlotte breathed, hoping to entice and impress him as she struggled to unhook her bra.

"Baby, if you've got a hole, I can fill it for you," Damien said, reaching up to help her with the clasp.

More breast meat than he had ever seen flowed from her cups and down to her stomach near her belly button. But the amount of Belvedere they'd been drinking all night made it all good as far as he was concerned.

"Well, I'ma show you something them little skinny girls only wish they could do," Charlotte boasted.

She reached down and stroked Damien's crotch, finally giving in to the urge she'd been fighting the entire time they were at the sports bar.

"Damn! You're loaded, huh?" she declared.

"You don't know the half of it," Damien beamed, unzipping his pants to free himself. When he pulled out his massive wand, he noticed the wide-eyed reaction from Charlotte and beamed.

"Good Lord!" she shuddered, smiling as a flurry of possibilities rushed through her mind.

"No, Goodlove, baby. That's Goodlove genes," he corrected.

They looked down at his own wetness, confirming he was excited and ready for some action. Charlotte eased down and positioned herself to take him whole. She licked his fluids from the tip, and then took his entire length between her chubby cheeks and sucked him like he was a tender piece of succulent rib smothered with her favorite spicy honey barbeque sauce.

Damien's toes curled, his eyes rolled up in his head, and his heart threatened to burst through his chest as she worked him over. She had set his body aflame with raw desire, and for the first time he could recall, he desperately wanted a big girl.

"Goddamn, girl!" Damien managed to say.

She was making him weak. Something very few women could do. The girl had vicious skills, but not to be outdone. He had a few tricks up his sleeves, too. First, he grabbed the back of her head when he couldn't hold it in anymore and released a hefty deposit.

Charlotte, being the true soldier she was, didn't bat an eye or gag, but instead, slurped and sucked until she had devoured every drop he had to offer. His legs got weak as an electrifying sensation quickly shot from the balls of his feet up to his brain so fast, he thought he might suffer an aneurysm. But it was all good.

"Whew!" he shook his head taking her in. Charlotte, he decided, had delivered an award-winning performance. He was impressed.

"You got any lube?" Damien asked, the minute his third leg showed signs of revival.

"Lube?" Charlotte asked, twisting up her face, offended. "Baby, I don't need no damn lubricant. That's for amateurs. I can handle mines. The question is can you hang with all this?"

Damien had to admit, she was a whole lot of woman—more than he had ever had before, but he had never been known to walk away from wet, wanting pussy, and he wasn't about to start now.

"I can show you a whole helluva lot better than I can tell you," he insisted.

Although he had heard what she said, Damien couldn't remember loving a woman who didn't need any coaxing when it came to back door action, so he thought he'd take it easy at first.

He positioned himself behind Charlotte's ample behind and used one hand to take his member and ease it up and down her crack. After a few minutes, he guided the tip of it in, then pulled out and slid up and down her crack again.

Charlotte sucked her teeth and looked over her shoulder at him, confused.

"C'mon, daddy, I know you ain't afraid to work with all that you got down there, are you?"

She was growing tired of all this procrastination. She'd long heard of his reputation floating around church and wanted to see what all the fuss was about. From what she could tell, Damien was either scared or had been messing with a bunch of women who didn't know what they were doing.

"Look, I don't need instructions," he snapped.

"Well, shit, I can't tell. I mean what you scared or something?" Charlotte snapped right back.

Damien had to admit, her fire had turned him on, and it didn't take long for him to snap out of it. When Damien thrust into her, she bucked her ass and matched his wicked moves stroke for stroke, quickly casting doubt about just who could hang with whom.

"Jesus, girl. Work it!" he screamed.

Slap! Slap!

When he spanked her large behind, then her thick thighs, the sensation just seemed to turn her on even more.

"C'mon, baby, take it like it's yours, baby. I'm yours. It's all yours tonight. Take it . . . take it," she encouraged, begged even. "Now that's what the hell I'm talking about!"

And he did, moving his hips and plugging away as he tried to blaze a new trail in Charlotte's insides. He couldn't believe the way she was keeping up with him. He thought because of her size he'd have to teach her a thing or two. But Charlotte proved it was he who was about to be schooled.

As he rocked his hips, dipping in and out of her, he kept marveling at the fact that if the back door action with her was this good, he couldn't wait to get inside her womb.

Since hitting her door, they'd been at it for nearly three hours, and he'd already cum twice.

"I could tell you ain't never had a big girl before," Charlotte said as she lay next to him while they caught their breath.

"What makes you say that?" he asked, finally getting his breathing back on track.

"'Cause I could see you trying to handle me delicately, like you think I might break. Baby, I ain't none of those little anorexics you probably used to. I ain't nowhere near fragile. I needs me a real man—someone who can knock my back out. I mean, you got the tools. I just need you to work 'em," she chastised.

Damien chuckled. He was a bit taken aback, but didn't want to say so. Never in all his years of fucking had anyone complained about his performance.

"So how many more of these breaks we gotta take?" Charlotte asked straightforwardly. "I mean, you ain't even been properly introduced to Ms. Kitty yet."

That's when the gravity of the situation dawned on Damien. Here he had put in all that work, and he still hadn't penetrated the hole that counts most.

Damien eased up on one elbow and looked down at Charlotte.

"What you tryn'ta say?" he asked.

"Look, all I'm saying is you got a lot more work to do. That is, if you're up for the job."

It had all come back to him, like it was only minutes instead of hours ago. The bed squeaked as Charlotte got up. "Keep it warm, daddy. I'll be back," she said over her shoulder as she sashayed into the bathroom. She was bold, not even trying to cover up.

He watched as her dimpled thighs rubbed together and carried her wide hips and massive behind into the bathroom. Damien surprised himself when his erection stood at full attention upon her return, his headache a distant memory.

"Shit, I think you done woke the dead," he said when she eased back in bed.

"Oh, baby you ain't said nothing but a word," Charlotte grinned. Before he could make a move, she shoved him back down then swung one thick leg over and straddled him.

"Baby, you ain't been in heaven until I've been on top," she promised as she sucked him up between her wet and throbbing walls. "This here," she wiggled her hips adjusting herself onto his large magic stick, "is Ms. Kitty," she smiled, then proceeded to rock Damien's world until his eyes fluttered back and forth between open and closed.

Chapter 10

"**N**ow, before I leave you today I want to share something for you to take," Assistant Pastor Isaac Roberts said. He looked out at the congregation.

"Jay Leno, host of The Tonight Show, did a 'man-on-the-street' type interview where he asked some young people questions about the Bible," he chuckled. Theola stifled a yawn and shook her head. She had already noticed Mama Sadie and the rest of the holy rollers watching her every move.

"Can you name one of the Ten Commandments?" Jay asked two college-aged women. One said, 'Freedom of speech?' Mr. Leno said to the other, 'Complete this sentence: Let him who is without sin...' Her response was, 'have a good time?' Jay Leno then turned to a young man and asked, 'Who, according to the Bible, was eaten by a whale?' The confident answer was, 'Pinocchio.'"

Members of Sweetwater tisked, grumbled, and a few even chuckled. Pastor Roberts continued.

"Is it any wonder morality is in trouble? Yet, I wonder how many of those who sit in this very church this morning could answer such questions. Better yet, even if you could answer the questions, I wonder how many of you understand the significance of the Bible's teaching in our modern world and how it applies to you." He looked around at the parishioners again.

"I must confess to you that on this latter consideration, I'm not too optimistic. I see a lot of Christians whose behavior is no different than those who don't know God. I see them making the same poor choices again and again and messing up their lives and the lives of those around them, sometimes to points beyond repair," he insisted, grabbing the edges of the podium.

Theola looked over at Mama Sadie and her crew and pursed her lips. She wondered if they realized she thought the pastor was talking about them. *Probably not,* she figured.

". . . We're told that the divorce rate is the same in the church as it is in the world. Many believers' behavior and morals on Monday through Saturday are really no different than those of their non-Christian neighbors. We're going to go to the Word of God today and learn from it. For learning to take place, we must have a preacher to preach and people to listen and take it to heart. I'll work hard to do my part. I hope you will, too."

Theola frowned and glanced at her watch. *Is he about to start an entirely new sermon?* she wondered. But she decided she'd better sit there and labor through it.

"I'm calling this message, Stupid Things Believers Do to Mess Up Their Lives. It's based on a portion of the life of Abraham and is part of our continuing study of his life. I hope that once you see these things, you will agree that they really are stupid. Then, I hope you'll make up your mind to remember and avoid each of them in your own lives." The preacher looked down at his notes, then back up again.

"Our lesson today comes from Genesis sixteen. We'll begin in verse one. I want you to know I understand that the various problems of the human race can be grievous in both their nature and effects. The truth is, emotional pain is very real. Childlessness, an unhappy marriage, loss of a loved one, disappointment in the children we have raised, and many similar issues, push us to the limits of our emotional stability. Sarai's inability to conceive children was a very real pain that she had lived with for a long time. As we enter this part of the account, she is seventy-five years old. All human hope of conception is gone."

Theola started nodding until suddenly an angry sounding voice rang out from the back of the church.

"You have got to be kidding me!"

Heads turned, the pastor looked up and out into the crowd as if he wasn't sure whether he should continue.

"Ah . . . having said that, I also want you to know that some of the schemes we cook up as desperate remedies for these problems can be even worse than the problems themselves—"

"Is this the best we can do, Sweetwater? I mean seriously! He's putting us all to sleep here. When are we going to get an update on Pastor Goodlove? I can't take this anymore!" Someone yelled from the back of the church.

This wasn't the kind of excitement, Theola was looking for in church, but she had to admit, things were beginning to liven up. Pastor Roberts just wasn't cutting it and despite the rudeness, she had to admit, she was glad someone finally spoke up.

By now, Pastor Roberts had moved away from the podium. Damien stood behind the mic and tapped it a few times. When he heard the feedback, he lowered his head and spoke. The church was in an uproar. People were arguing and talking among themselves.

"Sweetwater, I need your attention," he said, then looked around the room.

"I know your behind ain't about to try and talk. You're worse than Lucifer himself." Michelle stood up, shouting toward the front of the church. "Why don't you sign the friggin' papers?" she screamed.

Theola rushed a few rows back to where Michelle stood.

"I know you ain't 'bout to try and comfort anybody," a voice yelled at Theola. "Your husband's been laid up in the hospital for weeks and ain't nobody seen near hair nor sight of you! You got a whole lotta nerves," Ms. Geraldine, one of the holy rollers, screamed as she moved toward Theola and Michelle.

"Ladies, ladies . . ." Damien once again tried to speak.

Theola turned and came face to face with Ms. Geraldine. "Look, I don't need this mess from none of y'all right about now. If you know what's best for you, you'd step off!" She despised them, and she didn't care who knew it.

"You piece of landfill trash! How dare you speak to her like that?" Mama Sadie jumped in.

"I know your old gambling behind ain't talking about trash. Don't think I forgot what you and the rest of you holier-than-thou folks tried to do to my husband — you ol' broke down trick!" Theola spat.

"Did she say Mama Sadie tried to do something to Pastor Goodlove?" another member asked. Soon, that sparked a brand new argument.

Suddenly, Mama Sadie shoved Theola. She fell back onto a few onlookers. By the time Theola was able to pull herself up, Michelle jumped between her and Mama Sadie and her crew, but it was too late. Theola swung and accidentally hit another member who wasn't even involved in the scuffle.

"Sweetwater! Have you no shame?" a new voice boomed over the intercom. Only then did everyone stop where they stood and looked toward the front of the church.

"You are in the house of the Lord, yet you're cussing, fighting, and disrespecting yourselves and your brothers and sisters in Christ." Deacon Parker huffed as he spoke into the mic. "What would your pastor say if he could see how you behave in his absence?"

Eyes immediately cast downward. Some people returned to their seats. The choir started up with a song meant to calm the frayed nerves. But Theola had had enough. She ran up front, grabbed her purse and rushed outside. Michelle was hot on her heels.

In the parking lot, Michelle called out to Theola.

"Wait!" she yelled.

At first Theola kept walking, wondering where in the hell her driver had gone. When she turned to look toward the church doors and saw Michelle standing there, her features softened a bit.

"Oh, girl, I'm so through with these doggone people I don't know what to do." Theola sighed. She dug through her purse in search of her cell phone. "Shoot! I don't know what to do about this damn driver. I swear I can never find his simple behind," she hissed.

"Well, things could be worse," Michelle tossed in. She looked around. Your philandering tramp of a husband could be refusing to sign the divorce papers like there's a chance in hell of reconciliation. I'm about to lose my mind."

"What?" Theola frowned. She stopped digging in her purse. "I had no idea." She shook her head.

Michelle wiped fresh tears from her cheeks. "I can't begin to tell you how this man has ruined my life. A man of God." her lips quivered as she spoke. "I did every fuckin' thing right. I swear to you. I fucked him even when I didn't want to. I never denied my husband. Still, it wasn't enough to keep his ass at home. Girl, I just wanted his ass gone, out of my life. Now, I'm on probation, and he's just walking around scott-free — free to keep screwing everything that moves, and he refuses to sign the damn papers!"

"You want to go somewhere so we can talk?" Theola asked, realizing her problems may not be as bad as Michelle's.

"You know what? I may take you up on that offer some other time. I think right now, I just need to be alone," Michelle insisted.

"Okay, but understand what I'm saying. Anytime you want to get away, you just call me. You can come out to Blueridge. You know I'm there alone. Or, we could even go somewhere. You know, like a little tropical getaway, on me of course," Theola smiled.

"You know, I may just take you up on that, but for right now, I think I need to take my tail home before I catch another case." They laughed and Theola's driver finally pulled into the parking lot.

"Can I drop you somewhere?"

"No, thanks, I have my car, but I will take you up on that offer, even if it's just to come spend some time with you out at Blueridge," Michelle promised.

"Okay, well, I'm headed to the hospital, but you have my numbers," Theola said.

"Oh, how's the G-man?" Michelle asked.

Theola shrugged and smiled awkwardly. "Girl, you heard those old bats. I don't know — ain't been there in a week. I just got back from Belize last night," she admitted. "So, I'd better get over there." Theola did a finger wave and slipped into the back of the town car before her driver could get out to open the door.

Chapter 11

Michelle didn't feel like dealing with this at all, but she knew she had no choice. This was all his fault. She couldn't stop thinking about Damien. Here she was with her children, back home, living with her parents because she had no job, and money was now tight. And what was he doing? He was doing the same careless things he was when they were married. But it seemed like she was the only one suffering. He slept around. He broke their vows, and he lied and cheated. Her mind couldn't stop thinking about how he had done her so wrong, and here she was essentially paying for being his fool. She quickly killed those thoughts when the inmates shuffled into the room. They were loud and rowdy like a bunch of high school delinquents.

There were four men in the first ministry session. Her job was simple enough. She was to sign inmates in, pass out papers, pens, pencils, and then collect them after the session was over. She was also responsible for replacing Bibles and assisting the pastor in any way necessary.

Most of the time when the pastor preached to the inmates, Michelle sat thinking of ways she could kill her husband. Of course she had no plans to actually carry out the murder, but she relished in the thoughts of ways it could be done. At the end of the session, Michelle collected the pens and papers and stacked the Bibles on the proper shelves. She didn't pay any attention to the inmates as she worked. She wanted to be anywhere but there, even though she got immense joy from killing Damien in her daydreams. Every once in a while she'd look up at the pastor.

Pastor Raul Peebles was a tall and thick Hispanic man with salt-and-pepper hair. He was clean-cut and very well spoken. He wasn't shy about his past, saying before he had found the Lord, he had served a nine-year stint in prison for burglary. His ministry was his way of giving back. Pastor Peebles approached Michelle after their first session ended.

"How are you doing?" he asked pleasantly.

"I'm okay, I suppose," she answered as truthfully as she could, hoping the disgust she felt wasn't etched into her features.

"Well, I'm glad to have your help. We try to do three sessions a day. I promise not to wear you out. If ever you get tired or bored, don't be afraid to let me know. I want you to get something out of this, too," he said sincerely.

Michelle's heart wasn't in this, and she had no plans on changing. She just wanted to get her hours done so she could get on with her life. She had eighteen and a half weeks of this shit, and she cringed each time she thought about her punishment. It just wasn't fair. Here she was doing time, and he was probably out screwing everything that moved. What happened to his punishment? Yes, what she had done was wrong, but he wronged her first.

And she fully realized the whole two wrongs crap, but what about when the Bible said an eye for an eye? Michelle was truly conflicted. She questioned her walk with God and wondered why, after having done all the wrong Damien had done, it was like God wasn't even interested in punishing him—only her.

"You've got about twenty minutes before the next session begins if you want to go get some fresh air or grab a snack," Pastor Peebles told her.

"No." Michelle shook her head. "I'm fine, but thank you anyway."

She felt a pang of guilt for the way she was treating the Pastor, but she excused herself, saying she shouldn't be in this hell hole in the first damn place. The entire prison was a dark and drab place. The room was a large gray square with blank walls, no windows, and vomit-colored paint everywhere the eye could see.

The second session was made up of a total of five men. Again, Michelle passed out the pens, pencils, Bibles and notepads to those who needed paper. When she was done, she took a seat in the back of the room and began to think about what would've happened had the poison been effective. Damien would be dead and that was the best thought possible.

There were a few times when she looked up after feeling someone staring at her. When she glanced up, she wound up chasing a few eyes away. Michelle found that odd, but she wasn't about to start tripping. Tomorrow, she told herself, she'd have to bring a novel to read.

By the end of the first week, the church ministry had increased by two folds in all three sessions. Pastor Peebles smiled at Michelle at the end of the second session and said. "Word spreads fast around here." He chuckled a bit.

Michelle didn't know what he was talking about, nor did she really care. By the end of the second week, she had successfully killed her soon-to-be ex four different ways and had only been questioned by police once. She felt her time spent in the sessions were quite productive. The goal was to pull off the crime so well that she never popped up on the officer's radar, even though it was just a fantasy. Still, she told herself, she had a goal.

It was during the last session that Michelle finally understood what Pastor Peebles was talking about. Suddenly a total of twenty-two men were present for the session. They were busy chit-chatting with each other, but it was more crowded.

When Michelle went around the room to distribute the notepads she overheard two of the inmates talking. And they were talking about her!

"I told you her ass was fyne."

"Damn, dawg, you wasn't lying, huh?" the other one answered.

Michelle frowned. They couldn't be talking about her, she thought. How disgusting! Now she was really vexed about having to be in the company of such lowlifes. At first, it made her skin crawl to think about the thoughts that must've been running through their minds. Thanks to Damien, she could smell a dog a mile away. But as time went on, Michelle found herself becoming quite self-conscious about her appearance, the way she walked and even whether sitting in the back of the room, disconnecting, was really a good idea.

"Shiiit, I could work wonders with that," she heard one of the inmates whisper to another.

For the first time since she'd been surrounded by all of those men, she found herself looking at *them*. They were men after all, she told herself.

Chapter 12

Damien's eyes once again fluttered open. He had been on cloud nine for the last fifty-eight minutes and thirty seconds. He knew exactly how long because Charlotte had taken him into her warm, wet mouth at exactly nine o'clock, and the digital clock now read nine-fifty-eight. And Charlotte showed no signs of slowing down.

"Jesus, girl! Yess!" he coached.

As her head bobbed up and down, her eyes stayed glued on his. She stared at him intensely as she worked. Damien didn't know how she was able to work the magic she worked but however she did it, it kept him coming back for more.

When his balls began to tingle, signaling the inevitable was threatening to bring this pleasurable session to an end, he tried to wean her off. But she wouldn't budge.

"Okay, baby, you 'bout to make me . . ." he insisted, talking in such a husky voice, he had to do a double take to make sure it was his own.

Still, she remained fastened on to his member like a pit bull locked on a meaty bone. Damien shook his hips, trying to wiggle it from her jaws, but that didn't work.

The more he moved, the more she moved right along with him, sucking even harder. If he pulled back, she grabbed his behind and was all but shoving him into her face, moaning and groaning and that was turning him on.

"Damn, I'm about to . . . I'm not ready. I want to tap that ass first," Damien insisted.

Finally, he decided to stop fighting the feeling and go with the flow. He stopped resisting, quit trying to think other thoughts, and decided to ride the wave. And what a spectacular wave it was.

"Do your thang, girl. You know what I like," he sang.

And she did. Right when she felt his body jerk, she sucked harder, took his sack into her hands and squeezed, applying just the right amount of pressure and slight pain. Within seconds, his warm fluids filled Charlotte's mouth. When some ran down the side of her chin, she quickly used her fingers to sop it up and then licked them dry.

"Emmm, you are so damn delicious, Damien Goodlove," she testified. "I'm such a lucky girl."

Damien shook his head. "Oh, no, I'm the one who's lucky," he insisted before he fell back onto the bed, his heart threatening to explode out of his chest. He swore he saw colorful stars dancing before his eyes.

"Oh, no, buddy. I know you're not trying to back out on your responsibilities," Charlotte teased. He pulled her closer and planted wet kisses all over her face.

"Disappoint you and Ms. Kitty? Never, never, I tell you," he joked.

"You need me to bring him back to life?" she asked, hungry to feel him inside of her warmth. Since the last time they were together, she hadn't been able to think about another thing but his touch.

After their first night, they'd been together several times. Charlotte thought for sure she wouldn't see him so soon after the melee inside the sanctuary.

When Michelle launched her verbal attack against Damien, Charlotte wanted to run up there and stand by her man, but she knew better. Instead, she sat quietly in the hall of the overflow room and watched in horror as the drama unfolded.

Two days later, Damien showed up at her doorstep looking like a broken man. She didn't even care that he hadn't called. She pulled her door open, stepped aside and welcomed him into her apartment, and then hours later, into that warm and moist place he couldn't seem to get enough of. She was honored to invite him into paradise, and he rewarded her with that blissful combination of pleasure and just the right hint of pain.

Damien rolled on top of her, used one hand to pin her arms above her head and ravished her body until she squirmed beneath his strength.

"Please, please, please," she begged.

"Please what? What do you want? Ask for it," he urged.

"Please, Damien, give me some of that Goodlove of yours. Please, baby, please, give it to me," she whispered lustfully in his ear.

It was all music to his ears. Damien loved when women behaved as if they simply couldn't go on without him. Forget about those independent types. He liked a woman who wasn't afraid to let a man know how much she needed him. He took one of her hefty legs, lifted it over his shoulder, eased up on his knees and gave her exactly what she'd been begging for.

He entered her with such strength he nearly took her breath away. She stared at him wide eyed and in awe of him and the way he made her feel.

"You like that?" he whispered, sending chills up and down her spine. Damien had a way of making her feel sexier than she ever had. He loved her body with such careful and calculated precision, she couldn't imagine why any woman would ever leave him.

It had crossed her mind, but she didn't dare ask about the status of his relationship with Michelle. Charlotte told herself Michelle was probably just another one of those skinny girls who thought the sun rose and set between her bony-ass legs.

Charlotte didn't know if she worked so hard in bed because she always felt like she had to prove something, but she did know she always wanted to make a damn good impression on the man she decided to bed. Charlotte especially liked turning out guys like Damien. She knew he probably thought he was God's gift to women, but she also figured like others, he hadn't had a woman like her.

Just listening to their bodies slapping together was like sweet harmony to her own ears.

"Oh, shit, girl, you got some good stuff right here," he said, breathing hard and working his hips.

"Take it, if it's good, baby. Take it like you like it," Charlotte cried.

He loved her aggressiveness, loved the fact that she was so damn confident and sure of herself. Mostly, he loved the way she'd lift her legs and wrap them around him, squeezing until he thought he'd become lightheaded and explode at the idea of being trapped.

Charlotte knew how to work her jelly for damn sure and he loved everything she did.

After loving Charlotte three times, Damien finally dragged himself into the shower. He had to lock the bathroom door to keep her out, or he'd never make it to the hospital to see the old man. Each time they hooked up, they'd fuck, suck, slurp and have sex for hours upon hours. She was amazing.

When he had come for the fourth time, Charlotte turned to him and asked, "Hey, you have any fantasies?"

"Damn, you just a big ol' freak, huh?" Damien worried he might've hurt her feelings, but when he noticed the smile break out across her face, he knew he would be fine.

"Actually, I have a friend I thought you'd like to have with me," Charlotte offered.

Damien swore his heart was about to stop beating. Could she be *the* perfect woman or what? If she was offering what he thought he was hearing, he'd drop to his knees and thank the man upstairs for sure.

"You asking if I want a threesome?" Damien tried to clarify. He didn't want to misunderstand, or misinterpret anything she was trying to say. But he instantly felt a tingle in the spot that counts when he asked the question.

"What? Can't handle it?" she teased flirtatiously.

"Girl, please. Get real."

"So what does that mean? You wanna do us or not?" Charlotte inquired with an eyebrow raised.

Damien sat staring at her for a second. Was his dream finally coming true?

"Hell yeah," he quickly confirmed. "Your friend, what does she look like?"

"You remember her—Sam. We'll, we'd like to make a nice sandwich with you in the middle. I told her you could handle it. I mean, there's definitely enough of that magic stick of yours to go around," Charlotte commented.

As he stood beneath the steaming hot shower, he shivered when he thought about a threesome with two big girls. Damien was no stranger to threesomes, orgies and such, but never before had he even considered things like that with big girls.

"Shit, ain't nothing to lose in a threesome," he mumbled as he turned, filled his mouth with water and spit it out.

When Damien stepped out of the bathroom, he was on the lookout for Charlotte. The woman was like the energizer bunny. And normally he didn't mind her insatiable sexual appetite, but he really did need to get to the hospital.

"Hey baby," Charlotte said when he walked out to the living room fully dressed. "You coming back by later or what?" she asked.

"I think I will. My brother and his girl are having major issues with their wedding plans so I should probably crash over here."

Charlotte didn't want to react to the fact that he was talking about staying over. She didn't want to come off all needy, but there was a full fledge parade going on inside of her.

"Barry, right? I thought the wedding was postponed until your father gets better," she said.

"It was, but Amy still wants to keep planning," Damien said.

"Okay, well, just call me when you pull up outside so I can open the door for you," Charlotte said.

Damien gave her a peck on the cheek, and headed out the door.

About two hours later, when Damien finally made it to the hospital, he was surprised to see Theola sitting next to his father's bed. She looked like the ever-concerned and supportive wife he knew she wasn't. But he didn't want to overreact.

"How's he doing today?" Damien asked the minute she looked up.

"No change. It's just like he's sleeping, only he's not," Theola stood, shaking her head. She hated being there, hated seeing Ethan like that. Despite what many of Sweetwater's parishioners thought, she did love the old man. "Well, I was about to go home anyway," Theola said, rising from her chair.

Damien felt indifferent when it came to her. He wanted to say something about what happened on Sunday, but decided it was best if he just left well-enough alone. He knew people expected him to step into his father's shoes, but he also knew he was nowhere near ready for such a huge responsibility. For years, he had told himself, if he ever got the calling, or even an inkling of the calling, he simply wouldn't answer.

Besides, he didn't have the electrifying abilities like the old man. He couldn't take the Word and translate it into interesting sermons that kept people on the edge of their seats. No, God knew who to call upon, and He also knew who not to call.

As Damien looked at his father, he prayed God would work a miracle and help the old man wake up. Since his father had slipped into the coma, everything had started falling apart—for both he and Barry. When Amy was over to Barry's the night before, Damien couldn't help but over hear an argument.

"Didn't I tell you my cousin needs a bigger role in this wedding?" Amy had asked Barry. It wasn't just the question, but the way she asked it, like the question was about to be followed by a blow. "You hear me talking to you?" she snarled.

Damien wanted to burst into the room, but he didn't.

"Look, let's talk about this later," Barry's responded.

"Later my ass. I want you to pick up that phone, call my cousin, and do what I said," she demanded.

Much to his surprise, Damien heard Barry greeting Amy's cousin on the phone only a few minutes later. Damien couldn't believe his ears. Was his baby brother being punked by his own damn fiancé? The sound from the machine jarred hismind back to his father's lifeless body. Yeah, the G-man needed to wake up, and do it in a hurry. Damien had a feeling things would get a whole lot worse before they got better.

Chapter 13

Should she stay or go? That was the question. Theola had been thinking about it ever since she left the hospital. Doctors informed her there had been no change in her husband's condition. They didn't anticipate anything anytime soon, so why should she hang around? After the fight at church last week, she didn't really feel like going this week, but she knew she should. The only real reason she continued to attend Sweetwater was because she felt she had to in her husband's absence.

"If I go, I could stay for three days or even two just to help with this loneliness," she whispered aloud.

Theola wasn't the kind of woman who liked to be alone. She needed attention from men, and more importantly, she needed what only men were capable of giving women.

She wanted to see Stone Pier, but mostly, she just wanted some company. Theola dialed Michelle's cell number again hoping to convince her to come out to Blueridge for a couple of days. Blueridge was the sprawling compound Theola shared with her husband. And since he'd been hospitalized, she dreaded going there alone even more. But just like before, Michelle didn't pick up her cell phone.

Theola thought if Michelle came out, she knew for sure she'd be there for church. But the minute service was over, she was on the next thing smoking to Belize. She had no one else to call when Michelle didn't answer. Theola kicked herself for not talking to Michelle when she saw her at church, but there had been just too much going on.

Theola dialed another number then waited for the cheerful voice to answer.

"Yes, I have an event to go to. It's very upscale, and I was wondering if you could find someone to accompany me," she said before she lost her nerve. Her heart was beating so loudly in her ear, she could hardly make out what the woman was saying.

"If you decide you'll need this companion for more than a few hours you should be aware there will be an added charge, by the hour of course," the woman said nonchalantly.

"Of course," Theola answered. She was surprisingly shocked at herself for going through with it.

"So tell me: What does your perfect man look like?"

"Hmmm, let's see. I like a firm chocolate tower, standing about six-two to six-three, maybe six-four. I'm talking about a mass of chiseled perfection, if you know what I mean." Theola could hear the woman's acrylic nails on the keyboard as she spoke.

"Oh, I'm getting a vision," the woman chuckled and joked.

"I like my men cut in all of the right places. If you could picture him wearing skin tight swim trunks, you'd be able to get a good idea of his ample package. This may sound crazy, but I like a man who's not afraid to wear sandals, you know some men won't. Oh, also, I like a nice chest, the kind that leaves you hypnotized if you stare at it too long. A deep sexy voice and strong hands would be good, too."

Theola described Stone Pier as best she could. "Oh, also, I like back rubs," she chimed in.

"I think we have just the person for you," the woman said and Theola could hear the smile in her voice.

"Great." Theola beamed.

"So when is your event and where would you like your date to meet you?"

"Is this evening too soon?" she tried to mask the desperation in her voice.

"Ahhhhh . . ." Theola could hear the nails on the keyboard again. This time the pace was faster.

"Let me see. You mind holding for a sec?"

"Not at all," Theola said. She just hoped for some company. Maybe if they were compatible, her new friend could help her through this rough patch in between visits to Belize.

"This evening won't be a problem," the woman returned to the line and said.

"Great. Well, I have a room at the Double Tree in downtown."

"Near Dallas Street, right?" she asked Theola.

For the first time since her feet hit U.S. soil, Theola finally felt like she had something to look forward to and for that she was excited. She didn't have a damn place to go, but she was tired of being hold-up in a big fancy mansion all by herself. She decided she'd go through her closet, find a dress, go get the room and tell her date their event was cancelled at the last minute. As long as he was getting paid, Theola was sure it wouldn't be a problem.

Nearly four hours after placing the call, Theola was dressed and waiting in her suite overlooking downtown Houston. She had on a long, black, silk halter dress that dipped low in the back and showed off her ample cleavage. The dress had two splits running up both sides, showing off enough thigh to imply she was ready for just about anything.

Her hair was tied up with curly tendrils framing the sides of her face. She wore jeweled encrusted stiletto sandals and was proud of what she was able to scrape up at the last minute. The mini bar was full, and she looked forward to having someone to talk to.

Her heart nearly skipped at beat when there was a knock at the door.

"Just a minute," she yelled. Theola rumbled through her purse and removed a bottle of Beautiful. She sprayed some behind her earlobes, between her breasts, then said, "and one for the midgets," as she sprayed near her crotch and smiled. She tossed the bottle back into her purse and rushed to the door.

She pulled the door open and smiled at the heavenly vision standing before her.

"I'm Hunter Malone," he said with a voice so deep it made her insides tingle. He presented her with a single red rose and her heart nearly melted.

Hunter Malone was tall, about six-feet-four inches of firmness. His skin was the color of burnt wheat. He was clean cut with a fade haircut and a thin mustache above his beautiful pink lips. His dark eyes sparkled, and when he smiled, his dimples were so deep, she wanted to tweak them with her fingers.

"Hunter, I'm Theola. I'm glad you could meet me to-night. Unfortunately, I have bad news," she began immediately.

She swung the door open to let him in and locked it after gazing longingly as he swaggered in. He was bowlegged, her absolute favorite.

"It seems our event has been cancelled." She feigned disappointment and shrugged.

Hunter's eyes stayed at her cleavage. And she didn't mind because to her that meant they were definitely on the same page—none of that awkward wondering whether he would be down.

"Would you like a drink?" Theola asked him coyly. Her skin tingled beneath his intense gaze. She didn't mind his scrutiny at all. As a matter of fact, she welcomed it.

"I'd like whatever you want me to like." Hunter smiled and licked his lips as he sat down.

Theola's eyes lingered on his lips for a few minutes. When she felt that tingling sensation between her thighs, she turned and sauntered toward the mini-bar.

Theola returned with two miniature bottles of Crown and eased up next to Hunter with a wicked but inviting smile.

"Why don't you have a seat," he offered, licking his lips again. When he spoke, Theola felt her blood begin to boil, he even sound sexy. Theola flopped down next to him and extended a bottle toward him.

Hunter shook his head.

"I thought you wanted a drink," she said.

"I do, but what I really want is for you to come and sit right here," he insisted.

Theola's eyebrows crept together. She was confused. "I am sitting here—right here next to you," she told him.

Hunter pulled his jacket back and patted his thigh.

"I meant sit right here." He smiled.

Their eyes met. They both smiled and Theola got up. She didn't wait to be told twice. They downed the bottles, and Theola giggled. Once again, that feeling of freedom was creeping back up on her, and it felt good.

When their eyes met, her smile dropped instantly. He brushed her lips with his, and Theola confirmed what she thought the instant she had laid eyes on his pretty face. He wanted her, too.

His lips were succulent and soft. She wondered what they'd feel like on other more pressing body parts, but quickly shook that thought from her mind. *That*, she told herself, would come in due time.

"What?" Hunter asked. "What?"

Theola frowned. "What do you mean?"

"You were thinking something. What is it?" Hunter pressed.

Theola giggled again, confirming for Hunter and herself that she was just a tad bit nervous. Hunter took the bottle from her hand and placed it on the table. Once her hands were empty, he scooped her into his strong arms and carried her like a doll toward the back. She didn't put up a fight or struggle.

When Hunter stripped down to his silk boxers, Theola was in awe of his beautiful body. Muscles seemed at home all over his glorious body, and she wanted to take her tongue and glaze from his six-pack to his package and up to his pretty rippled chest.

He untied her dress and manhandled her breasts. She enjoyed the feeling, pushing them out so he could work it out. Hunter grabbed her breasts and slopped over them recklessly.

She threw her head back and squealed at the sheer pleasure she felt.

"Oh, God." She trembled.

"How do you want me?" Hunter asked. "I'm here to please you."

"I wanna ride."

Hunter stepped out of his boxers, and she was glad he was so well endowed. Hunter was hung and Theola looked at him hungrily as he put on a condom.

He eased back on the bed, already stiff and hard, and pulled her onto his lap. She straddled him as he sat upright.

"Come on. Ease it up in there," he urged. Theola followed instructions and wiggled her hips, then scooted all the way into his lap until his wand was nestled comfortably between her walls.

"Yeah, that's it," Hunter moaned as Theola grinded her hips deeper into his lap. Theola contracted her walls, taking his swollen shaft and trying to squeeze the life from it. Hunter thrust his hips as Theola pulled him deeper and deeper into her wetness.

"Shit, it's all wet and warm, inviting, just the way I like it," he mumbled through gritted teeth.

Theola wanted him to be quiet so she could concentrate. He felt good, like he was moving things around up in there.

"Oh yeah!" he squealed, his eyes tightly shut. "Work it out."

Finally frustrated by his constant talking, she started squeezing her breasts and took one and stuffed it into his mouth.

He got the hint and grabbed them, shoving them together, taking her nipples and suckling them both at the same time.

Theola made sure she got her money's worth. She ravished Hunter three more times before she paid him. She finally turned him loose just before the sun inched up welcoming a new day.

Chapter 14

"So what are you going to do to fix this?" Michelle screamed into her cell phone as she pulled into the jail's parking lot.

Her attorney had just told her that Damien was still refusing to sign the divorce papers. A bolt of panic raced through her veins at the thought of him prolonging her misery, and she was too through. She hadn't seen him since the blow up at church last week, but she was hoping something would've happened to make him change his mind. Sadly, nothing had.

"Look, I need to go check in. I'll call you when I get off or go on my lunch break," Michelle said.

She hissed and pressed the end button before he could respond. She couldn't believe the way Damien was trying to drag this thing out. Maybe he found out about the money. She shoved that thought from her mind and stepped into the gate once the miserable little guard checked her name off his list. The way he slumped there guarding the gate like someone might want to sneak in, made her stomach churn. Everything about the damn place made her want to puke.

The moment she stepped into the part of the building that housed the room they used for the prison ministry, she noticed two inmates were already standing outside the door.

"Here she comes," she heard someone attempt to whisper.

What now? she thought as she took weary steps toward them. Just then, a guard walked up to the duo. He looked at the inmates, then at Michelle.

"Whassup?" The guard greeted the inmates.

Michelle's eyebrows went up slightly, but she didn't say anything.

"Ma'am, you lost?" The guard, a beefy Hispanic man, asked.

"No, uh, I'm with the Prison ministry," Michelle stammered.

"Yeah, she cool people's, Juan," one of the inmates said. The guard looked at Michelle, then back at the inmate who spoke to him. They seemed to exchange knowing glances before the guard moved on.

"How are you today, Miss Goodlove?" the inmate who had chatted up the guard asked politely.

"I'm fine. Thank you." Michelle wondered what they were up to, and why he was so buddy-buddy with the guard. She was not in the mood for foolishness.

She couldn't remember which session the inmates had been in, but she knew they were a part of the new batch that had suddenly caught religion since word spread about her being there. The attention didn't bother her in the least. Actually, it was kind of flattering, but still, she remembered the warnings she and the others had received.

"Is Pastor Peebles here yet?" she asked.

"He is, but he's counseling right now. It's why we're out here," the other one answered.

"So, you married or what?" Before Michelle could answer, the inmate who had talked to the guard said, "I'm Raymond, and that's my buddy, Scott." He smiled. "Oh, and don't trip on Juan. We homies," he added.

Michelle simply nodded as she eyed him suspiciously.

In the outside world, Raymond would've been the equivalent of a sexy rough neck. He was a darker version of the sexy rapper, LL Cool J. Raymond was a bit taller, but he still had that sexy body and handsome face. Scott was a weasel of a man, short thin and scruffy looking. He was light with curly hair and an incredible acne problem that the prison obviously couldn't help correct. He was also obviously the Robin to Raymond's Batman.

Michelle nodded. "Nice to meet you both," she said. "If you must know, I'm getting a divorce," she answered through gritted teeth.

Michelle wasn't sure why she was taking her anger out on them. It certainly wasn't their fault her bastard of a husband was being difficult. She tried to check her attitude until they said something else.

"So you're looking for a new man, huh? Well, I'll say you came to the right place." Raymond chuckled.

Scott laughed like he was being paid to back Raymond up.

Michelle frowned and snickered. "A new man, huh? Let's just say I've had enough. I want to get rid of this one then get on my way. I'm through with y'all for a while."

"Oh, c'mon now. Don't be so mean. Just because that brother didn't know how to treat a queen, you can't put us all in the same category. Some of us understand the needs of a woman and are prepared to step up to the plate and handle *said* needs," Raymond preached.

He was so fine, she thought.

"Yeah, until something better comes along," Michelle challenged with a snicker.

"Oh, naw, it ain't even gotta be like that," Scott co-signed.

Michelle could feel Raymond's eyes washing over her from head to toe, then back up again. It was as if he was undressing her with his eyes. She had even noticed him licking his lips a few times. Michelle was glad when the door swung open and Pastor Peebles asked her to come inside.

She blinked a few times trying to understand the feelings she desperately wanted to deny. How could compliments from some inmates have such a visible impact on her? She didn't know the answer, but she did know for sure something had awakened deep within, and she wasn't sure how long she'd be able to ignore that nagging feeling or whether she even wanted to.

Michelle played with their comments and questions in her mind as she went through her daily rituals of passing out pens, pencils, Bibles and notepads. Each time she passed by someone's desk, she noticed an extra smile here and there. There were a few winks, and if eyes could perform, she'd probably be moving around naked. That's just how many times someone looked as if they were trying to find a way to undress her with their eyes. Thoughts of the probation group leader's words crept through her mind once again.

You've been warned... the voice in her head mocked. *If he's handsome, irresistible and you just must have him because your pathetic lives just don't lead you to anyone in the free world, wait until you've finished serving your sentence!*

"Aw, shoot!" someone complained, breaking her train of thought. The culprit started looking toward the back of the room where Michelle sat buried in a novel.

"Miss Michelle, my pencil lead broke. You got another one?" He smiled, looking guilty.

She jumped from her seat and swore all twenty-two heads turned to watch her every move. Michelle sashayed as she moved up the aisle to switch out the pencils. Every eye stayed on her until she reclaimed her seat. Michelle wondered what kind of attention she'd get if she wasn't forced to dress in the drab pants and smock-like top.

"Damn," someone whispered as she passed his desk.

It was kind of funny when she thought about it. There were so many men locked up she often thought about how she could probably find exactly what she wanted if she didn't mind love on lockdown.

Michelle chuckled to herself and tried not to be distracted by the little attempts the inmates made to try and get her attention. And they seemed never-ending.

"Miss Michelle, uh, you got an eraser?"

"Miss Michelle, I need more paper."

"Miss Michelle, um, this pencil doesn't seem to wanna work!"

On this day, Raymond attended all three sessions. And every chance he got, he whispered something sweet to Michelle. She knew then she'd have to keep extra close tabs on him.

Chapter 15

Damien was all messed up and frustrated with the doctors responsible for his father's care. He felt they weren't doing a damn thing to help his father's condition. He and Barry had just wrapped up yet another meeting meant to keep them updated on Pastor Goodlove's condition, but just like the ones before, this meeting had netted no results. Damien was still hot at Reginald. Here the old man was, laid up in the hospital, and it felt like everything was on his and Barry's shoulders.

They didn't even bother to question why Theola wasn't present. They had grown accustomed to her lack of interest when it came to their father since he was now incapacitated.

"Damn," Barry muttered as they stepped off the elevator.

"What's up, li'l bro? You seem really wired lately," Damien said.

Barry shook his head. "Well, there's this thing with Pops, and not to mention we can't move forward with the stupid wedding plans. But my real problem is, Amy is still planning away like nothing has happened. You know if it was her old man lying up in there like that, I wouldn't even see her," Barry hissed.

"You know how crazy women are, especially when a wedding's involved," Damien reminded him.

"Yeah, I hear you, but still."

"Besides, whatever happened to that crazy girlfriend of yours," Damien asked, realizing he hadn't heard a sound about the woman who was possessed with taking his baby brother from his current fiancé.

It had been a mess, but one day the girl just vanished, or maybe Damien had been so wrapped up in his own drama, he had no time to think about that of his brothers. Reginald still hadn't been seen nor heard from.

Barry shrugged. "One day calls just stopped coming from her. I wasn't about to go investigate. I was just glad she found something else to occupy her time, besides me of course. But boy I tell you, I really wish Pops would wake up so I could figure out what to do about this wedding."

Damien wanted to tell Barry to run and hide while he still had a chance, but he decided against offering up that advice. Marriage might just prove good for his little brother.

As he slid behind the wheel of his car, and Barry buckled up, Damien's cell phone rang.

He dug for it, checked the caller ID, and pressed it up against his ear. "What's up, Sam?" He sighed and rolled his eyes.

"Michelle's attorney called again. Wants to find out what it would take to get you to sign."

"Sam, you're not going soft on me, are you? I want half. It's just that simple. That's what we agreed on, half. So half is what it would take for me to sign," Damien insisted. He couldn't believe Michelle. Did she really think he was that stupid? Obviously she did.

"I know, I know, but as your attorney I have to advise you about all offers that come through," Sam said.

"Yeah? Well what's the offer now?"

"She says she just wants you to sign. You can share custody of the girls, and she just wants her freedom," Sam sang.

"Well, you tell her ass I said, she's not gonna use my kids as a pawn in her little game to try and keep half of what's rightfully mine," Damien hollered. "And quiet as it's kept, she better be glad I didn't fight her for custody."

"Hey look. We're on the same team here, buddy. I'm just keeping you abreast of what's going on. I'm still trying to figure out when this case of hers is going to settle. Give me a few weeks, and I'll have a better idea of how we need to proceed."

"Good job, Sammy boy," Damien said.

"Well, you be good and stay out of trouble until we get the information we need. I'll be in touch," Sam informed him.

"Yeah, but Sam, next time you call make sure you're calling with good news, how about that?" Damien said with all seriousness.

When he got off the phone, Barry turned to him and said. "What's going on? I thought you were on easy street since that Jazzlyn decided to leave Sweetwater. I mean what's going on with you and Michelle now?"

"You don't even wanna know bro . . . trust me on that."

"You're probably right. You know what? I'm just trying to stay drama-free myself. Once Sissy vanished, I promised God I'd do right, so that's my new mission—get back on track and stay there. I want Pops to get better, and then I want to decide whether marrying Amy is the best move and go on with my life," Barry said, shaking his head.

Damien thought back to Jazzlyn. When she had first switched her membership to Sweetwater nearly the entire deacon's board wanted to be first to see who would have the pleasure of finding out if he could live up to her reputation.

Of course Damien hadn't wasted any time hitting that, but once Michelle found out what was going on, that was the beginning of the end of life as he knew it. Unfortunately for him, Jazzlyn was wrongfully arrested inside the church for the attempt on his life, and she grew horns and began to make his life even more miserable.

Despite that, he was still able to hit it a couple of times after that mess, but the damage had already been done. There really was no way for them to recover.

Besides, Damien never wanted to be tied down with Jazzlyn. She wasn't that type. The deacons all wanted her, but her hideous face all but ensured no one would ever admit to hitting it much less wanting to.

Even after Michelle left him, and Jazzlyn thought that was surely her *in*, things became even more miserable between them. Finally, Jazzlyn decided she wouldn't find a husband at Sweetwater and switched to a church on the North side. He last heard she was kicking up drama over there and that didn't surprise him in the least.

"Yeah, that Jazzlyn was a bonafide trip," Damien commented about twenty minutes after his brother had forgotten about his question.

His phone rang again. "Hold up a sec," he said to Barry.

It was Charlotte. Damien smiled when he saw her number pop up on his caller ID.

"Hey, big daddy," Charlotte cooed the second Damien answered.

"Hey, what's going on?" Damien whispered softly.

"Where are you?" she asked.

"'Bout to drop my brother off. Why? What's up?" Damien wanted to know.

"You know that thing we talked about doing with me you and Sam?" Charlotte reminded him.

Damien's eyes lit up and his member immediately stood at attention.

"Yeah, what's up with that? I remember. So what? Is she down or what?"

"It's going down tonight. I mean, we're trying to take care of you for real. She was hyped when I presented the idea, so what's up? You free or what?"

"Am I? What time do you ladies want me there? And what do I need to bring?" Damien laughed.

He didn't mind being a part of their little sandwich experiment at all. He had never met a woman like Charlotte, and if her big friend was just as freaky, he knew he was in for a real nice treat. He marveled at how Charlotte had single-handedly changed his views on the girls with curves. Visions of being sucked, fucked, and ridden until they rendered him dry was an enticing thought, which brought a naughty smile to his face.

"Why don't you hurry on over, and we'll be waiting," Charlotte sang in his ear.

Not in his wildest dream could he ever imagine that he'd be this excited about a big girl, but he was. Damien wished he could drop Barry off at the nearest bus stop so he could see just exactly what Charlotte and her girl had in store for him. But the truth was, he had to drop Barry off at his apartment, then fight traffic to get to the other side of town.

They wrapped up their phone call and an intense smile quickly spread across his face.

"Dang, that must've been one heck of a phone call," Barry commented after the visible shift in his brother's demeanor once he hung up and pressed the pedal toward his place.

"Aw, man, it's just this girl I know," Damien grinned again.

Barry flashed him a knowing look and shook his head. Barry knew, regardless of what problems Damien suffered, he knew his big brother wouldn't be suffering for long.

Damien couldn't stop thinking about all of the glorious things Charlotte was able to do with her mouth, body and hands. All the things that made him feel so damn good. He couldn't wait to get himself sandwiched between Charlotte and her friend, Samantha.

Chapter 16

When Theola breezed into Sweetwater PG Sunday morning, she had sauntered in like she didn't have a care in the world. She wore a skintight leopard print mini-dress made of rayon. Her wide brimmed hat, with three different colored feathers protruding from the side, added an extra four inches to her height. With her four-inch Marc Fisher pumps clinking as she strolled to the front pew, Theola was a visual feast for every eye that followed her, and there were many.

As she sat, she tossed a nasty look in Mama Sadie's direction, like she dared the old woman to try her today. Theola was just biding her time. Once she visited her husband immediately following service, she was headed back to paradise. By her calculations, she had just discovered the perfect plan. She'd go to Belize every two weeks, and in between visits, she'd have Hunter to ease her sorrows or anything else that might make her heart ache.

The choir had just wrapped up another one of its toe-tapping, hip-shaking renditions of "Jesus Is My Rock," and members of the congregation were preparing to dig deep into their pockets.

"It's time to give," a jubilant voice roared through the sanctuary's speakers.

"Sweetwater! I said, it's time to give." The choir started back up again—this time with a tempo so uplifting, church members smiled as they passed their envelopes into the large baskets.

Visitors who didn't know better would've thought they'd just walked into a church made up of good prayed-over Christians who had nothing but the utmost love and respect for their brothers and sisters in Christ. This week's visitors at Sweetwater would've had no way of knowing about the big brawl that broke out only seven days prior.

Theola sat reminiscing about that day. Afterward, she thought about all of the things she should've said, and what she could've done. Normally, she wouldn't even think to hit a woman old enough to be her grandmother, but Mama Sadie had been so out of line, Theola was certain the term laying on of hands had nothing to do with the vicious words that spewed from Mama Sadie's lips that day. Days after the incident, Theola would wake from her sleep swinging and kicking at the ol' bat, involuntarily imitating what she'd done in her dreams.

Minutes before service wrapped up, Theola jumped from her seat and headed for the door. She didn't have time to waste today. If she could get to the hospital by two, she could be at the airport in time for her seven p.m. flight.

"Theola!" a voice called. "Theola!"

She sighed upon hearing her voice. There was no way she could act as though she didn't hear it. When she turned to see Michelle standing there, she slowed her pace a hoped Michelle didn't notice the look of disappointment across her face. Of course Michelle would reach out now, when she had plans, Theola thought.

"Hey girl. What's up?" Theola asked.

Michelle walked up. "Well, I don't know. I wanted to see if you had plans later. I was thinking I could come out to Blueridge."

Theola frowned. Now here she'd been calling this girl for days, with not as much as a return voicemail, all but tracking her down, then on the very day she was headed to paradise, Michelle wanted to come talking about a "girlfriends" night?

"Ooooh weee, I sho' wish you would've said something sooner. I tried to call you several times yesterday, and got your voicemail. Girl, I'm trying to rush over to the hospital now," Theola said. She looked around the parking lot for her driver for good measure. She flicked her wrist and checked her watch then frowned again. "I need to go spend some time with Ethan," Theola added.

"Oh yeah, well, I can certainly understand that," Michelle quickly agreed.

Theola looked beyond her, finally seeing her waywardly driver. *Note to self,* she thought, wondering why Michelle was still standing there. She'd have to have a word with this driver and remind him about his responsibilities because she was growing weary of all the damn time she had to spend waiting on a ride. She wouldn't even have had to go through that uncomfortable situation with Michelle if he would've been on time.

"But that's why I was thinking I could come spend a few days with you out there. I mean, I remember you saying how bored you were being in that big ol' house all alone."

Yeah, Theola *had* said that many times before, but that was before she had mastered her coping techniques.

Theola put a hand up to stop her. She shook her head. "Again, girl, bad timing on your part. As soon as I leave Ethan this evening, I'm headed to Belize." Theola's head was still shaking. "I've been trying to tell you to get with me, girl. I found this spot over there . . ."

When the driver pulled up and got out to open the door for Theola, she sighed, elevated her eyebrows and shrugged her shoulders. "Girl, I gotta get with you later." She slipped into the back seat and got comfortable.

Theola absolutely despised hospitals. She's never liked them one bit. Everything always had to be so sterile and quiet, and then, not to mention the fact that the damn place reminded her of the dead. Her grandmother, grandfather, two uncles, and her mother had all gone into the hospital and never walked out. They all wound up dead.

She eased into her husband's room and saw someone hovering over him. Instantly, Theola started to get angry.

"Who the hell are you?" Theola snarled.

When the woman turned, Theola noticed her uniform and her cheeks got warm. "Ah, I'm Veronica Smith. Pastor Goodlove's nurse," the woman said.

"Oh, my bad, I thought you were one of those busy bodies from church," Theola said.

The nurse's cold gaze rolled up Theola's length beginning at her feet, moving up to her head then back down again.

"No one was here, so I thought he could use some company," the nurse said, her mouth turning into a sharp frown.

"Any change whatsoever?" Theola inquired.

She sure hoped the heifer wasn't trying to insinuate anything by her comment about no one being there. Taking that mess from the holier-than-thou group at Sweetwater was one thing. She'd be dammed if she'd take it from the hired help, too.

"Nope, he's still sound asleep." The nurse fluffed his pillows, fussed with the sheets that covered his body and made some adjustments to things on his night stand.

Theola rolled her eyes. It really didn't take all of that, she thought as she watched the nurse work. She didn't know what this nurse thought she was doing, but Theola knew she was in no mood for any crap. She did have a plane to catch.

"Okay, honey, I think I got it from here," Theola said, popping her gum hard and loud. She tossed a hand to her hip and gave the nurse a look that said she should find some other patient to fuss over.

The nurse frowned then sucked her teeth. Theola stepped up to the head of Ethan's bed and gave the nurse a knowing look, gum still popping.

"You should be ashamed of yourself," the nurse snickered beneath her breath as she motioned away from the pastor's bed.

"What the hell did you say?" Theola asked, her voice dripping with attitude.

But the nurse tossed her a dirty look and pulled the door open. She rolled her eyes at Theola before stepping outside. Theola was sick and tired of being disrespected—first, at church, and now, at the damn hospital? She told herself to simply brush it off. Once she was gone, Theola had to admit, she was bored. Outside of the sound coming from the TV, all she could hear was the constant humming and buzzing from the various machines connected to her husband.

Theola first sat next to his bed, then moved her chair back a bit. After about ten minutes, she got up to stretch her legs and walk around the room. Restless doing that, she soon stretched out on the sofa near the window. The room was decorated nicely enough. Plants, flowers, roses, balloons and tons of get well soon cards were all over the room.

"Shit! I can't take this," Theola said. She snatched her purse, walked to the head of her husband's bed, looked at him trying to see if she could notice a flinch, movement behind his eyelids, or anything that might indicate he was still among the living.

When nothing happened, she turned to leave. She had a plane to catch.

Chapter 17

Michelle was growing accustomed to her time at the prison, and she didn't know whether that was a good thing. Raymond was also becoming a staple in her life as he now attended all three of the prison ministry sessions.

"You just be walking up in here teasing us, like you oblivious to the power you possess, ma," Raymond had said to her the moment she walked up one morning.

A grin appeared across her face.

"You say the sweetest things." Michelle smiled.

She was also getting used to the compliments and sweet words the inmates showered upon her. She couldn't remember a time in her life when men had been so complimentary, and she liked it.

"Look, I'm really digging you," Raymond whispered and licked his lips for good measure. Michelle felt something wake inside as she watched him.

It had been more than a year since Michelle's feminine parts had been tingling with such anticipation. Thanks to

Raymond and his crew, that sensation was no longer foreign to her. She wondered if he was all talk or whether he packed some action behind those words.

"Say, why don't you take a bathroom break twenty minutes into the next session. I can meet you. You know nobody's gonna be walking the halls. I've been monitoring all week. Besides I could get Scott to look out. You ain't gotta answer me now. Just think about it in this session. Then meet me in the bathroom for this wing."

He was talking so fast Michelle could hardly keep up. One thing for was sure though: Her heart was beating a mile a minute, and sheer excitement was pumping through her veins.

"But what if someone sees me going in there?" Michelle asked.

"Look, you 'member Juan, right? He's cool. This is his area, and don't trip, seriously," he urged.

What would she do in that bathroom with him? What if they were caught?

"Just trust me. It's all good. I promise. I'll make it worth your wild. Fine ass woman like you, shiiiit. You oughta always feel good. I can see the stress in your face. Trust, I can help you with that. Believe it, baby!" he boasted confidently.

Michelle had to think fast. She was curious. It had been so long, and she had so much to lose. Raymond had been sweet and caring. He'd inquired about what was on her mind when she seemed distant and worried, and she had to admit he had become somewhat of a confidant. She had all but forgotten about her relationship with her girls.

And, when she had approached Theola the week before, she was hoping to have someone to share these conflicting feelings with, but Theola was too busy. Besides, Michelle wasn't even sure even Theola would understand. She had her own issues to deal with.

Michelle still had a few hours to think about Raymond's proposal before she had to make an actual decision. Michelle went about her duties, but she was only going through the motions. Throughout the session, inmates and Pastor Peebles had to call out her name a few times before she acknowledged them.

What the hell? Michelle thought. When the first session wrapped up, she watched as the inmates shuffled out of the room. She and Pastor Pebbles shared small talk for a little while then they prepared for the second session. Although there were a few new faces and a large number she recognized, Raymond was missing. *Oh God! He was serious,* she thought. Michelle felt her insides come alive. Electricity rushed through her veins, and curiosity was driving her mad.

When Scott smiled at her, she knew he was in on it. Michelle kept looking at her watch. She did her duties then at seventeen minutes into the session, she walked up to Pastor Peebles, whispered something in his ear and headed for the door.

Now when Michelle walked, she felt like she was on a runway. All that was missing was the camera flashes. But with all the eyes that followed her, she felt like she was always the center of attention. She took a deep breath, pulled the door open and peered out into the hall. Noticing the coast was clear, just like Raymond said it would be, she stepped out and tried to tiptoe toward the end of the hall.

"Why am I tiptoeing?" she mumbled under her breath. Michelle found the bathroom door, looked around again then finally stepped inside the small room. Her stomach quivered the moment she closed the door and flicked on the light.

Her heart nearly stopped when she saw Raymond sitting there on top of the closed toilet.

"Jesus! You nearly scared me to death," she barked.

"I'm sorry," he whispered. "Fear is the very last thing I want you to feel from me. You should never be afraid. You're so beautiful, I just want to make you feel good," he admitted, staring deeply into her eyes.

His words always came right on time. "Shush," she said stepping between his open legs. He tilted his head upward, and when their lips touched, Michelle felt like she had finally found home. His lips were so succulent, tender and sweet.

Raymond ran his hands up her back, rubbing her thighs and stroking her with such power, she melted with every breath she took.

Suddenly he pulled back, both of them breathing heavy and hard. "We've gotta hurry," he said, licking his lips in that sexy way she'd grown to love.

"We don't have a lot of time. I want you to sit on my face. I just want to give you some pleasure. I want to be responsible for the smile on your face," he said sincerely.

"But how?" Michelle asked, looking around their closed and cramped quarters. "It's so small in here," she insisted.

"Here." He took her by the hand. "Move to the side." Raymond eased his body to the floor and extended his legs so that they were placed atop the toilet seat. "Okay. Now take off your pants and come sit here on my face," he said.

Michelle hesitated for a flash of a second, but as she watched him lying on the floor, she quickly unzipped her pants. She couldn't remember a time when she felt so excited, so alive. The fear of being caught worked like an aphrodisiac and seemed to fuel the passion even more.

"Just remove one leg. I can move your panties to the side," he told her as he watched her fumbling with her pants.

She did, leaving one leg in the pants. She put the other leg on the side of his head and lowered herself down, close to his face.

Raymond reached up, grabbed her hips, used his lips to suckle the skin on her inner thighs, and then he moved her panties to the side.

"Oh, God," Michelle squealed trying to remain quiet.

He didn't relent.

"Oh, Jesus!"

At first, she felt awkward as she lowered herself down on his face. But he clutched her by the hips, holding her still and steady and explored her silken slit like a famine victim who had been denied food for far too long. When his tongue made contact with her flesh, she began to move her hips.

"Emmmmm." She gyrated her hip, grinding her body down onto his face. His tongue moved with such precision, he kept pleasuring her, working like there was no end to what he had to offer.

When Raymond reached up and found her nipples, Michelle had to chew on her lower lip to stop herself from screaming out loud.

It had been so long since she'd experienced such pleasure. Her heart raced. She didn't know what to do with her hands as she twisted her hips. She felt sweat gathering in her armpits. Her scalp was searing hot, and Raymond was working his tongue like he was auditioning for a job. He moved back and forth between squeezing her nipples and palming her behind, shoving her onto his face even more.

"Oh, yes! Yessssss!" she cried. "Right there. Right there, Raymond!"

Michelle felt the glorious sensation racing from the bottom of her feet, up her legs, through her thighs and up to her brain. She quickly stuffed her arm into her mouth to muffle a scream she couldn't contain. She hadn't felt like that in nearly two years.

Soon, she had to fight to get off Raymond's face because he was trying to suck up the juices he caused to gush out of her like free-flowing water.

When she scrambled to grab tissue to sop up the excess wetness, Raymond pulled himself up, smiled and said, "You were just as delicious as I imagined." He eased out of the door, leaving her alone to catch her breath.

Chapter 18

"**I**'ve always watched you in church," Samantha said as she eyed Damien in awe. He had been at Charlotte's for about twenty minutes, and they were talking each other up a bit before the real action could begin.

"Is that right?" Damien asked, his eyes moving back and forth between the two.

"Emmm-hmm." Samantha's head bobbed up and down. She had been so giddy with excitement the moment Charlotte called and told her the plan.

A tiny part of her didn't even believe it. Having been members of Sweetwater PG for years, she knew all about the Goodlove men's reputation. Although the middle brother, Reginald, was just plain weird, they found out just how much Barry had been working his mojo, on the low. They remembered how that crazy stalker put all his business out there to church members with that juicy email and those salacious billboards. That was some good dram. And of course they couldn't help but know all about Damien's reputation with the ladies. And in all those years, she couldn't remember a single one of his conquests being remotely shaped like either herself or Charlotte. But she was just happy he wanted to experiment because she was becoming quite envious of all the great loving he bestowed upon Charlotte.

Lately, when she'd called to talk about how Damien had worked that massive wand of his, Samantha was secretly wishing he and his wife would reconcile so that she and Charlotte could return to their usual discussions of what they would do if they had men like him at their disposals.

"Did you tell him?" she looked at Charlotte and asked coyly.

Charlotte dismissed her with the wave of a hand. "Girl, no! Why would I?" she asked, her face filling with dread. She was unable to believe her girl was about to embarrass her right in front of her man.

"Tell me what?" Damien asked. He had dropped his little brother off, barely stopping so Barry could get out before he took off, rushing to get to Charlotte's house.

"It's nothing, really. It's nothing," Charlotte said unconvincingly.

"If it was nothing, you two wouldn't be exchanging funny glances and giggling." Damien tried to hide his building frustration with the girls.

"I'll tell you myself," Samantha chimed in. "We used to sit in the back of the church and fantasize about all the naughty things we'd like to do to you on that stage your daddy preaches from." She giggled.

Damien looked at her, then at Charlotte, but didn't say anything.

Charlotte waited with baited breath. She didn't know what to think as Damien sat there looking between her and

Samantha. Had she gone too far? Why would she say something so damn stupid anyway?

The smile had long faded from Samantha's face, and judging by the look on Charlotte's, she figured she had fucked up. She just hoped she'd be able to help salvage the evening because she had no idea when they'd get another chance at a Goodlove man again.

"Well, why don't we go and find out," Damien said finally breaking the silence that hung over the room.

Samantha's eyes grew wide, and her mouth fell open. She looked at Charlotte, whose eyes were even wider. Charlotte's head snapped in Damien's direction the moment the words fell from his mouth.

"Are you bullshittin' us?" she wanted to know.

Damien did a half shrug with one shoulder and said, "Why would I do that? I mean, I've got the keys to the building. I can come and go as I please," he answered easily.

Charlotte and Samantha exchanged glances. Their faces broke into big silly grins.

"You bet' not be playing Damien. That ain't even funny," Charlotte hissed. When Damien stood, she didn't know what to do. "You cannot be serious," she finally screamed.

"Why not? It's like an athlete doing it on a football field. Who doesn't dream about getting it on at work?" he asked.

"Yeah," Samantha quickly co-signed, shaking her head for good measure. "Think about it, teachers on their desks, doctors in their offices, flight attendants . . . where do you think the term mile-high club came from?" she asked.

Charlotte still wasn't sure about it. She figured they were right, but just the thought of doing such forbidden things in church of all places. Something just seemed so extra-sinful about it. But she figured if anyone did, Damien definitely knew what he was doing, so she was down if he was.

"So what's up? Y'all ready to take this show on the road? My escalade is right outside," he said, motioning toward the door with a slight tilt of his head.

The outside of Sweetwater PG definitely had curb appeal, Samantha thought as Damien pulled to the back of the large building and pressed a button to open massive gates that housed the employee parking lot. He drove the truck into an underground garage that neither Samantha nor Charlotte knew existed and parked near the elevators.

"I had no idea this was even here," Charlotte said as they got onto the elevator.

"Private quarters," Damien informed the two.

When the elevator doors closed, he punched in some numbers, and they zoomed upward almost seamlessly.

Stepping off the elevator and into the dimly lit halls, Charlotte gazed around the eerily empty building and the hairs on the back of her neck stood up.

"Man, this is a trip," she mumbled, looking around.

They followed Damien to the main sanctuary, and he pushed a button that brought up just enough light for them to see each other and look around.

Samantha ran down to the front pew and sat there, stretching out.

"I don't think I've ever been this up close," she said, gazing back at the empty church. She held her head up and saw the balcony with the two theatre style boxes on each side, and she was in awe.

Charlotte was still on the main platform, moving around as if she was examining the area for just the right spot. Damien took a seat, leaned back and watched them inspect their surroundings.

"Do you know how long we've been coming to this church, and we've never been up front like this?" Charlotte said to no one in particular.

"Guess it helps to know people in high places," he joked. She turned to him and smiled. Charlotte pulled several scarves out of her Coach duffle bag and started moving toward him.

"We've got plans for you, Mr. Goodlove," she said, dangling the scarves in front of herself. Samantha quickly ran up onto the platform to join the party.

"Do tell, ladies. Do tell." He smiled as he prepared himself for an outer body experience or a different kind.

Chapter 19

Theola had been under Stone Pier's mystical spell for three days, and she was starting to go raw. Their flesh had rubbed together so vigorously and so frequently, she was afraid some permanent damage may have been done.

When he inserted three fingers inside of her, and noticed her flinch and wince at the same time, worry lines eased onto his otherwise perfect forehead.

"Am I hurting you?" He stopped moving his fingers just to be sure.

A reluctant Theola slightly bobbed her head up and down to confirm what she'd been trying to conceal for the past forty-five minutes.

"I don't know what's wrong, but yes. It's like I'm sore," she whined.

"Too much of a good thing?" he frowned.

Theola shrugged.

"Here, let me see," he said, spreading her legs as he moved downward.

Theola shrugged her shoulders. They had been humping each other like rabbits the moment she checked into her cabana. She had been there for thirty minutes, putting things away when his knock sent a jolt of electricity running through her veins. She didn't even have to ask who was there. It was as if his body had called out to her the moment her plane touched down.

"Come in," she had yelled.

Theola held towels as the door eased open and Stone Pier stepped inside. He stood clad in a tight pair of trunks, leather sandals and carried his duffle over his chest.

His eyes immediately lit up as if he was looking at a ghost.

"You're here? You came back to me, just as you said you would!" he exclaimed excitedly.

"Yes, and I'll be back again and again," she assured him.

Stone Pier dropped his bag at the door and rushed across the room. He scooped her into to his muscular embrace and squeezed her tightly. Her feet dangled off the ground as he twirled her around the room.

"I've not stopped dreaming of you since you left weeks ago," he whispered.

That was music to her ears. Theola understood she was paying handsomely for his adoring attention, but she couldn't care less. It still made her feel incredibly good. She'd pay whatever to share his company. The small earthquakes that made her entire body quiver proved hers had been money well spent.

"I'm just glad you're back. It's like how do you say?" he searched for the right words, putting her down to her feet. "Like living my dreams, only I'm not asleep, and you are really here." He beamed.

"I am! I am!" She smiled.

For the first three days, they never left the room. Stone Pier had explored her body like he was trying to test his memory. Theola laid back and allowed him to handle her his way, enjoying every bit of his careful inspection.

The first seventy-two hours of their reunion consisted of food, hot steamy sex on every piece of furniture in the room, and on the patio, along with body rubs and even more sex. Theola had truly found heaven on earth, she was convinced.

Now on the fourth day, after they'd returned from breakfast, Theola and Stone Pier sat on the bed talking with words for a change.

"I've thought of you every moment you were away," he said sincerely. Her hand was nestled between his. He moved it to his lips and placed a delicate kiss there.

"You're always on my mind, too," Theola said.

At that instant, Theola wondered why she ever decided to go back to Houston. No one there cared about her. Her church family did very little to practice the Christian ways they preached about, and she really had no true family to speak of. And despite Damien technically being her stepson, Theola had tried to be there for Michelle with the divorce. But it seemed like Michelle ignored every attempt she made at reaching out to her, and Ethan's kids didn't respect her one bit, so why should she even bother going back to Houston?

"I wish you could just stay here," Stone Pier said sadly.

He was all she needed to keep the tongues wagging at Sweetwater. Theola stood, smiled at him, and chuckled to herself about his comment.

Chapter 20

A hint of a smile touched Michelle's lips. She was giddy for no damn reason. Or at least none she could tell anybody else about. Michelle could hardly believe how lucky she was. It had been a little more than a month since she discovered the impossible. Raymond had single-handedly restored her faith in men. But she was convinced she had found the second coming and had been floating on cloud nine ever since she discovered the possibilities of Raymond's magnificent tongue.

But the wonders of his tongue had nothing to do with what was causing ripples of pleasure to flood through her body in time released waves. She used the back of her hand to wipe sweat from her forehead.

They were at it again. By now, Michelle was already hooked on the fantablous sex.

"You oughta be with me," Raymond's sweet succulent lips moaned in her ear. She buckled at the sensation, arched her back, released a cry and wiggled against his movement. The sound of her voice, slow and passionate only fueled his mission.

He groaned as she pulled him closer and deeper and deeper. She was completely caught up in the rapture and couldn't think of a single thing that could compare to the sheer bliss she was experiencing.

She'd inhale, close her eyes and release that deep guttural groan that had been trapped in her throat. Michelle rotated her hips, grinding down on him in slow motion.

"Ooooohhhh weeeee," she oozed, slapping the sides of his head in an attempt to grab a hold and keep him in place.

Raymond clamped his own rugged hands down on her hips, pulling her into him. As he painstakingly moved with such precision, he was sure she'd be back for more.

They had been hold-up inside the small bathroom, which now doubled as their love nest. The toilet had been rocking since the moment he sat down and had her straddle him. Michelle rode him like she wasn't sure when she'd have another opportunity. She had to try and make the best of this ride.

Their coupling had always been so fiercely intense, they'd tear at each other, kiss, suck, and bite, trying to take more than enough to last until the next time.

"Jesus, Raymond! You hittin' my spot. You hittin' my spot! Right there, baby," she cried and shuddered as waves of pleasure washed over her.

"You like that?" he breathed before smothering his face into her breasts.

Raymond pulled back and saw one of her stiffened nipples, screaming out to be touched. He caught it between his lips and suckled it. Michelle swore she had discovered a higher calling. She pulled her head back to see his eyes fluttering. His mouth was agape, and he was in a world all his own. She just hung on for the ride.

"Good . . . real good," he groaned incoherently and palmed her breast, squeezing it so hard she winced from the pain then smiled at the surge of pleasure she was now experiencing.

When they were apart, all she could think about was him easing the fire that burned so deep inside of her.

It was their third time this week alone, and she was beside herself. She couldn't imagine how something this good could be caged up. But then it dawned on her, maybe this was a good thing. At least she didn't have to worry about whether he'd be dipping into anybody else's honey pot.

"Oh God!" she cried, screaming a bit louder than she intended. When he exploded, she was on fire, right at the edge of ecstasy.

She shook her head, trying to get rid of the pounding sound that was ringing in her ear.

"Ooh, God!" Michelle cried.

"Ssshhh." When Raymond's hand cupped her mouth, she realized for the first time the knocking sound was not in her head but at the door.

"Who's in there?" a voice called out.

Michelle looked at Raymond, her wide eyes as they filled with horror and tears. She jumped when the knock boomed at the door again.

"I said, who's in there?"

Michelle's heart dropped to her feet. They'd been caught.

Chapter 21

Having a woman squatting on his face and wiggling her hips was nothing new to Damien. But having a three hundred pound woman on his face, doing her thing while her best friend rode him backward on the podium inside his daddy's church was definitely a first for him. And words couldn't begin to express the sheer joy he felt.

The freak show between Damien, Charlotte, and Samantha was getting steamier by the second. He already knew Charlotte was talented between the sheets, and her friend was working it as if she was trying to compete.

Damien shoved his tongue into Samantha like her flesh was dripping sweet syrup. He used his fingers to poke at her walls and his tongue to launch a sweet assault against her panic button. Meanwhile, Charlotte tilted her body to the side, grabbed his ankle and rode him relentlessly. These girls moved better than any skinny woman he'd ever experienced, and he was quickly becoming hooked.

"Sssss, yes . . . yes," Charlotte moaned.

The feeling that nearly swallowed Damien was unexplainable. He had no idea why he hadn't done this before now. The sound of skins smacking and slopping together echoed through the sanctuary, bouncing off the walls and vaulted ceiling. There was just enough light in the semi-darkness for him to make out the sex-induced expressions on his lovers faces.

"Oh, Daamien," Samantha cried. But when she clamped her thighs around his head, he wasn't sure if he'd be able to make it out from under her alive. The action was thrilling nonetheless.

The girls switched positions and Damien was just fine with that. Just when Damien was about to hit the grand finale, a bright light flashed on them. He had to flinch to make sure he wasn't being called home. The voice that roared at them assured him he wasn't.

"What the he—" a voice yelled.

Another light shown down on them out of nowhere, and it took Damien a minute to realize just what was going on.

Charlotte was first to tumble off of him, shuffling to grab clothes in a haphazard attempt at covering herself. Samantha sat frozen with the deer-in-the-headlights expression plastered on her face. She couldn't even think much less move.

"Mister . . . ah, I mean, Deacon . . . Goodlove? Is that you?"

Damien couldn't see a damn thing. He wanted them to turn off those flashlights so he could try to readjust his vision.

"Who—" Damien started to fume. "Turn off that fuckin' light," he snapped.

One light flicked off. That's when he noticed the two security guards.

"I think you guys need to get decent," the female guard snickered.

"I can explain," Samantha stuttered. She finally moved to cover her body.

"Explain?" Damien spat. He stood up, picking up his clothes, and slipped on his boxers. "You ain't got to explain a damn thing," he barked. But he was not the least bit shame-faced. As a matter of fact, he was pissed by the disruption.

"What the hell are you guys doing in here?" Damien snarled.

"I think we should be asking the questions here" the female guard stated. "How dare you commit such blasphemy, and in the Lord's house! While your father... umph, umph, umph, may God have mercy on his soul!" She gagged like she was sure to puke.

"Blasphemy?" Damien screamed. He moved closer to her. "You don't even know what the word means. How dare *you* talk to me like that," he hissed as he hovered over her as he quickly tried to pull up his pants.

That's when the other guard stepped up.

"Mister . . . um, I mean, Deacon Goodlove, look. I, too, have indulged in the sins of the flesh." He cut his eyes over to Charlotte and Samantha who were huddled in a nearby corner. "I must say, never to the extent of this, but all we're trying to say is we need you to get a room. I mean, isn't anything sacred anymore?" He shook his head in disgust.

Damien looked at him with pure evil eyes. "Why don't the two of you rent-a-cops give us some privacy." He snarled.

"That's where this becomes a problem," the male guard said. He scratched the side of his head. "Unfortunately, we can't just leave so the three of you can keep this going. As a matter of fact, we're gonna have to issue you a ticket. You're trespassing," he insisted.

The frown that appeared on Damien's face was as good as a lethal threat. "Trespassing? A ticket?" He scowled. Damien shook his head. "Do you know who the hell I am? My daddy owns this damn church," he snapped as if he'd been vindicated in anointed oil.

The female guard had already started pulling out her ticket pad. "You see, when you referred to us as rent-a-cops, I think that's what you called us. Well, you were wrong. Not as wrong as you are for the sins you're committing here in the Lord's house, but still wrong nonetheless. We're actually off duty HPD officers, and no, the church belongs to the members of this congregation, not your daddy! If I were you, I'd take this ticket, put on my clothes and scurry on out of here with your two friends over there," she warned.

But before she could start scribbling with her pen, Damien's hand swung and knocked the thing to the floor. "I don't give a damn who you are . . ." he began.

The other guard wasn't sure what Damien was doing. When he saw the quick movement, it was like his reflections kicked in. He rushed between Damien and his partner. In that attempt, he inadvertently pushed Damien into the female guard, who as a result, bumped into the podium and the three of them tumbled to the floor.

A scuffle quickly ensued. Charlotte, who was right out of ear's shot, noticed what was going on and rushed over to Damien's aid. Soon, the four of them were tumbling around on the floor.

"Officer down! Officer down! We need back up!" the female guard yelled into her radio.

Chapter 22

Theola and Stone Pier enjoyed a stroll along the beach. The aqua-green water had such a calming effect on her, she was already trying to think of ways to make a home for herself in breezy Belize.

"I was so glad to see you," Stone Pier said, taking her hand into his. "And you came back, just like you promised."

As the water splashed at their ankles, and the sun beamed overhead, a light breeze hugged their bodies. Theola was certain this was true paradise.

"I know . . . I know. You would not believe my life back in the States." Theola shook her head. "I'm so lonely there. I have no one. No one who cares about me. That's for sure," she continued.

"Well, why do you stay?" Stone Pier stopped walking and turned to face her. "I mean, look at this place. Look at the beauty here. Why would you want to go anyplace else? Every-thing you need is right here at your fingertips. And me," he pointed at his bare, glistening chest, "I'm here, and I care about you," he insisted.

"Ooooh, you're so sweet," Theola cooed.

"No, I'm serious. You should take me seriously," Stone Pier insisted.

Theola reached up and took his head into her hands. She placed a kiss on his lips. "Oh, baby, I know you are, but it's not quite that simple. Me just moving . . . I can't really. I have responsibilities in the States. I'm um, well I guess you can say I'm a somewhat important person over there," she admitted modestly.

"You are important here," Stone Pier challenged. "To me," he added with a pout so sexy, Theola wanted to ravish him right there on the water's shore.

"I know, babe, I know. And you're important to me, too, but you know what I mean," she smiled and waited for him to do the same. After a few minutes, he did and they continued their stroll.

"I say we enjoy lunch in some of the common areas. I didn't even leave the room last time I was here," Theola mentioned.

"But was it not the best vacation of your life?" Stone Pier wanted to know.

"Hands down!" Theola testified.

She pulled him by the arm and started running toward the main building of the resort. People frolicked near the massive, sparkling, freshwater pool. It was outfitted with a swim-up bar and a grand view of the Caribbean Sea just at the pool's edge.

"I'll go get drinks. You get us a seat under the blue umbrellas," Stone Pier said to Theola.

"What's wrong with the red umbrellas?" she queried.

"Nothing's wrong, but when the sun shifts, if you're over there, you won't get any shade," Stone Pier informed her.

She smiled at him and rushed over to the rows of blue umbrellas. Beach towels were already stacked on the small tables that sat between the chairs. The small intimate couples only resort was nestled amongst six lushly landscaped acres right on the water's edge.

Theola eased back in the chair and closed her eyes. She had already started drifting off to a peaceful sleep only to have the noise from Stone Pier's sandals clanking against the wooded boardwalk snatch her from serenity.

"Here you are—a cool tropical drink. I think you'll enjoy it," he smiled and eased onto the patio chair next to hers.

"Emmmm, this really is paradise. It's so calm and serene here." She took a dramatic deep breath, holding the fresh air in her lungs before releasing it. She reached over and took a sip from her drink. Theola closed her eyes and savored the taste, willing it like her vacation, to last forever.

"The air agrees with your skin. You're glowing," Stone Pier commented.

Theola opened her eyes and grinned at him. Her soreness had subsided, and once again, she felt herself wanting his touch, wanting to feel him buried deep inside of her.

"Are you tired?" Stone Pier asked, wearing a worried look on his own face.

"No, no, I wouldn't say tired. I'm just trying to relax, that's all," Theola looked around at the three or four other couples scattered around the resort. "Where is everyone?" she asked.

"You won't see massive crowds here. It's why people come. How do you say . . . discreet—"

"Discretion?" Theola asked, then wondered what the likelihood of her running into anyone she'd know.

She shook the thought from her head and sipped from the massive drink Stone Pier had brought. She felt so free in this beautiful country. Even if she ran into one of the holy rollers, she daydreamed about how she'd treat them in front of Stone Pier. She knew one thing for certain, she wouldn't take shit from any of them, not the way she did back in the States.

"Would you like a back rub?"

Her eyes lit up. "Would I ever deny you access to me?" she asked.

Stone Pier frowned a bit, as if he didn't understand. At times she forgot that his English wasn't exactly perfect. She nodded her answer and quickly flipped onto her belly so he could work his magic.

When he unclasped her bikini top then untied it from the neck, she jumped up and her breasts dangled freely. She pulled a hand up to shield herself.

"What are you doing?" she looked around the resort, nervously.

"I was giving you a back rub," he said, looking confused. "Was it not good? Pleasurable?" he looked at his hands as if they'd failed him.

"No, I mean, you were taking off my top," Theola looked around again. "You want everyone to see me?"

Stone Pier looked at her and chuckled. "We're at a clothing optional resort," he said. "You didn't know?"

As if being let in on a secret, she glanced around and saw a couple of women in thong bathing suits, but still that didn't mean she was ready to let it all hang out.

"Really?" she asked, frowning.

"Yes. No one will complain if you reveal a little more skin. No worries here in Belize. You are free to be free in our country—no laws against nudity here." He smiled.

"Yeah, but still." She winced.

"If you wish to keep it on, no problem." He bowed his head. "Whatever makes you happy," he acquiesced.

Theola eased back onto the lawn chair. She didn't make him retie her swim suit top, but she didn't resist when he pulled her bottoms over her hips and onto her thighs either.

"Would you like to go dancing tonight?" Stone Pier asked. "Each night they have a party at the club here. I think you would enjoy it."

"Really? I had no idea," she said.

"We'll go tonight," he said. "You'll have a good time. I'll see to it."

The resort transformed the water's edge to an outdoor style restaurant with a massive bonfire in the center of tables and chairs.

Theola could hardly believe all she'd missed out on the first time she visited. She and Stone Pier feasted on the freshest seafood she'd ever eaten. Everything was complimented by red beans and rice and fried plantains.

Before they finished dinner, the DJ had started preparing for the party. She marveled at how much was actually going on around her.

After dinner, they slipped back into her room so she could change. Stone Pier added a wife beater to his shorts and sandals. Theola used a sleeveless terrycloth mini-dress as her outfit, threw on a pair of wedged sandals, and they left for a night out—their first since she'd been a guest at the resort.

The moment they arrived at the edge of the cabana rows, soca music drifted in the air. Theola liked the music so much, it kept her energy level high. "Is this Soca music something like Salsa music?" she asked. "I love it!" she exclaimed.

He chuckled. "Something like that, but with more of a Caribbean twist. It's a dance music, which is claimed to have originated in Trinidad from Calypso," Stone Pier answered.

Whatever it was or wherever it originated, its pounding sound sent chills up her spine and made her want to shake her hips.

They walked into an open space at the end of the boardwalk. There were now several large speakers positioned atop the deck's cover. Theola watched as half-naked sweaty bodies gyrated on the wooden dance floor. She eased closer to the two large industrial-sized fans that were positioned near the seafront. Theola liked the way the water's cool breeze blanketed them.

"I love this place!" Theola screamed. She had no idea there were this many people even at the resort. She tugged on Stone Pier's arm. "Do all these people stay here?" she asked.

Stone Pier shook his head. "No. They're allowed to come at night and party—mostly invited guests of the owners or friends of VIPs who've been coming here for years."

Theola shook her head. She knew all these people could not have been staying at the resort. They'd been secluded, but not that secluded. "What's back there?" She motioned toward the three offices toward the back of the massive room.

"Oh, that's Binky's office," Stone Pier said. When confusion spread across her face, he quickly said, "Brian."

"Oh," Theola said. She sipped from her drink and moved her hips to the fast-paced music.

Nearly two hours after dancing and partying, Theola and Stone Pier stumbled back to her cabana.

When she unlocked her door, she nearly died at the sight she saw before her. Not only had the bed been tossed, dresser drawers overturned, and clothes and other belongings strewn across the room, but someone was still in her bathroom.

She went cold.

"OhmyGod, Stone Pier . . ." she whispered. When two men walked out of the small bathroom, Theola fainted.

Chapter 23

Michelle's head pounded hard and her heart raced. What to do? What to do? She looked at Raymond who had eased himself up and placed a warning finger over his mouth.

He reached over and turned the faucet on, "Sssshhh," he whispered then kissed her lips. "Just calm down. If we need to, we can just say I took you hostage." His eyes pleaded with hers for cooperation.

Wide-eyed fear stared back at him. Michelle began to tremble. A tear slid down her cheek. If they had to go that route, it could mean big trouble, if not more time on his sentence. She shook her head.

"No!" She wept quietly.

They were caught and she didn't know what to do.

BOOM! BOOM! BOOM!

She jumped when the knocks began at the door again.

"I know someone's in there, now open up," the now angry voice demanded.

"Just open it," Raymond quietly begged. "I'll get behind the door, trust me," he whispered. "I'll be okay."

Michelle started sobbing softly now. Finally, Raymond positioned himself behind the door. She took a deep breath, turned off the water then slowly pulled the door open.

"Is everything okay in there?"

Michelle looked at the guard with worried eyes. He had one hand on his radio. She was petrified. More tears tumbled from her eyes, she didn't even attempt to stop them.

"Um, yes. I'm so sorry," Michelle sobbed. She was glad the tears had come when they did. "I'm not feeling too well. I was throwing up. Is someone looking for me?" she asked now blinking back her tears.

Raymond was hunched down behind the door. He was trying to place the guard's voice, but couldn't.

"Well, I thought I heard moaning in there," the guard said. He tried to look beyond Michelle. When she noticed what he was trying to do, she moved her body from the door allowing it to open wider.

The reflection in the mirror behind her showed there was no one there, so he looked down the hall in both directions and said, "Well, you might want to keep it down a bit. Besides, I don't think it's a good idea for you to be walking around here by yourself. You are in a prison, remember?" he warned her.

"I just need to pull myself together," Michelle offered. "I'll be out soon."

The guard's eyes wandered the length of her body. He looked back at the mirror again before pulling on his radio and speaking into it.

"I found her . . . must be on the rag or something, but she's good," he said and turned to leave.

Michelle rolled her eyes and watched him walk down the hall until he turned a corner. She couldn't stand when men assumed all female problems were related to PMS. After a few minutes, when she thought he was gone for good, she closed the door and turned to Raymond.

He stood, and she fell into his embrace. Raymond wrapped his arms around her, squeezing tightly. When her shoulders convulsed against his chest, he squeezed her tighter.

"Aw, baby, it's okay," he tried to console.

Michelle pulled back to look up at him. "No, it's not. How are you gonna get out of here?"

"Oh, girl, I don't want you worrying about that. I'll be fine. Trust me. I know this place like the back of my hand. As a matter of fact, I'm gonna duck out now, and I'll see you tomorrow, okay?"

"But what if he's still lurking around?" she asked.

"No," Raymond shook his head. "Don't worry about it. Trust me, these guards aren't running around here looking for trouble. Trouble means more work for them, and they damn sure don't want that. So look, I'm 'bout to bounce up outta here, and I'll see you in the last session tomorrow."

Michelle didn't know what to do. When Raymond reached over to kiss her lips, she didn't want to let him go, but she knew she had to.

A while after he left, she made her move. "Better late than never," she said to herself, slipped out of the bathroom and shut the door.

By the time Michelle arrived, the last session was just about over. Pastor Peebles looked up from the Bible he was reading aloud and made eye contact with her.

"Class, I need a minute," he said. He closed his Bible and walked to the back of the room to where she stood.

"Are you okay?" he whispered. "I asked the guards to check on you, make sure everything was okay."

"Oh, I'm so sorry. I'm just not feeling well. I didn't want to puke all over myself in here. I hope you didn't need me," she said.

"I was just making sure you were okay, didn't lose your way back. This place can be confusing until you learn your way around," the Pastor added, "especially if you wander over to the main lock-up, which I don't recommend"

As he spoke, Michelle couldn't help but relive the moment Raymond made her body shiver with tantalizing little earthquakes. Now that they had made it out okay, she was relieved, but just as hungry for more of him.

For the first time in the six weeks that she'd been there, she was excited, and actually looking forward to going back to jail the next day.

Chapter 24

Once again Damien woke inside the frilly room and didn't feel an ounce of alarm. He marveled at how comfortable he had become in Charlotte's space and how quickly it had happened.

He looked down at her sleeping body then thought back to all they'd been through in their short time together. Instantly, his mind took him back to the arrest, his time in jail.

Damien couldn't believe he was sitting up in a holding cell at the Harris County jail like some common criminal. He had called Barry the moment he was given the green light to place his one phone call. But still, he was vexed. He'd have both the police officers' jobs if he had to die getting them. How the hell is *he*, of all people, going to be arrested in his own daddy's church? Didn't they realize who *he* was? It was just crazy thinking about it.

Six hours after making the call, he was being processed and released. But that didn't ease the fury he felt inside. When he had the bail bondsman Barry brought to inquire about

Charlotte and Samantha, he was informed that they had been released three hours earlier.

"What exactly happened?" Barry asked as he slid behind the wheel.

"Man, this shit is wild."

"Yeah, but why were you arrested for trespassing and resisting arrest?"

"Okay, what had happened was, this chick I was seeing and her friend wanted to get an up-close look at the church. You know, wanted to see what it was like to be in the pulpit, that kind of thing. All of a sudden, security comes, starts tripping, and next thing you know, we're all tumbling around on the floor." Damien shrugged his shoulders. "It was just one big ol' misunderstanding," he insisted.

"Didn't you tell them who you were? I mean, how could you be trespassing? You're like nearly the owner of the church," Barry said.

"You know how it is when you pull somebody's card and they feel a little like they got punked. I don't know why the guards started tripping. Before I knew it, they called for backup, and one thing led to another."

Barry shook his head. "Man, it's like everything is falling apart since the G-man has been in this coma. I just want him to wake up." He pressed.

"I guess I haven't really been doing the best job of stepping up, huh?"

"It's not just that. I mean, we haven't heard a word from Reggie, all this stuff with this stupid wedding, you and Michelle, and what's up with your stepmother?" Barry chuckled.

"That tramp ain't my step nothing!" Damien growled.

"Seriously though. What? Does she just visit once a week or something? I went by the house and talked with the staff there. They say she goes away like every other week for about a week, then comes back in time for church. They can't reach her, and she doesn't bother calling them."

"She's the last thing on my mind. I mean, I got my own issues. Whatever she's doing, I just want her to stay out of the way."

"Man, you see what she wore to church the last time she showed up?" Barry turned to his brother. "What the heck was she thinking?"

"That's *your* stepmother," Damien laughed, remembering the dress Theola strolled in wearing. He also remembered the warm embarrassment he felt when he realized the other deacons were staring at her.

"Nah, man. That's all you." He laughed. "Seriously though. You think we'll ever see Reggie again?"

Damien shrugged his shoulders. "You know what? I really don't even care," he said.

"What?" Barry balked. "How could you say something like that, man? About your brother?"

"Man, he was always a weirdo. I mean think about it. He acted like he didn't like us when he was around." Damien shook his head. "I don't miss anybody who don't want to be around."

"Well, it's kind of sad if you ask me. I mean, he don't even know the G-man is in a coma." Barry shook his head again. "Where you headed?"

"What do you mean?" Damien answered.

"You coming to my place, or you hooking up with one of your mystery friends?"

Just then, Damien's cell phone began to ring. "Hold up a sec." A smile curled at his lips when he looked down and noticed Charlotte's number on the screen.

"Hey you," he said in a voice lower than the one he just used to talk with his brother.

"I'm so glad you're out. I still can't believe we got arrested. This is so wild," Charlotte said.

"I'm sorry about this mess. I'm gonna take care of it," he promised sweetly.

"No, it's me who should be apologizing. I should've never got involved. But when I saw what looked like them jumping on you, I just . . . I don't know. I had to help."

"It's okay, baby, you did the right thing. I'll talk to the lawyers and see what they have to say about this mess. And don't worry about it."

"Okay."

There was silence between the two. When suddenly, Damien asked, "What are you doing this evening anyway?"

"You, if you'll let me," Charlotte said.

Damien giggled like a girl then caught himself once his brother shot him a knowing glance.

"Um, okay. I'm about to get some clothes from my brother's house, and I'll be by later. Cool?"

"I'll be waiting," Charlotte cooed.

Chapter 25

When Theola finally came to, she felt like her near-perfect dream vacation had turned to nothing short of a horrific nightmare. She rubbed her eyes and struggled to remember what was going on. Theola shook her head, trying to change things, but that didn't work.

"W-w-what happened?" She eased up from the bed, glancing around the room with a quizzical look.

Stone Pier stood at the left side of her bed. But it might as well have been a ghost on the other side of her. The sight of him now made her jump. She couldn't believe *he* of all people was standing there. No one had seen nor heard from *him* in at least a year. Now he stood over her? But how? She was bewildered.

"How the hell did you even find me?" she snarled, wrinkling up her nose. "What are you even doing here? How'd you know I'd be here?"

"I don't think you're in a position to be asking any damn questions," he answered with narrowing eyes. He had always looked down on her as if he had the right to stand on some higher moral ground.

Theola rolled her eyes at him then turned her attention back to Stone Pier. "Um, I need to . . . there are some things I haven't told you about myself," she stuttered.

At first Stone Pier stepped a bit closer, but suddenly his stare looked to the opposite side of her bed, and he reluctantly pulled back a bit. When he did, Theola snapped her head to her left.

"What do you even want?" she hissed. "Who told you I was even here?"

"I need you to shut the hell up! Like I said: I'm the one asking the questions here."

Reginald Goodlove had all but vanished more than a year ago, wiping out a substantial amount of money from one of the church's bank accounts.

Looking at him now, Theola instantly revisited the night her husband came sulking home. He had just barely regained the confidence of his congregation and should've been rejoicing. But instead, he acted as if he had been plummeted with a ton of bricks.

He had looked up about to say something to Theola, but then shook it off and lowered his head.

"What's wrong, daddy," Theola had asked her husband that evening in his study.

He was sitting there, his face buried in the palms of his hands, and a drink sat nearby. His shoulders convulsed as he released a huge sigh. At first, Pastor Goodlove didn't even acknowledge her presence, much less her question. But eventually he did look up and answered her question.

"It's Reginald. He's gone," Pastor Goodlove said, now removing his hands from his sunken face. "And so is more than a quarter of a million dollars from the church's general funds account."

"What?" Theola shrieked. Her eyes became saucers, and she stumbled back onto a nearby wing chair. "So, he stole from you?" she asked in bewilderment.

"He stole from the church!" Pastor Goodlove screamed. He shook as he spoke. "The bastard stole from the church, and that's like stealing from God!"

She allowed his words to linger in the air. When they had realized his middle son had been cooking the books all along, the gravity of Reginald's betrayal was so sickening; Theola thought she'd noticed her husband aging right before her eyes.

"So this is gonna be something else for Mama Sadie and the holy rollers to attack you about, huh?"

"I'm not as worried about her and her crew. I think I've taken care of them for the time being. But this is not gonna fare well with the parishioners." Pastor Goodlove shook his head.

"How are you gonna find him?" Theola asked.

"I've got someone on it, we'll find his ass, and God help him when we do," Pastor Goodlove had vowed.

When Stone Pier dropped her hand, it snapped her back into the current situation.

"I know what you did," she hissed at her stepson, a man older than her.

Reginald was wearing a sinister smile. He shook his head at her. "I've done nothing wrong. But you, on the other hand, I know exactly what you've been up to here in paradise and tisk, tisk, tisk, Theola." He abolished her with a shaking index finger. "I think the old man would be more interested in what you're using his money for than me. Not to mention just what you've been doing over here in your little slice of paradise. You wanna bet on who's in the most trouble here?" Reginald said, as he looked over at Stone Pier then back at Theola. He shook his head as if he were disgusted by them and what they'd obviously been doing. Reginald even behaved as if he was put out that he was being questioned.

The smirk on his face never wavered. Theola couldn't believe this. Then it suddenly hit her! She looked at Stone Pier then back at Reginald. Had Stone Pier been a part of this plan all along? A mortifying shiver shot up her spine, and she felt her blood begin to boil.

Could this have been a setup from the very beginning? She swallowed back the bile that was building up in her throat. How could she not have known? She glared at her paradise lover then back at her stepson and began to seethe.

Chapter 26

When an inmate slipped her the note, she had a look of sheer confusion across her face. The number of inmates attending the Bible sessions had started to taper off a bit. She figured word must've spread that she was spoken for, so to speak.

Michelle was bored and longed for the days when the place was crawling with men. She opened the note and had to reread the words. I'M IN THE LIBRARY, NEAR THE LAW BOOKS. HURRY AND COME. A small R was scribbled at the end of the note. Michelle's heart stuttered. A smile stretched itself across her face as her eyes glazed over the brief note.

She looked around the room and noticed Pastor Pebbles was still reading from the Bible. She tried to summons him with her eyes, but the little man wouldn't look up.

Michelle didn't like to cause a disruption, but she had no idea how long Raymond would be in the library, and she didn't want to waste a moment's time. She pulled herself up from her chair and made a quick dash to the front of the room. She stood a good minute before Pastor Peebles even looked up at her.

"Oh, is everything okay?" he asked, his voice laced with concern.

"Yes, everything is fine. But I was thinking since we've got such a small group here in this session, maybe I could spend some time in the library?" she told, more than asked him.

Pastor Peebles looked around the room as if to verify what she had said. He brought his gaze back to her and shook his head. "I think that's a fabulous idea. Things have quieted a bit around here, so I can imagine you're probably bored." He shook his head. "That would be fine, Mrs. Goodlove. I just ask that you check back in at the beginning of the last session. Who knows? Things may pick up." He smiled.

Michelle doubted they'd see the kind of crowds they saw when word had spread around the prison that new meat had arrived. Now it was as if she wore a label saying she was off limits, reserved only for Raymond. She didn't mind either. As she shuffled her way across the courtyard, she avoided eye contact with any of the guards. Being too friendly with them might make things hard for her and Raymond, and she couldn't run the risk of that.

The prison library was nothing more than a bedroom-sized space with two massive floor-to-ceiling bookshelves dividing the room into three separate sections. As soon as she walked in, she was stunned to see Raymond behind the desk.

"Oh, hi," she managed. "Your note said you'd be near the law books."

Raymond waved his arm behind him, and that's when Michelle noticed the neat rows of books. She couldn't hide the disappointment on her face when images of what she thought they'd be able to do in a dark corner raced from her mind.

"I'm glad you could come," Raymond told her. There were two rows with two desks and chair combinations lined up in front of each side of the massive book shelves.

"It's not much in here, but this is where we come to do research or try to escape to other worlds," he joked.

"So, you have to stay behind this desk?" she asked, finally looking around the room. Two older white men had their heads buried in massive books on opposite sides of the room.

"Not always, but for the most part this is my job, so I kinda gotta keep an eye on things," Raymond said, hoping his revelation didn't turn her completely off.

"Oh, I didn't know you had a job. I mean, how were you able to attend all of the sessions the way you did?"

"Someone owed me a favor, and that's how I collected," he answered truthfully.

"And they don't mind? The guards, I mean," she clarified.

Raymond leaned into her as much as he could over the counter that separated them. "I told you: These guards really don't give a shit what we do as long as we keep the trouble down. Besides, I'm cool with most of 'em anyway."

Michelle felt awkward just standing there. She looked around at the two other inmates who hadn't peeled their heads away from the books.

"What should I do?" she asked Raymond.

"Just talk to me. I mean, I know we don't usually talk using words, but I thought we could get to know each other better. I ain't never been married, and never want to if a wife is anything like my crazy ass baby mama! She's off the chain! And she got this skanky friend, Jewels, who be all up in our business. My boy is seven. I know you married. Y'all got any kids? And besides that, what brings a fine-ass educated woman like you up in here anyway?" His eyes rolled up and down her body.

"Usually we only get the junkies and occasionally we'll get some check fraud broads, but they're into the Iranian brothers, so it's like only the junkies are free game, and who wants that shit?"

Michelle didn't like the way he classified women into categories the inmates picked and chose over sampling. She also didn't like the fact that he had a baby mama because she was in no mood for drama. And she knew, where there was a baby mama, drama wasn't too far behind. But still, a part of her was glad Raymond was essentially saying she was the crème of the crop, sort of.

"We have two girls—eight and six—and well, let's just say I got tired of my husband using me and making a fool of me. One day, I simply snapped and laced his food with rat poison," she admitted easily.

Raymond flinched. "Damn! That's cold," Raymond said before he could catch himself. "I mean, like that?" He frowned.

"You don't know what he put me through," she stated, ready to defend her actions. Back in her dating days, Michelle had a strict rule against talking about her exes to a new prospect. But something about Raymond made her want to open up. "We belong to this church in Sugar Land, Sweetwater PG, and well, my husband, soon-to-be ex, is a deacon there. His daddy owns the church, and he just used his position to run through every new piece of flesh that came his way," she reported.

Raymond's eyes were wide. "What? Like a man of the cloth?" he chuckled.

Michelle shook her head. "Well, he's something like that, but what he did, it was just so embarrassing. Here he is, basically in line for the pulpit at one of Houston's most successful houses of worship, and he was nothing but a filthy dog!"

"So, what did you do? I mean, how long had he been dogging you?" Raymond asked.

Michelle told Raymond the entire torrid story. She began with the first time rumors had started to fly around Sweetwater and brought him up to date with the arrival of Jazzlyn.

"She was already known for her whorish ways at another church. It's why she left there and came to ours," Michelle said.

"And lemme guess: Your boy wasted no time in hittin' it?"

"I heard he and the rest of those nasty-ass deacons even had a bet going to see who could run up in the tramp the fastest. Well, you know my dog was already barking up that tree."

"Ol' boy was out of order for real," Raymond agreed.

"I can't believe he had other women wearing your panties and shit. Now that's real foul."

Michelle shook her head at the memories that wasted no time creeping back up as if they were as fresh as yesterday's news. She started feeling heated.

"But the very last straw was when my doctor's office called to say I had been infected with HIV." The words fell from her mouth without much thought.

When she noticed the deer-in-headlights stare she got from Raymond, she rushed to clean it up. "Oh, it was a mistake, but at the time I didn't know it," she offered.

"A mistake?" Raymond cringed. In that split second his own heart had nearly stopped. They hadn't had time to find a condom. In their rushed passion, he had no choice.

Raymond remembered the moment he felt her warm flesh, and he vowed to do whatever he could to experience that feeling over and over again. Could it have been his impeding downfall?

"I don't have HIV," Michelle clarified, but still, she noticed the shifty expression still on his face. "It was all a mistake. My doctor's office had made a mistake because of the health department's lab results," she explained.

"Wait. You know what? I read about something like that in the paper about a month ago . . ." Raymond's voice trailed off.

Michelle's expertly arched brow heightened on her face.

It seemed as if Raymond's mind had been stuck in one place because he came back with, "But that article said those people were supposed to get like millions because of that mistake," he murmured slowly.

Chapter 27

Damien couldn't completely see the patch between Charlotte's plump thighs, but he knew exactly what to expect when he dove between her legs face first. He had attacked her nectar like a famished man presented with a three course meal. When his tongue caught a hold of her swollen button, he held it captive and sucked her unmercifully.

Charlotte had been squirming like a trapped animal the moment he made contact. When she could no longer endure it, she released a strained yelp as if she'd been socked in the gut and fought to push his head away. She simply couldn't take it anymore. Spasms rushed through her body as ripples of pleasure flooded her veins.

"Oh, Damien," she shrieked. "Oh God! Oh God," she added as he continued to work that magic she had grown accustomed to.

He had marveled at just how attached he was becoming. She wasn't his type that night they met. He thought he'd have some fun in his drunken stupor, trying something new for a hot second. But never did he think he, of all people, would or could be happy with a big girl. But Charlotte was not just the best big girl around. He was sure she had to be the best woman he'd ever had. And that was saying a lot.

Once round two wrapped up, Damien lay on his back, struggling to regulate his breathing. She had managed once again to satisfy him like the king he was.

"That was hot," Charlotte exclaimed. She was breathing hard and heavy herself. She loved when Damien put it down with such passion. The man had skills, she thought.

"Yeah, hot it was," Damien added, remembering a few new moves he had used to get the job done for sure. Charlotte was good for his ego and good to him. The thing he liked most about her was her talent between the sheets of course, but also the fact that she did everything to the fullest, with one goal in mind: keeping him happy.

"What do you think is gonna happen with what we did in the church," she asked, seemingly out of nowhere. Damien turned his head and gave her a quizzical look.

"Happen with what we did?" he questioned. "I don't understand."

"Well, you know—the way we were caught up in the church. What's gonna happen?"

"It already did, sweetheart. We were arrested, bonded out, and first thing Monday morning, I'm gonna talk with my lawyer and see about getting the charges dropped."

Charlotte flicked a surprised glance at him. "You mean it? For me and Sam, too?" she asked excitedly.

"You're my girl, aren't you?"

It was as if the world had stopped its spin. Charlotte's stomach did a flip. An unfamiliar feeling rushed through her veins, and she allowed her eyes to openly linger as her mouth sat agape.

"D-d-did you just say I was your girl?" she asked, pointing at her chest and barely believing the words the second time she heard them, despite the fact she was merely repeating what he'd said.

Damien grinned and raised his eyebrows. He thought it was cute the way his comment excited her. He laced his fingers behind his head and looked up dramatically.

"Well, let's see. Do I not spend most of my free time either here with you or someplace else with you?"

"Yeah," Charlotte confirmed.

"And, when I need some lovin' do you not break me off some until I can't muster up any more energy?"

"Ah, you damn straight I do," Charlotte let it be known.

"Okay, well, do we not go out to eat at least once if not twice a week together?" Before she could answer, he tossed in, "And where do I lay my head at least four out of the seven days a week?" He waited for her response.

"All of that is nothing but the God-given truth," Charlotte testified.

"Then I think that makes you my girl," Damien said. "Wouldn't you?"

When Charlotte leaned back so she could snuggle up next him, she was truly outdone. She couldn't remember a time when she'd been happier.

Charlotte raised her head after a few minutes of cuddling. "Is it a secret though?" she wanted to know.

Damien didn't answer right away. He thought carefully before answering this one. "You know what? If you think about it, everyone pretty much knows Michelle and I are getting a divorce, so I don't know if I'd say we have to be a secret. But because I am still married, and I don't wanna be all in her face with us, maybe we should try to be careful. But I mean, the minute Michelle and I work this thing out, you can go to the highest mountain and shout it loudly," he informed her.

Charlotte's eyes lit up. She couldn't believe it. Many women had talked about what they'd do given a chance, a night with the infamous Damien Goodlove. And boy had she taken full advantage of her chance. She had worked her jelly like nobody's business and her efforts had paid off.

"So that means what for now?" she asked.

"Well, for now we just keep chilling like we do, and we keep making each other happy, you give me time to get through this divorce, and it's all good," he said.

"Okay, so um, I mean, why's it taking so long," Charlotte asked uneasily. Since she was his girl, she felt she could ask, but she didn't want to get carried away.

"It's Michelle," Damien lied. "I mean, she knows it's over, but she just doesn't want to let go—like she just doesn't want to see me free." He sighed.

"Are you serious?" she asked, easing herself up on one elbow now.

"Yeah, it's sad, really. The way she keeps trying to hang on. I keep telling her what we had is over—long gone, but some women never want to let go. We're just not good together," he added. Damien liked Charlotte, quite a bit, but he didn't know if he should trust her with news about his expected millions just yet.

Charlotte knew why things were over between Damien and Michelle. She had attended Sweetwater long enough to hear the gossip and rumors. And although she didn't work on any of the ministries or even hang with the in-crowds, good gossip traveled fast, but church gossip seemed to move faster than the speed of light. And even though she knew what he'd been up to, it was still interesting to hear his side of the story.

"I never really understood what you saw in her," Charlotte admitted sheepishly. "She just seemed so," Charlotte shrugged as she searched for the right words, "so not your type."

"What do you mean by that?"

"You're a freak. I know 'cause I'm a freak, too. I picture you with some fun loving chick who loves to have a good time. Not some prude like her," Charlotte said, wrinkling up her nose.

Charlotte and Damien talked into the wee hours of the morning. When he saw the time glowing on the digital clock, he couldn't believe it was after three. She had been so easy to talk to, and he loved the way she hung on his every word, like nothing but importance could ever spew from his lips.

And the way she set his loins ablaze was enough to drive him mad.

"We'd better get some sleep. Gotta get up early for church," he reminded her.

"You're right," Charlotte said. "But all this talk about sex got me feeling . . ." Charlotte cocked a provocative eyebrow and used her little pink tongue to trace the lines of her lips.

Damien couldn't begin to pull his gaze from her mouth. He felt himself go from soft to steel-like in less than sixty seconds flat. Unable to take her sweet torture anymore, he pulled her head into his lap, and Charlotte did what she knew he wanted.

Chapter 28

"If you help me out, I can help you," Reginald had finally said.

"What makes you think I need your help?" A bitter lump lodged in Theola's throat as she looked at Reginald.

"Well, let's see," he began easily. "You've been running through church money like it was water, and I've got proof that shows exactly what you've been doing. I think you may need my help a lot more than you're willing to admit," he answered with his chest stuck outward.

That's when Theola started thinking back to the first time she'd even laid eyes on the brochure. It had been buried between stacks of bills and seemed like such a common sense way to get her mind off Ethan and his condition. Never once did she stop to think she was being set up. But the proof stood right in front of her. Not only had she been set up, but she shuddered to wonder why.

Knowing when she was on the losing end of a battle she never chose, Theola cast her gaze downward and asked, "What do you want?"

"I want to come home," Reginald admitted. "I've been here for over a year, and I'm tired. I want to come home, but I don't want to go to jail for *anything*," he said.

Theola shrugged. "I think that's up to a judge, not me. Where do I fall into this?"

"I don't know why, but the G-man will listen to you. I want you to convince him that it was you who took the money. You blew it, and that way he'd be more likely to forgive me." Reginald had it all planned out.

"And why should I?" Theola asked in defiance.

"Well, I don't know." Reginald looked at Stone Pier. "Maybe because I know what you've been doing here in your little slice of paradise. And, I'm sure all of your fans at Sweetwater would be just as thrilled to learn how their first lady relaxes," Reginald said sweetly.

Theola didn't respond or react right away. Instead, she sat there as if she was contemplating her next move. When Reginald tossed the stack of pictures onto her lap, she cringed.

Images of her and Stone Pier twisted like pretzels on the patio, in the bed, in the ocean, and on the shores, were enough to make her try to repress her scowl. She wouldn't fall apart in front of them. She wouldn't give them the satisfaction. By now, Stone Pier had moved away from the bed. He was outside on the patio smoking a cigarette like he'd rather be anywhere else but there.

"Don't worry. You don't have to decide right away. You can give me your answer when you come back. Ah . . . ." Reginald snapped his fingers. "When are you due back here? Oh, yeah! Next week. I can wait for a week to find out what you're gonna do," he offered sweetly. "Besides, I'm sure you need to get ready for your flight."

Theola continued to flip through the pictures, each one more graphic than the other, but the memories were priceless.

Reginald turned to leave her room with Stone Pier in tow. "Oh, and if you decide to go back to Houston and not come back here, thinking this will just go away, well, let's just say each and every member of Sweetwater will have their own copy of that stack along with an itemized list of your activities here," he warned before leaving. Theola grabbed a crystal vase and flung it toward the door.

She looked at the shattered pieces lying on the floor and vowed not to allow her life to crumble into a similar pile. How could she have been so stupid?

The flight back to Houston was the longest few hours she had ever endured. Reginald had set her up good. She couldn't believe Stone Pier had been part of Reginald's twisted scheme, but the truth had slapped her like a ton of bricks.

Her pretty little Belizean hunk was nothing more than a paid worker doing his job. It was enough to make her stomach churn.

Theola's driver pulled up to Blueridge nearly two hours after her plane landed. She didn't want to go inside, but knew she had to. She figured she'd go through the motions, bypass the staff, and stay in her master suite until she had time to think this thing through. She had come too far to slip back to where she'd risen from. No, that was not an option.

When the alarm clock screamed, Theola was still drunk and stupendous from sleep. She wanted to yank the thing from the wall and toss it out a the window, but she knew she couldn't. She reluctantly pulled herself up from her bed and padded her bare feet into the bathroom. It hadn't been a nightmare. Her problems were all too real, and she still didn't know what the hell she was going to do. Church would be a struggle for her today. She couldn't get her mind off of Reginald and his looming threat.

A knock at her door rubbed her the wrong way, but she figured most things would today.

"What is it?" she snarled.

"Uh, Mrs. Goodlove, just wondering if you're going to church today," one of the housekeepers asked.

What business is it of yours, Theola wanted to say, but instead she answered, "I'm getting ready now."

When her driver pulled up at Sweetwater, Theola needed a minute to prepare and try to shake Reginald's threat from her mind. All morning long, from the shower to the car ride over, she still hadn't been able to come up with a plan.

"I'm gonna need a moment," she informed the driver with a heavy sigh. She really didn't want to go inside the church. She had so many other things she needed to do. First and foremost was trying to figure a way out of this mess. Ethan Goodlove had been the best thing to ever happen to her. There was no way in hell she could afford to lose him and the lifestyle she'd quickly become accustomed to. And that's what Reginald's threat meant to her. Yes, she needed to find a solution, and she needed one fast.

Once she gave him the signal that she was ready to go, the driver walked around and opened her door.

"He's a way maker, a burden bearer. My God is a mighty, mighty God!"

Theola's pulse slowed. Her eyes widened, and she stopped momentarily in her tracks.

How could it be? she wondered as she listened to the voice booming from the outdoor speakers. There was no mistaking who she was listening to. It was her husband's voice.

Was Ethan back? *OHMYGOD!* Theola became nervous and excited all at once. Gone were the thoughts of the problems she had. Gone were ideas that her relationship, her marriage may be in jeopardy.

"The healing is not in the medicine," her husband's voice screamed. His dramatic pause brought back so many memories. As she walked up, the lines were winding nearly around the corner, and people were waiting to get inside. Many of them had their eyes closed and had their arms waving in the air.

"Jesus," she hissed as she tried to see the front door over a mass of people who stood waiting to get inside.

Theola thought about summonsing her driver to tell him to take her to the back entrance, but she, too, was getting swept up in his electrifying sermon.

"I saaaaid, the healing . . . it ain't in the doctor or even the research. Naw! The healing is in *His* touch!"

A thunderous roar blasted through the speakers. "Amen, Pastor! Amen, amen! Preach, preach," parishioners responded zealously.

It *was* her husband. He was back. He had recovered. *Oh, God!* she thought as she frantically fought her way through the crowd. He was finally back.

"Oh, I saaaid . . . My God is a mighty, mighty God! You see: You can ask God for a clean heart . . . because we all know it takes a clean heart to do good," Pastor Goodlove sang.

Theola had finally made her way inside the church. The smile she had been carrying suddenly faded when she realized she had walked into darkness. Once she made her way to the main sanctuary, she realized just what was going on. There before her very eyes stood her husband larger than life.

His image was plastered across the massive projection screens located at the front and back of the sanctuary. Plastered up there, Pastor Goodlove stood at least fifteen feet tall. Through the projection image, Pastor Goodlove shook his hips, bent his legs at the knees and moved his body like a skilled dancer. With his arms flailing, he hopped on one leg much to his congregation's delight.

"You wanna to talk about unspeakable joy?" Pastor Goodlove asked as he winked one eye shut. "It's so good, I can't even talk about it . . . I can't even speak about it. I mean, you've asked God to clean you up, but you need to know something," he said and cupped his ear. "Hello, somebody," Pastor Goodlove screamed toward the congregation.

"What the hell?" Theola said as she stood in the middle of the aisle staring at her husband's larger than life image.

The thunderous call roared through speakers. "Preach, Pastor! Preach!" parishioners screamed enthusiastically.

"When God cleans you up, He's gon' clean you from the inside out. I mean, you'll be good to go! God can wipe your slate clean. He can make it all better. So when you talk about unspeakable joy, the kind of cleansing that only my God can do, you'd better be ready!"

With that, Theola watched as her husband did his famous strut across the stage then rushed off into one of the wings. When he did, the room went completely dark. Everyone around her jumped to their feet and applauded.

Theola looked around, wondering what the hell was going on.

Chapter 29

Damien was glad the tribute went off without a hitch. Ever since word spread around town about how the members of Sweetwater had treated its last two guest preachers, they'd been hard pressed to get anyone to help them out.

It was actually Mama Sadie who came up with the idea to do a tribute to Pastor Goodlove. When she pleaded her case, he started thinking she was on to something.

"I don't know 'bout y'all," Mama Sadie said, wrapping up. "But I miss me some Pastor Goodlove. Can't nobody deliver the Word like our pastor. So I think we oughta do it up big." She waved her frail arms around herself as she spoke.

"We could do press releases, send each member a fancy invitation, and do a phone drive to make sure we have a full house. Who you know wouldn't wanna come back if they knew for sure they could hear one of Pastor Goodlove's good ol-fashioned, tell-it-like-it-is sermons?"

Ms. Geraldine said 'Amen' to that.

"So what are you proposing we do exactly?" Damien had asked.

"We can do a tribute. Give an update about his condition, circulate the visitation list, and continue our goal to make sure at least five visitors stop by every day. Then, we play on the massive wall a taped version of his sermon and end with testimony of how the good Lord has help others through the storm!"

Damien knew it was a good idea, and he liked it.

"Okay, but we need to put a cap on the testimonies. I mean, we could be here all night," Damien chuckled.

Mama Sadie looked at him and nodded slightly. She didn't want a fight, but her mind kept thinking about the rumors flying around about him. She and the other holy rollers had decided not to say a word because they knew how close those boys were to their daddy, and they figured they were losing their minds while he laid up in that coma.

But rest assured, the moment Pastor Goodlove opened his eyes, as God is her witness, she and the rest of the women's auxiliary would get to the bottom of "the incident" as she'd heard it referred to as quickly as possible.

As if his womanizing ways weren't enough, he allowed that ol' nasty Jazzlyn to ruin his marriage, then he still didn't learn! Oh yes, she'd demand Pastor straighten him out promptly before he leads himself and the rest of the Deacons straight to hell with their britches on fire!

Chapter 30

"**G**irl, that was such a good idea. Pastor Goodlove tore up that sermon today," Michelle commented. She was so glad to be back with her friends. Since things had gone downhill with Damien, she tried to avoid other Sweetwater members, fearing they'd side with him somehow, but she should've known better.

"Oh, he did do good today, but did y'all see that ol' Theola," Tammy spat. "You see her running up in there looking all confused, like she had no clue what was going on?"

Michelle placed her glass back on the table. She and her girls were meeting at the bar in Pappadeaux's Seafood Restaurant after service, like the good old days. And just like those days, they were standing there waiting for their other friend, Kim, since the restaurant preferred to seat complete parties only. Moments later, Kim strolled in and they were being led to a table.

"I'm running to the ladies room. Be right back," Kim said as she rushed toward the back of the restaurant. Tammy and Michelle took their seats.

"Girl, don't even tell me you think our first lady didn't know what was going on" Michelle said as she looked around the bustling restaurant. She didn't want Theola to sneak up on them while she was talking about her.

"She ain't none of my first lady," Tammy insisted. "I've said so from day one, and I still mean it today. Besides, she ain't even been by the hospital all week. I just think it's wrong."

"Don't tell me—y'all must be talking about that ol' nasty-ass Theola," Kim snickered as she approached the table. "As usual," she added. She pulled out a chair and joined the conversation like she'd been included from the very first word.

"All I'm saying is think about how many times we called her to talk about the tribute and she never bothered calling back. I mean, it was like the bitch was saying 'to hell with y'all!'"

"Kim, hursh your mouth, cussing like that! Didn't you learn a thing from Pastor's sermon today? Church ain't even been out a good hour yet, girl," Michelle mocked, like the good old days.

She had missed her time with her girls. But she couldn't tell them all that she'd been up to since her community service began. What would she look like admitting that she was risking her own freedom by screwing an inmate? At times, she could hardly believe it herself. She shook the traitorous thoughts from her mind and tuned back into the conversation.

"Well, if you ask me, I still say the heifer had no idea what was going on," Kim said as she looked around the busy restaurant, obviously searching for their waiter.

"Well, I've tried to reach out to her, but we keep missing each other's calls," Michelle admitted. She tried to say very little as it dawned on her that one day, in the not so far future, they might be holding court and talking about her.

"I don't care what anybody says. She had no clue what the hell was going on until the lights flicked on," Kim hollered.

"I can't say. I mean I got there late myself. Besides, it was hard for me to believe that Mama Sadie was the one who spearheaded the tribute," Michelle said. "How are they getting along with Theola anyway?"

"Girl, Theola ain't around until you see her at church. Period. She ain't even been hanging around the hospital. Now you know that's tacky, right?" Tammy leaned in closer.

"Well, you didn't hear it from me, but somebody told me, she runs off to be with her real man and shows up just in time for church. From what I hear, that's why her ass didn't know what was going on with the tribute. She probably thought that was her man in the pulpit until she realized what it was."

"No shit?" Kim asked.

"I don't know. I mean, it ain't like I've been hanging around much myself either." Michelle shook her head.

Kim sipped her drink.

Michelle marveled at the good time she was having with her friends. After she'd been sentenced to her probation, it was her who didn't want to be around them. She felt embarrassed by her punishment. They talked about everyone, so she didn't have to ask whether they would talk about her. And she did admit it was much better to be on this end of the talk instead of the target of those wicked tongues. But deep down, she knew her day was coming.

"Girl, did you hear about Barry and Amy? Now, I don't know if this is true," Tammy continued, "but I heard Barry suddenly decided he didn't want to get married. Now you know damn well her family was planning a big huge shing dig, right?"

"Well, his daddy is connected to a bunch of tubes. What's the big news there?" Kim snickered.

"The big news is when he said he wanted to call things off, at least until his daddy gets better, Ol' Daddy Big Bucks had an intervention. He actually met with Barry and talked with him for something like four hours."

"What?" Tammy balked.

"Can you imagine being forced to marry someone you don't want to marry?" Kim asked with a shake of her head as their waitress approached.

"So you're saying Amy's father, Bishop Blackwell forced Barry to marry his daughter?" Tammy questioned.

Michelle's blood suddenly went cold. Suddenly, she shot up from her seat. Was this déjàvu or what?

Kim tugged on her arm, motioning for her to sit back down. Once seated, Michelle's head cocked to the side. She frowned a bit but the girls had already noticed her stare and followed it.

"Who the hell is that with Damien?" Michelle asked out loud although she didn't mean to. Or at least she didn't mean to make it sound like she was really pressed over seeing him with another woman.

She hated that this restaurant was so close to the church. It was almost like an extension of it. Besides, Michelle wondered why couldn't he take his skanks to another place to eat? She knew he'd say he needed to be close to rush back, but seriously?

Tammy and Kim exchanged awkward glances then quickly turned their heads back to their plates. That's when Michelle knew for certain something was going on, and her two so-called friends hadn't been talking.

"I heard he's turned into a chubby chaser," Tammy snickered as she tried to stuff her mouth with food.

Michelle frowned and looked at Tammy.

"A what?" she asked, frowning, more out of confusion than anything else.

"You know: That's what they call a man who likes big girls. He's been kicking it with her for more than a minute," Tammy confessed sheepishly.

"Yeah, I heard the same thing," Kim offered up reluctantly.

They both gave Michelle a sorrowful glance. It was like the pity was written all over their faces.

"Um, you didn't hear about the tape?" Tammy asked, never bringing her gaze up to meet Michelle's.

"What tape?" Michelle wanted to know as she watched her husband treating the big, oversized woman like she was some kind of queen. A ping of jealousy shot through Michelle momentarily. He rarely pulled out chairs for her when they were together, even in the beginning.

But she shook it off and pulled her gaze back to her friends.

"I said, what tape?" Michelle asked again, using a more firm and stern voice.

"Well, apparently there's a tape of your husband," Kim began, wiggling like she was receiving blissful pleasure from dishing the dirt.

"Soon-to-be ex-husband," Michelle corrected crisply. She could feel the vein at the side of her neck threatening to pop.

"Okay, soon-to-be ex-husband, getting it on with his extra-large girl and her friend inside the main sanctuary," Kim reported with a wicked grin.

Michelle's light eyes turned into saucers. "What?" she asked, disgusted by what she was hearing. *How nasty and utterly disrespectful,* she thought. "Are you trying to tell me that he and his girls were having a threesome in the sanctuary? As in, inside the church?"

"You didn't hear it from me," Kim began, "but word is, it's the security tape. The guards released it to get back at him." She half shrugged. "I don't know how true it is, but I'm just telling you what's going around."

"Girl, I heard it's quite a sight to behold. It's floating around on the Internet now," Tammy added. "Can you imagine? Who would want to be wrapped up between two nasty-ass fat people? Their thighs probably rub together every time they move. Eeeewwww," she shrilled, her body shaking for good measure.

"You shouldn't talk about overweight people like that." Michelle frowned at Tammy's exaggerated reaction, and then pushed her chair back from the table. She wondered why their friendship even meant so much her.

Tammy sucked her teeth but she didn't say anything about Michelle's comment.

The sight of Michelle approaching halted Damien's actions immediately. He held a slice of buttered bread mid-air as Charlotte's mouth hung agape. Not the way she wanted to see her new man's soon-to-be ex-wife.

"You nasty-ass, disgusting bastard. Why won't you sign the freakin' divorce papers?" Michelle spat as her hands flew to her hips.

"Ah, Michelle, this is not the place to have this conversation," Damien stood and tried to block her view of Charlotte.

"You son-of-a-bitch! You don't tell me what the fuck to do. Sign the goddamn papers," she hissed. "Why are you trying to hang on? It's over between us!"

"Let me see my kids," he countered, nonchalantly.

His eyes shifted nervously around the restaurant. He wanted her gone. She wanted him dead. "Don't think I don't know what you're up to with the money. The shit ain't gonna work," he hollered at her. "You need to let me see my kids, and you need to pay up," He yelled with spittle gathered at the corners of his mouth. He had gone from zero to sixty faster than she'd ever seen. His eyes were on fire, and Michelle wondered what she ever saw in him.

"Pay up, hell! Just sign the damn papers you filthy loser," she snickered.

"You know, Michelle," Charlotte interrupted. "I really think you should let us enjoy our brunch, and maybe the two of you could talk about this at another time," Charlotte offered.

Both heads snapped in her direction. Michelle's nostrils were flaring and her pretty brows furrowed in the middle of her forehead. Damien didn't even try to hide his stunned expression either. But it was Michelle who went in for the kill.

"You fat, sloppy-ass bitch! When someone wants your opinion, they'll ask for it. Why don't you sit there and keep stuffing yourself," Michelle barked.

"Who are you calling a bitch?" Damien asked before Michelle could launch another attack.

By now, Charlotte had risen from her seat. Her hands flew to her hips, and she stepped from behind the table.

"I've got your, bitch! And I also have your man. Now I suggest you move your ass away from here, and let us enjoy our meal. I don't want any trouble, but it would take me less than five minutes to snap your twig-ass in two!" Charlotte warned.

Michelle looked her up and down and scrunched her nose up like a foul order had suddenly invaded her space. She didn't doubt Charlotte could probably do just what she was promising. But her beef wasn't with Charlotte. Michelle took a retreating step backward.

"My man?" she chuckled. "He ain't nothing but a nasty-ass snake in the grass. You can have him. Just get him to sign the divorce papers! Besides, he'll fuck around on you, too," Michelle assured Charlotte.

"I don't know about you," Charlotte began, "but I've never had a problem keeping my man interested. Damien has never cheated on me," she bragged.

Michelle chuckled. She looked at Damien. "Sign the damn papers," she warned through narrowing eyes."Oh, and you'll have to grab that money from my cold clutch before I fork anything over," she added then turned and looked at Charlotte. "You've got a lot to learn, sistah," she said as she spun around on her heels and stormed away from their table.

When Michelle made it back to her table, she was suddenly disgusted with herself for meeting with Kim and Tammy. She knew without a doubt, this little episode would be all over Sweetwater by the time they came together for Bible study classes on Wednesday evening.

"Girl, you okay?" Kim asked.

"Okay? Of course. I just want his ass to sign the papers. I'm tired of being hitched to him," Michelle retorted as she tossed a dirty look in her husband's direction. He had the nerve to be all out in public with his new plump girlfriend, like he was already single. *They need Jesus and a room,* Michelle thought.

"Can you believe he's been kicking it with *her*?" Tammy wrinkled up her nose, gazing toward the couple. "I mean, how does that make you feel?"

Michelle's head snapped toward Tammy. "What is that supposed to mean?" she asked, not even trying to hide her displeasure.

"Well, all I'm saying is, if Steve left me for a— what's the politically correct term these days?" Tammy searched for just the right words. "I mean, she's so big. She's fat," she finally balked.

"I don't care who he crawls up into. I just want him to sign the friggin' papers so I can move on with my life. Besides, Damien left me long before she came along. He's just a dog. Every few months they look for new spots to piss."

"Umph," Tammy grunted. "Well, I hate fat people. They're so gross and disgusting. I mean, why can't they just stop eating. If I looked at myself in the mirror and I looked like her, I swearfoGod, I'd swear off food forever!"

"She's cute," Kim said, looking toward Damien and Charlotte.

"I don't care how cute she is. All fat people are lazy and nasty. Her ass shouldn't eat another thing," Tammy said adamantly.

"They can have each other," Michelle said matter-of-factly. As Tammy went on and on about how disgustingly lazy all fat people were, Michelle knew then she could never tell her so-called friends about her relationship with Raymond.

How would they react if they knew she was carrying on with an ex-con who still has at least two years left on his sentence? Better yet, how would they react to the fact that he was wrapping up a seven-year stint for possession with the intent to distribute? She shuddered to think what they would say.

Chapter 31

Damien couldn't believe his ears as he exited the elevator in his brother's apartment. He could hear the argument all the way down the hall, and he wasn't sure going inside was the smart thing to do.

He had never heard Amy curse the way she was cursing at his brother Barry. Instead of retreating back to the elevator, he moved toward the door even faster.

"Hey, what's going on in here? I hear you guys all the way down the hall," he said, letting himself into the apartment.

Neither Barry nor Amy responded. Instead, they remained at an apparent standoff, both breathing hard and glaring at each other with narrowed eyes.

"Seriously. What's up?" Damien asked, looking between Amy and his brother.

"I'm just sick of this shit," Barry spat.

"After what you've done? You should be willing to do any and everything I ask of you. You embarrassed me to no end. My daddy is still asking me if I can really trust you. Do you know what that's like?"

"Oh, we're talking about daddies now? Is that what we're talking about, because it seems to me, you only care about your own! What about the fact that my father is in a hospital clinging to life, and all you want to talk about is this damn wedding?"

SLAP!

Barry's hand flew to his face. Had she just slapped him, and right in front of his big brother? Instinct caused him to flinch in her direction, but Damien pushed him back.

"Hey, hold up a sec," Damien interjected, trying to hold Amy at bay.

"I have told you about putting your fucking hands on me!" Barry screamed.

Amy reached around Damien and clocked Barry upside his head.

"You cheating bastard! You should be glad I'm still marrying your ass."

"Whoa! Hold up a minute here, Amy! Keep your hands to yourself!" Damien screamed at her.

She walked away from them both, steaming mad.

Damien turned to his brother, still stunned by Amy's sudden outbursts. He had never even heard her raise her voice in his presence. Now, not only was she screaming like a mad woman, but she was actually throwing blows like her last name was Ali.

"You two should just calm down. We're all under a lot of stress right now, but this is not the time to turn on each other," Damien said to them both.

Barry stood off to the side, looking like he was deep in thought. Amy was huffing and puffing in the opposite corner.

"Now I don't want to get all up in your business or nothing like that, but I sure hate to see you two carrying on like this."

All of a sudden, Amy looked at Damien and said, "How dare you try to tell us anything? You should be ashamed of your nasty-self!"

Barry's eyes grew wide. He stepped toward the center of the room. "See, this is the kind of stuff I'm talking about. The way you disrespect my family, it's like you think you're better than us. My pops is laid up in a fucking hospital, and all you wanna talk about is this wedding. Then, my brother is trying to help, and you haul off and disrespect him?"

"Oh, I'm disrespecting him?" Amy yelled. "None of you know anything about respect. You know what?" She sighed hard and closed her eyes. "Look, the cake guy will be here in less than ten minutes. I'm gonna go to the car to get the pictures. Can you at least act like you're interested in the samples he's bringing?"

Barry took a deep breath. And when Amy reached into her purse for her car keys, he simply shook his head. Damien stood by quietly as she walked out the door.

When he was sure she was gone, he turned to his baby brother. "Look, I know I'm not perfect—nowhere near, but that bitch is crazy, and you shouldn't marry her."

Barry was outdone. He couldn't believe what he was hearing. "Are you serious?" Barry asked sarcastically.

"Dude, she swung on you twice. What the hell was that all about? I mean, shit!"

"DUDE! You are about to get a divorce. You couldn't stop fucking around on your wife, and you're giving me advice?" Barry behaved like just the mere thought was enough to make him chuckle.

168

Damien threw his hands up in mock surrender and shook his head. "Hey, I'll be the first to stand up and say, perfection," he pointed at his chest, "not over here. But that broad," he pointed toward the door, "she's crazy, and you're gonna end up in jail behind her ass. Mark my words!"

"Look, I'm stressed. She's stressed. Things got a bit out of hand. I just need to remember how emotional women get when it's time to start talking all this wedding stuff, that's all."

Damien shook his head at his brother's stupidity. He wasn't about to try and shove advice down the boy's throat, but he didn't like the way things were going between Barry and Amy. He knew he had neither no right nor ground to stand on, but his years of running around had taught him how to spot a crazy woman. And Amy was downright certifiable as far as he was concerned.

Before Damien could issue another warning, Amy eased back into the apartment beaming as if she hadn't just roughed up her fiancé. "Okay, he just pulled up when I walked back in. Are you ready, baby?" she asked sweetly.

"Yeah, I'm good," Barry said, tossing Damien a warning glance.

Damien walked into the back bedroom and started packing a bag. He was going to spend a few days with Charlotte. After that scene in the restaurant with Michelle, he figured he needed to pay extra-attention to Charlotte.

He had been waiting for her to say something about the divorce papers, but she never brought it up. At first, he was worried Charlotte would fire off questions about why he made it seem like it was Michelle who was refusing to sign, but the woman hadn't uttered a single word.

By the time Damien walked back out to the living room, he had to look around to make sure he was in the right apartment.

Amy and Barry were on the couch, laughing and loving all over each other like nothing happened. The cake man was explaining the ingredients in one of the many options he had for the happy couple to sample.

"So you can see why this remains one of our most popular selections," the salesman said.

"Ah, excuse me," Damien interrupted. Barry looked in his direction. "I just wanted to let you know I'll be gone tonight and tomorrow. I'll see you at church Sunday?"

"Oh, Barry is coming to my church on Sunday," Amy interjected. She smiled as she sat poised with perfect posture, her pearls glistening when sunlight bounced off them. "So I guess he'll catch up with you Monday."

Damien wanted to tell her that he wasn't talking to her, and that his brother could speak for himself, but he thought better of it.

"What about seeing the G-man Sunday evening?" Damien purposely looked at his brother when he spoke, but that seemed to matter very little to Amy.

She said, "Yeah, we're going to look at locations for my bridal portrait, and we've made several appointments for Sunday evening." She smiled perfectly then took a delicate bite of the cake she held on a small saucer.

"Uh, I'll call you," Barry added.

Damien felt sorry for Barry as he walked out of the apartment. But soon he reminded himself, he had problems of his own. There was no need to waste emotions on his baby brother who seemed too oblivious to consider the mistake he was about to make.

Chapter 32

Theola never thought she would dread the day it was time for her to board a plane and head back to Belize, but that's exactly what was going on. Suddenly her little slice of paradise had turned into a real life nightmare and there was very little she could do about it.

Days had passed, and still, she had no idea how she was going to get out of this mess she was in. Her flight was leaving the very next afternoon, but she was no closer to a solution than she was when she was stunned with the realization of what was going on.

She thought about trying to pay both of them off, but Reginald had made it clear he wanted to come home, so she knew that wouldn't work. Besides, she was already running up a hefty bill with all the traveling and escort services she was using. Theola didn't know how she'd explain that to Ethan once he came home. She chuckled at the memories. She used to think that would be her biggest problem. Then, all of a sudden, she's face with a mountain that seemed so high she knew she couldn't scale it alone. Things always seemed to go from bad to worse with her.

Sure she could call the police, but then how would she explain *what* and *who* she had been doing in Belize in the first place? No, that was simply not an option.

She had even considered not showing up at all, thinking, *What's the worst they could do?* But the more those type of thoughts crossed her mind, the more she knew none of those were viable options either.

"Mrs. Goodlove?" the housekeeper called out to her from the other side of the door.

Here we go. What now? Theola thought.

There was a soft knock at the door.

"Mrs. Goodlove, are you in there?"

"Yes?" Theola could never get used to the hired help they employed. Someone was always bothering her about something, and she didn't need the pressure. She didn't even bother telling the woman to come in. At first, she wondered how long she would stand there if she didn't answer, but she decided it was best to see what the woman wanted.

"I just had a question," the woman said, talking from the other side of the closed door.

Theola sighed like it was all she could do to have to listen to whatever was on the woman's mind.

"You can open the door," she said dryly.

The woman did, but only stuck her head in. Theola knew they were probably wondering when she would be leaving again. She had quickly fallen into a pattern, and she was sure they'd become accustomed to it. And she wished like hell her only dilemma was which two pieces to pack. Oh, how she wished she hadn't fallen for the ploy.

"I was wondering if you would need anything else this evening?"

Theola looked at the woman like she had already grown bored with her intrusion, but she didn't answer her right away.

An awkward silence hung between the two.

"Why do you ask?"

"Well, some of the staff wanted to go by the hospital," the woman said, her voice trailing off as her stare cast downward.

Theola rolled her eyes. So what if she hadn't been by to see Ethan. Shit, she had problems of her own, and she needed to figure something out before he woke up. Sitting up in that damn hospital room wasn't going to solve anything for her.

"Oh, well, I will be here, and I'm going to need the staff around in case I have company," Theola offered haphazardly. What did she care if the excuse wasn't believable? They didn't need to be holding vigil next to their boss's bed anyway. How would that make her look? No, she wasn't having it.

The woman's expression said she was stunned.

"Company?" she stammered, as if she knew to tread lightly.

"Yes, company. Now, I need to get back to my meditation. Let everyone know I don't want to be disturbed," Theola hissed with her neck twisting as she spoke.

"Uh," the woman began then started to retreat. Theola shot her a look. "Um, I was just wondering what I should do..."

"Do about what?" Theola questioned, now irritated beyond words.

"Err, about your uh, company?"

"Just leave me alone!" Theola screamed, forcing the woman to jump and slam the door shut.

She wasn't in the mood. She had too many nagging issues to deal with. Why did the tramp have to even mention the hospital. It was as if she was trying to mock Theola right to her face.

She knew where she needed to be, but she had so many other things that needed her attention. Besides, she didn't need any hired help trying to make her feel bad.

"Maybe I should just pray about all of this," Theola whispered.

She quickly shook the thoughts from her head. What could God do to fix this mess? He had already failed her so many times before. What happened when her mother's drunken boyfriends would wander down the hall and into her room? Or better yet, what about when she was married, and her drug addicted husband would plummet her with his fists because the people at his job wouldn't get off his back? And what happened to God when she was out there living on the streets, struggling to turn tricks just so she could eat? No, God was no friend of hers.

Theola got up and walked over to the closet. She pulled her suitcase from it and started to pack.

"God didn't create this mess, so I guess it's up to me to fix it on my own," she decided as she pulled items and stuffed them into the suitcase.

Chapter 33

Michelle was in a foul and funky mood. She sat at the back of the room with her face twisted in the second session. And she couldn't help but wonder what was going on. The classes had finally returned to their normal numbers, but that wasn't what was pressing on her mind. She hadn't seen Raymond, and they only had one session left for the entire day. Usually, he was there by the end of the first and trying to stay for all three. She told herself not to panic, but it was hard to listen to that inner voice of reason.

Oh God! What had she done? What if Raymond had just been using her, finally had his fill, and was tossing her to the side because he was finished? She knew her head was filled with negative thoughts lately, and she knew the source of those thoughts, but it was so hard to remain strong. Seeing Damien fawning all over that big, fat girl did very little for her own self esteem, although she'd never admit that to anyone.

Lately, all she could think about was why he would want a woman like *that* when he had her? How could she hold his interest when he cheated on her at every turn?

By the time Scottie came stumbling into the session, Michelle perked up a bit, thinking Raymond was sure to be right on his heels. "Hey, Ms. Michelle," he said cheerfully as he grabbed a Bible and flopped down into a chair.

But when the door closed behind Scottie, it might as well have been a steel chamber slamming shut on her broken heart. Where was Raymond? He didn't even call her over the weekend like he had started doing either. At first, she thought she'd have to take a bunch of collect calls, but once Raymond told her about the illegal cell phones he and other inmates had, Michelle figured they could talk freely and as often as he wanted. But now, she wondered whether he wanted to talk to her.

She slumped back into her chair and started thinking thoughts worse than those that had been haunting her lately. She didn't know why she simply couldn't pull herself up out of the dumps.

"Are you okay?"

It wasn't until Pastor Peebles touched her shoulder that Michelle realized the room was completely empty, and he had been talking to her. She looked around. Had the session ended already? She must've really been zoning out.

"Uh, I am. Uh, I'm sorry. I guess..." she started looking around the room in panic. "W-what happened?"

"It's okay. I didn't mean to startle you. Calm down. Are you okay? I noticed you seem a bit unlike yourself today, so I just wanted to make sure you're okay." He smiled.

He always spoke to her with such kindness in his voice. He was a gentle little man, and his concern seemed genuine. But how could she look up into his big, brown puppy dog eyes and admit she was down and out because Raymond appeared to be missing in action?

"Oh, I'm so sorry," Michelle stammered, trying to ignore the tears that were burning in the corners of her eyes and trying to overwhelm her voice. "I just . . . I'm having trouble sleeping at night, and uh, I guess it's just kind of seeping into my days," she offered with a sheepish smile. But even she didn't believe the words pouring from her own mouth.

Pastor Peebles didn't have a chance to respond. Just as he was about to, the door flew open and a couple of inmates came bustling through, laughing and talking among themselves as they filed in for the third session.

Before long a few more inmates trickled in, then a few others, and even more. As they walked in, Michelle's heart rose and fell with each face that wasn't Raymond's. She was literally on the verge of being sick.

Pastor Peebles had to clear his throat a few times before she finally sprang from her feet to pass out the pens, pads and Bibles. She was seriously zoning, and her emotions were on a fierce roller coaster. Then, at times, she felt worthless for being all down and out over some two-time con who was serving yet another stint because he didn't know how to obey the law. He was so beneath her, she couldn't even fathom the way she was carrying on over him. How could she be that desperate? Didn't she know she was worth so much more than what she had reduced herself to? Michelle ignored the logic. Instead, she told herself the heart wants what the heart wants.

"Miss Michelle, uh, this pencil is..." before the inmate could finish his sentence, Michelle was up, had snatched it from his hands and slammed another one on the desk. Every eye in the room was on her, but she had already spun on her heels and stormed toward the back of the room.

"Today's message will focus on the Seventh Commandment," said Pastor Peebles as he told the group which verse to turn to in their Bibles.

Michelle sighed. She didn't have a Bible, nor did she ever read along as Pastor led the class. But she couldn't help but sit and try to run down in her mind a list of the Ten Commandments. Thou shall not steal… Thou shall not lie… just as she was going over the list in her mind, Pastor Peebles looked up and made a point of clarification. "Did he say adultery?" Michelle questioned.

"Yup, sure did," an inmate turned around to answer her question. Michelle was mortified. She didn't even realize she had said it out loud, and she certainly wasn't talking to him. She sat with her arms crossed at her chest.

"People today tend to define it as any act of sexual intercourse outside of marriage, or perhaps a bit more narrowly, any act of sexual intercourse between a married person and someone who is not their spouse. That is appropriate in contemporary society, but it isn't how the word has always been defined," Pastor Peebles said.

Michelle was hot. "Where is Exodus in the Bible," she heard the same inmate turn to whisper. But Michelle was too stunned to even move much less pay attention to him and his question.

Why had Pastor Peebles decided to do a sermon on adultery of all topics? What was he trying to say to her? She just felt like his comments were directed at her. Michelle's throat suddenly went dry. Before she knew what was happening, she felt warm and her pulse raced wildly.

"I can't..." she managed, barely audible. The last thing she remembered was sliding from her chair and a loud painful thud when her head hit the ground.

Chapter 34

Damien struggled not to pull rank. But as he sat in his deacon's meeting listening to one complaint after another, he wanted to remind these men of a few things.

Number one: This was his daddy's church. Number two: Until his daddy walked up out of that hospital, technically he was in charge as far as administrative purposes. And number three: He shouldn't have to sit through these mind-numbing meetings. It was worse than listening to a nagging wife.

"So, Deacon Goodlove," one of the other deacons turned to him. "What is the real story behind this mess we hear about you and Sister Charlotte in the sanctuary?" He chuckled.

Damien was pissed. He couldn't believe the man had stepped to him like that, and in front of everybody? Like they were just discussing another agenda item? He couldn't believe the hate.

"Deacon Gerald, my bad, did I miss this item on the agenda?" Before the deacon could answer, Damien continued,

"Yeah, how about we just stick to the agenda. We ain't got all night to be here."

Deacon Gerald was a tall and lanky man with bad skin and an even worse sense of style. There had long been this rivalry thing going on between the deacons, but lately it seemed like more of his brothers in Christ were stepping to him in the wrong way. And Damien wasn't sure how long he'd be able to turn the other cheek.

"All I'm saying is, considering all that's going on with Pastor, I would think we'd all want to keep the drama to a minimum," the dejected deacon mumbled, but no one else was biting.

"If there's nothing else to talk about, I say we adjourn this meeting," Damien offered, not wanting to give Deacon Gerald's comment any more attention than it deserved.

As they filed out of the meeting room and headed down the hall, Damien's heart nearly stopped. He looked up then around to see who was standing near. Everyone else was pretty much rushing off to their destination.

"What are you doing here?" Damien asked, still looking around nervously.

"Is that any way to greet your long, lost lover?" Jazzlyn asked with a smile that was just as jacked up as Damien remembered.

"What do you want, Jazzlyn?" Damien didn't even stop walking.

"I forgive you for everything that happened between us," she said triumphantly.

He didn't want any trouble, and that's all Jazzlyn had been from the moment they'd hooked up. She was part of the reason he had been caught cheating on his wife. Before Jazzlyn tried to make their little fling more than it was, he kept his game going strong for a very long time and was able to operate beneath the radar.

Then Jazzlyn came along. From the neck down, she was the perfect woman. But for whatever reason, she decided she needed to have Damien all to herself. Needless to say, things didn't end well, especially once Michelle got hip to what was going on.

"But I do want to know something: Why did you do it?" Jazzlyn asked.

"I don't know what you're talking about, and I don't have time to listen right now. Someone's waiting on me," he said as he strode passed her.

"So are you trying to tell me that you didn't tell Greg all about my past here at Sweetwater?"

That's when Damien finally stopped walking and looked at her. He laughed. "What the hell would I do that for? I don't even know who Greg is, and why the hell would I go and tell anybody anything about you? It's been more than a year since you left Sweetwater."

Looking at Jazzlyn now, he couldn't imagine why he even decided to pursue her in the first place. She wasn't even a little bit attractive. But that was in the past, he didn't have time to linger on old stuff.

"It's been over between us for a long time now, and I don't believe in going backward. So tell me, why are you here?"

"Damien, I have finally found the one. I never told him about, well, my time here at Sweetwater, and I just can't imagine anyone who would have, especially if you say it wasn't you."

"Why would I?" Damien asked, exasperated. "I mean, do you remember how things ended with us? I wasn't trying to hang on to what we had, so why in the world would I go gossiping about you to anybody?"

Jazzlyn stood there as if she was trying to think of her next move. "I can't lose him," she yelled after Damien who had taken off again and was now near the door.

Damien shrugged, but he kept walking.

"So, what's up with you and Michelle?" Jazzlyn yelled after him.

"Nothing. We're getting a divorce. She's moved on, and so have I. As a matter of fact, my new girl is probably waiting on me now." He was even closer to the door.

"You guys really are getting a divorce?" Jazzlyn asked. But the sound of her voice was more hopeful than surprised.

By the time Damien realized he may have said too much to a woman who's mental stability was questionable, he was already pushing the door open. Jazzlyn had obviously moved on, too. Now she was someone else's problem, so he figured he didn't have anything to worry about.

The moment outside light poured in to the building, he noticed Charlotte pulling up. He smiled when their eyes met.

Damien did a brisk jog to the car, hoping he would've been able to outrun Jazzlyn. But by the time he slipped into the passenger's seat, buckled up, and reached over to kiss Charlotte's lips, he caught a glimpse of Jazzlyn standing at the doorway looking at them.

"Is that who I think it is?" Charlotte asked, unable to pull her gaze away from Jazzlyn. Damien didn't like the fact that Charlotte seemed to know about everything that ever happened at Sweetwater.

"Well, it depends on who you think it is." Damien tried to make light of the situation. But Charlotte hadn't cracked a smile.

"That crazy broad you used to fuck around with," Charlotte said with her eyes still on Jazzlyn.

"That's her," Damien confirmed.

"Hmm, what's *she* doing here?"

"Dunno. I mean, she was going on and on about somebody telling her old man about her past or some shit like that," Damien said.

"But why would she be telling you that?"

"I don't know, and I really don't care."

Damien wasn't in the mood. He didn't feel like allowing Jazzlyn's reemergence to be a problem for him, and he hoped Charlotte wouldn't either.

But as Charlotte pulled out of the parking lot and looked through the rearview mirror, she could see the cold stare from Jazzlyn, and something about it told her the special relationship she and Damien had been sharing was about to take a turn for the worse.

Chapter 35

When Theola stepped off the plane and into the humid tropical air, she tried to suppress the rumbling in the pit of her belly. She was anxious, but not the least bit excited. She hated not knowing how this visit was going to turn out.

Reginald thought he was doing her a favor by giving her another week to come up with an answer, but here she was back in Belize and no closer to a solution to her problem. Why couldn't he simply come back and take his chances? Why did he have to pull her into this mess? And better yet, how was she going to get out of it?

The biggest shock came when she arrived at her room only to find Stone Pier waiting.

"Can I rub your shoulders?" he had the gall to ask, all sweetly like nothing was wrong.

"Why are you even here?" Theola asked, irritated.

Gone were the butterflies that once sprang to life when she heard his voice. Now him standing in his little swim trunks, wearing sandals and clutching the duffle bag was enough to make her want to puke on him.

"I want to help you feel better," he said softly.

She had soured on him from the moment she learned of his involvement in luring her there. Theola rolled her eyes dramatically.

Was he serious? What a coward. Why couldn't he say no when Reginald approached him about betraying her? How could he try to go on like nothing had happened and like she even wanted to be in his presence.

"I want you to leave," she shouted.

"That cannot happen," Stone Pier said softly. And was he trying to use his sexy voice on her, like that might help her forget the betrayal?

"Oh, but yes, it can. Just open the door, step out and don't come back," she suggested, motioning toward the door.

"It's not so easy. I must stay here with you," he said.

Now when Theola looked at him, she noticed things that weren't so apparent before. Did he have a lazy left eye? And his teeth, when was the last time they had been cleaned?

"You don't have to stay. Actually, I'd feel better if you left. I kinda wanna be alone," she tried with a calmer voice.

He didn't move to leave.

Theola closed her eyes and sighed hard and deep. She was so sick and tired of going off on people, but for whatever reason, she noticed many simply didn't understand unless she flipped out and got all mad-black-woman on them. It was obvious this would be one of those cases.

"I said I want to be alone," she hissed, her gaze aimed at the floor.

Man, how could she have missed those hammer toes? And was that fungus living in his toe nail beds? Theola marveled at all she had missed when lust had clouded her vision and obviously her judgment.

Stone Pier sighed as if *he* had the weight of the world bearing down on his shoulders. Everything about him seemed to be at the root of her irritation.

"I do not have a choice. I must stay here," he finally said.

Theola wanted to spit on him. What did he mean he didn't have a choice? Now Reginald had him guarding her? Oh, how she had fucked up this time.

"So you trying to tell me that you've gotta stay here, watching me?" she snarled.

"I can do whatever you may want. I can make you feel good. I know this is a time of immense stress for you, and I want to help," he offered.

Well, there was one thing she could say about him. Stone Pier was one hell of an actor. He had thoroughly fooled her, and that was not easy to do. To imagine, she thought theirs had been a special and unique connection. She had even considered trying to come up with ways to sneak him to the States for a visit.

Suddenly, her emotions got the best of her. She looked at him, and then simply asked, "How could you do this to me?"

"It is not as easy as it seems," he admitted.

Theola sucked her teeth and looked at him with pure disgust. Her stomach felt like it was twisted into all sorts of knots.

"So, lemme get this straight: You've gotta stay here— to watch me while I'm here," she got up. "But you know what: That doesn't mean I have to be sitting up here all in your face," she spat, then stormed into the bathroom and slammed the door.

The truth was, despite how angry she was, how disappointed she felt over falling for their ploy, she was most disgusted with herself. Because in spite of the fury she felt, when she thought about the way he had loved her so carefully and precisely, there was still that small part of her that longed to feel his touch again. It was almost as if it was instinct, the way she hungered for the pleasure he gave.

Stone Pier may have been a snake in the grass, but he had the kind of talents between the sheets that made her want to forgive him, if only for one more taste.

On the other side of the bathroom door, she felt safe. She was still no closer to a solution, but at least she didn't have to sit there remembering how his powerful tongue beat her swollen button into sweet submission.

Another round would've done wonders for the knots lodged in her neck and shoulders. She knew it was stress, and unfortunately, the best stress reliever was toe curling and gut-wrenching for her. Well, not this time.

Theola shook her head. "No, that bastard betrayed me, and I had tipped him well."

When there was a knock at the door, she sighed again. She wanted to yell for him to go jump in the sea and sink to the bottom like cement. At first, she ignored him and his knock. But when he knocked again, she rolled her eyes and asked nastily, "What do you want?"

"Your cell phone. It has been ringing. I thought you should know," he said.

What now? Theola thought.

She wasn't ready to face him again, but she was also curious about who was calling, and what they wanted. When she finally opened the door, she was glad to see that Stone Pier hadn't unpacked his duffle bag. He was still wearing his sandals and trunks, and he looked like he could leave any minute.

Theola didn't utter a word to him. She walked over to her purse, which was near the door. The phone started ringing again. Whoever wanted her seemed desperate, she thought. She dug into the bag and plucked out the phone.

When her Caller ID popped up, her head tilted ever-so slightly, and she frowned in confusion. Now what the hell was Damien calling her for?

She pressed the button and said, "Hello?"

"Oh, Theola. I'm so glad I finally got you. It's the G-man," he started.

"Theola felt her heart drop. "W-what is it? What's going on? Is he... Oh, God!"

Chapter 36

By the time hump day rolled around, Michelle was truly in a bonafide funk and nothing seemed to offer her a ray of sunshine. It had been two days of sessions and no Raymond. She thought she simply needed to will herself to die and end the misery. If it wasn't bad enough that upon her return after the fainting spell, Pastor Peebles sat her down for a long talk. It was mind-numbing, but she wanted to put his mind to ease, so she engaged him in conversation, assuring him that everything really was fine.

She thought back to the previous Friday, when she opened her eyes and realized she had passed out. She knew things would go downhill from there. But she wasn't prepared for the depth of rock bottom she would soon hit.

As she walked through the gates to what had become her living hell right here on Earth, she didn't even bother greeting the inmate who checked her name off the list.

"Miss Michelle," he said.

She waited for her driver's license back and strode away as if he hadn't even acknowledged her. She wasn't in the mood to talk to him or anyone else. If things weren't right with Raymond, nothing was right in her immediate life.

Now she was even more disgusted by having to be at the prison. Michelle was conflicted all the way around. Yes, she was mad at herself for getting all sprung off some lowlife thug, but he had made her feel so damn good. And after seeing her soon-to-be-ex-turned-chubby-chaser, loving all over that barracuda in public, well, she was fit to be tied.

Thoughts of ways that she was going to completely rock Raymond's world on Monday was what kept her going after seeing those two together. But here Michelle was three days in, and she hadn't seen any signs of Raymond, nor had he called. Yes, something was definitely wrong.

"Michelle." Pastor Peebles smiled as she walked into the room. She put her things away and gathered the pens, pads and Bibles. She turned to him and plastered on a forced smile.

"Yes, Pastor?"

"Well, I appreciate your dedication. I mean, after what happened last week, I didn't think you'd be back so soon. But, I wanted to know if you needed to talk. The last couple of days," he shrugged, "seems like something's on your mind."

Again, his voice was just as sweet and caring as ever. Her eyebrows inched upward, and she shook her head releasing a sigh.

"Oh, Pastor, I'm so sorry. I'll really try to keep my energy level up."

"So, we don't need to talk then? I'm a great listener," Pastor Peebles assured.

"I'm sure you are, but really I'll be fine. I just need to stop watching all that reality TV and go to bed earlier," she laughed.

The pastor simply smiled and reluctantly turned away.

"Okay, well, you'll let me know if I can help in anyway. And if you're not comfortable talking to me, I can always refer you to someone just as capable." He smiled.

"I appreciate that so much," Michelle said sincerely.

Just as she started to pass out the items, the door swung open and the inmates filed in. She didn't even bother looking up. She told herself she was not about to play that game today.

If Raymond's ass was through with her, well, she was through with him. A few new faces filed into the room and Michelle gave them the items she had given to everyone else.

She retreated to the back of the room as Pastor Peebles began his sermon. By the time they were midway through the second session, she had resolved to the fact that she and Raymond were through. Nothing else explained his no-show.

Michelle looked around the room, and once she decided everything was fine, she figured she'd sneak out to use the bathroom. She eased up from her chair, put down the novel she was reading and turned to come face-to-face with Raymond.

She nearly fainted, again. His gaze held her frozen momentarily. Pastor Peebles still hadn't looked up from his Bible. A few of the inmates were no longer reading along with the Pastor. Their eyes were glued on Michelle and Raymond.

"I'm sorry," he mouthed.

Michelle felt her eyes swelling with tears.

"Excuse me," she said with a shaky voice.

Raymond mean-mugged the inmates who couldn't mind their own business, then stood for the right amount of time after Michelle had walked out of the door. He noticed that instead of turning right, she made a left, which meant she was going to their spot.

He didn't even knock. He bomb-rushed his way into the small bathroom and pulled her into his strong embrace.

Michelle didn't resist. She gave in, surrendered like a lightweight up against the ropes. She had no power to deny him. As his hands roamed her body, she felt all of the ill feelings she had for him evaporating into thin air.

When they finally came up for air, tears were running down her cheeks. "What happened to you? Where have you been?" she whispered loudly.

"I'm so sorry, baby. I'm dealing with a lot of shit right now. I was . . . my head was all messed up," he said.

"But what about me? I mean, I haven't seen you for the past two and a half days," Michelle whined.

"I know, baby, but I'm tryna tell you: My head was all fucked up. I wasn't feeling up to..."

"Well, what happened? I mean, you were just fine Friday."

"Yeah, but after you left, my baby mama called, and that bitch is like..." Raymond started shaking his head.

Michelle could see the anger in his features. She just wanted to help. She wanted to make it all better for him.

"What's going on, babe?" she asked, genuinely concerned. Didn't he know things weren't right for her if they weren't right for him?

"You know what? I don't even want to get you all wrapped up in this shit? The bitch is straight skitzo," he said, shaking his head for good measure. "And it don't help that she got this friend who ain't never had a man, but still she be dishing out advice like she Oprah and shit!"

"Wow, baby, if she's got you this worked up, so much so that you didn't even come see me for two whole days, don't you think I deserve to know what's going on?"

Raymond looked at her for a long time, not saying a word. She could now see the hurt in his eyes. She just wanted to love all of his pain and misery away. He had done so much for her, and they were going to be together when he got out anyway, so it was like his problems were hers.

"Maybe talking about it will help you feel better," she pressed.

"I dunno," Raymond said, releasing yet another loaded sigh.

"I hate that she's got you feeling like this. You know our time together is so limited. To have to see you clearly suffering, it just doesn't sit well with me," she said.

He kissed her again. It wasn't a deep passionate kiss, more of a thoughtful one, and that's when she realized just how much she had missed the taste of his tongue.

"She's just a real bitch," he complained. "She's nothing like you. You all classy and shit—sophisticated, and fine as hell. LaUnique is just a trifflin' skank that trapped me with three kids."

"Oh," Michelle said with a frown. The truth was, she loved knowing that he realized how much of a step up she was. He appreciated her.

"Do you know she's talking about reporting me to the judge for back child support? Talking 'bout making sure they extend my sentence for non-payment," he huffed, completely dejected.

Michelle's heart thudded. "She what?" she exclaimed.

193

"Yeah, see, that's why I didn't even want to tell you. I don't need you worrying about shit like that." Raymond shook his head.

Michelle could see it wasn't easy for him to share this with her.

"Why would she want to do something like that?"

"'Cause she a money-hungry-ass ho who just wanna sit on her ass and have me take care of her," he surmised.

"Well, how are you gonna pay her if she keeps you locked up?" Michelle tried to reason. "It makes no sense. She should want you out so you could work."

"That's what I'm tryna tell her stupid-ass, but she real dumb—dropped out in the tenth grade. I told her, if I had the fucking money, I'da gave it to her ass," he stressed.

Michelle sighed. She didn't even know LaUnique, and she couldn't stand her. She didn't understand how the woman thought keeping the man in jail would get her paid. Finally, she looked up at Raymond and asked, "Well, how much money are we talking here?"

"Eleven hundred," he said. "I only fell behind because I had to start buying my mom's medicine when her job laid her off, but you think LaUnique cared about that shit? Hell, naw!"

Michelle shook her head at LaUnique's lack of consideration.

"You know what," she said, staring into Raymond's hopeful eyes.

Just then, there was a knock at the door, and Michelle's heart nearly came up her throat.

Chapter 37

"**W**hat the fuck is *she* doing here?" Charlotte's narrowed eyes were fixed on Jazzlyn.

Charlotte and Damien were walking down the hall inside the hospital. They had just walked out of Pastor Goodlove's room together. Charlotte had gone in under the guise of wanting to see her Pastor and not as his future daughter-in-law as she had hoped to one day be.

At the sound of Charlotte's outburst, Damien turned to see Jazzlyn at the nurse's station carrying an extra-large floral arrangement. They watched as Jazzlyn headed in their direction.

"Hi, Damien." She smiled. She ignored Charlotte all together.

"What are you doing here?" Damien asked. It wasn't like he really cared. As a matter of fact, if Charlotte hadn't brought it up, he would've ignored Jazzlyn all together.

"Why, I'm here to see Pastor," Jazzlyn flirted out right.

"Oh, that's awful nice of you, uh, I mean, considering you're no longer a member of Sweetwater." Damien felt the need to make that very clear.

"Well, it seems I'm headed back after all," Jazzlyn beamed. "Let's just say something about the other day made me realize just how much I have missed my real church family. You know, there's no place like your church home," she said and winked flirtatiously.

Damien gave her a quizzical look. Jazzlyn allowed her gaze to roll down Charlotte's body, stopped at her midsection, and then back up again. Still, she didn't acknowledge her presence. Charlotte stood close to Damien, clutching his arm as if she feared he might slip away.

"But I thought you were thriving at your new church," Damien exclaimed.

"It wasn't a good fit. Especially once I realized everything I want is right here, um, at Sweetwater," she cooed.

"Mr. Goodlove," a nurse interrupted.

Damien's head snapped in the nurse's direction. She was coming out of his father's room.

"A moment?" the nurse motioned for him to come back to the room.

The three of them rushed over. But at the door, the nurse looked at the two women then said, "Ah, just immediate family please."

Jazzlyn looked at Charlotte, and Charlotte looked right back at her, letting it be known she could give much attitude as good as she received.

Damien turned to Charlotte and said, "Just wait right here for me. I'll be back soon."

The nurse walked him into the hospital room as Jazzlyn and Charlotte faced off.

"I don't know what you're up to, but I should warn you, I'm not in the mood for any drama," Charlotte spat.

Jazzlyn hissed, then again allowed her gaze to size Charlotte up, and then she twisted her face.

"I'm not sure what you're talking about or what you're afraid of, but I don't take kindly to threats."

"Oh, it's not a threat," Charlotte promised coolly. "See, Damien and I are working toward something here, and we don't need any more distractions, so if you think you're about to move back to Sweetwater and pick up where you left off, I'm warning you, you're wasting your time."

"Sounds to me like you're scared," Jazzlyn teased.

There wasn't a trace of a smile on Charlotte's face. She looked at Jazzlyn and sighed.

"I'm sure you're fully aware of my history with Damien, and obviously that scares you," Jazzlyn explained, "and honestly, you should be."

"Oh, darling, I'm not the least bit scared. Don't even get it twisted. But let me make something clear to you: When you left Sweetwater, you lost your place in line. So, if you think you're about to pick things back up, you just need to know we're a package deal, and I've already got a partner for our threesomes. So, you need to find someone else's husband to stalk."

"Oh? Well, last I checked, Damien wasn't married to you, so that tells me he's free game," Jazzlyn chuckled. "And I can tell you this: There's no man alive who can resist all of this. You see, this wicked body of mine has brought many-a men to their knees," she boasted with pride.

"That was then. This is now, and just remember you've been warned," Charlotte retorted.

As Charlotte turned to put some space between Jazzlyn and herself, she bumped into Barry.

"Oh, I'm so sorry. Are you okay?" he asked, then suddenly stopped cold in his tracks at the sight of Jazzlyn.

"Hey, Barry," Jazzlyn said cheerfully. "You doing okay?"

Barry looked at her, then back at Charlotte. Confusion was etched into his features.

"Uh, yes, I'm good. How have you been?"

"Real good now that I'm coming back at Sweetwater," she said, then motioned for him to take the arrangement. "Can you take these in?" she asked sweetly.

"Ah, yeah, and I uh . . . I need to get in there. They called for me, uh, us," Barry said.

"Yes, your brother is in there now. Okay. So, I won't hold you, but it's so good to see you again." Jazzlyn smiled. "I'll be seeing you around."

Charlotte rolled her eyes.

When the room door opened, they heard voices. Barry let out a yelp and what sounded like laughter.

"Yeah, I could tell I've been missed around here. Did you see how Barry looked at me?"

Charlotte was bewildered.

"I don't know why I even left," Jazzlyn commented.

"I'll tell you why," a voice boomed.

The two women turned to see two church mothers, Mama Sadie and Ms. Geraldine, approaching. "You left because we told you to. We don't need no more Jezebels at Sweetwater," Mama Sadie said. She turned her stare to Charlotte and said, "Lord knows we've got enough already."

Charlotte ignored Mama Sadie and Jazzlyn. She decided she needed to wait further down the hall. She wanted to be there the moment Damien came out, but there was no way in hell she was about to stand there in present company.

Just as she was trying to ease further down the hall, Pastor Goodlove's room door opened. Damien emerged. He looked around and smiled.

"God is good," he declared. "Pastor Goodlove is up, and he is talking!"

"Praise the Lord!" Mama Sadie sang loudly. "We fell to our knees the moment we got your call."

Jazzlyn flew into Damien's arms and planted a wet kiss onto his lips. "I am so glad to hear that," she squealed, pulling back.

Charlotte couldn't make it back to the door fast enough. Damien pulled Jazzlyn off of him, frowned, and said, "I need to get back in. I just wanted to share the wonderful news."

"Just sinful," Mama Sadie hissed, shaking her head.

Charlotte was fuming, and if she wasn't in a hospital, she would've made good on her promise and shown that bitch just how much damage a big girl could do.

Chapter 38

Theola thought she was going to be sick. Why did it seem as though her entire world was suddenly crashing down around her? She paced back and forth, waiting for a call from the airport.

"Oh, Jesus!" she mumbled as she paced.

Her cell phone had been ringing nonstop since Damien's phone call. After a while, she simply had to stop answering. Just as always, news spread through Sweetwater like a wild Texas grass fire burning through a dry field.

"Are you okay?" Stone Pier asked as if he really cared about her and what she was going through.

At first, Theola simply ignored him. She wasn't in the mood. That phone call from Damien just raised the stakes for her. She needed to leave, hop the next thing smoking, and get to that damn hospital. Although the flight from Belize to Houston was just a mere two hours, leaving the country was her newest challenge.

She was supposed to meet with Reginald the very next morning for brunch, but that wasn't what she was most concerned about.

Her husband was awake, and she could not get to the hospital. Theola was like a magnet to trouble, and she didn't need this shit right now.

"Can I do something to help you feel better?" Stone Pier asked calmly.

Theola turned to him. There was fire in her eyes as she gazed at him. "Yes, I need you to leave, and that's all I need right now."

"You know I cannot do that. I can't leave you here alone. I am to stay in this room with you, until you leave."

Theola frowned. "Well, you should get your things and get ready to go because I'm about to leave."

"You just arrived. Why not relax? Let me fix you a drink. I wish the phone would stop ringing," Stone Pier said.

Every word that came out of his mouth was igniting fury in her. She needed to think. She needed to try and figure out how she was going to get back to Houston.

When her cell phone rang again, she spied the caller ID. The second she noticed the airport's number, she picked up.

"Hello?" Theola released a huge breath.

"Mrs. Goodlove, I'm afraid we cannot accommodate your request. All flights leaving to the States have concluded for the remainder of the day. Your next opportunity to leave will be at 10:25 tomorrow morning," the airport director said.

This was not what she wanted to hear. What did he mean she couldn't be accommodated? "I need to charter a plane or do something. It's crucial that I get back to Houston, and I have to go tonight," she said frantically.

Stone Pier walked over and placed a soothing hand on her shoulder. The moment his touch registered, Theola pulled herself beyond his reach. She didn't want him touching her. Bastard!

"Ma'am, that would be a hefty price," the director was saying.

"I didn't ask you how much it would cost. Is it something you could arrange? That's all I need to know!" Theola screamed.

"I can look into that for you. When would you want to leave, Mrs. Goodlove?"

"I need to leave as soon as you can get clearance. Please, this is an emergency, and I've got to get back to Houston."

Stone Pier stood in awe as he listened to Theola's conversation. He had heard of people chartering planes before, usually wealthy white tourists who came to the country to dive in its pristine Caribbean waters.

All of a sudden, it was as if he realized he may have been on the wrong team. When Theola ended the call, he looked at her, his features softening.

"You are able to hire a jet?" he asked in awe.

Theola looked at him with hopeful eyes. Did he know anything? Was there anything he could do to help? It would surely help redeem him in her eyes.

"That's what I'm trying to do. Do you think it can happen?" she asked.

Stone Pier stood, looking at her like he was trying to decide whether to help.

"Listen, I need to get back to Houston. There's been an emergency, and I cannot wait until tomorrow morning. It may be too late then."

Theola was desperate. And although this man had betrayed her in the biggest way possible, she needed help now, and she didn't care where it came from.

"My cousin works at one of the deep sea diving resorts. Sometimes they arrange trips for important people from the States. They don't fly commercial."

Her eyebrows flew up.

"Do you think this cousin could help get me on a chartered jet?"

"You can afford such a trip? Ah, I mean, it is very costly," Stone Pier corrected himself.

"Can you please try to call him? Ask if I could charter a jet."

Stone Pier grabbed the phone and started dialing feverishly. After a while, he was able to get his cousin on the phone. He spoke in a native language that Theola could barely understand. She was as nervous as a streetwalker in church.

Theola could make out a few words here and there, but not enough to piece together what was going on. All of a sudden, Stone Pier flopped onto the bed, picked up a pen and notepad then started scribbling something down.

Struggling to contain her excitement, Theola just wanted him to get off the phone so she could figure out what she needed to do next.

Before long, he was hanging up. She did make out that someone was going to call him back.

Stone Pier took a deep breath and turned to Theola when he was finally done. "Okay, there is a jet leaving out this evening in about an hour and a half," he said. Theola released a huge sigh of relief. "But, my cousin has to call back. We don't know how many seats are aboard the plane, and we don't know if there would be a seat available for you. The jet is owned by a Houston oil company," he reported.

"I have got to get on that flight. I don't have a choice. Is there anyway we can go to the resort?" she asked him.

"I will have to wait for my cousin to call back," he said.

Theola hoped he wasn't playing with her. There was no way she could wait until the next day to be by Ethan's side.

When the phone rang, Theola nearly jumped. Stone Pier answered before a second ring.

"Yes," he simply said.

"I see," he turned and looked at Theola.

"Okay, wait a minute. Let me check," he covered the phone and whispered to Theola. "He says the cost will be nine thousand Belizean dollars," he reported.

"What does that mean?"

"Uh, forty-five hundred U.S. dollars," Stone said.

"Okay . . . okay. Tell him yes."

Stone Pier went back to the phone call. "Okay, yes. She wants the seat." He reached for the pen again.

Theola felt a wave of relief washing over her.

"Okay," she heard Stone Pier say. "We can get there," he added. When he hung up he looked at Theola. "Okay. We have to get the driver to take you to the resort. From there, you'll go to the private airstrip and board the plane. But they want you to have the payment before you board the jet," he said.

"Oh God! Bless you," she cheered. "Bless you!"

Stone Pier smiled. "Let me call the driver because you've got to be out at the resort well before this evening. I have no idea where the airstrip is located.

Theola sat back and watched as he called down to the lobby and spoke to someone about having the driver ready.

Now, she felt better. Now she could rush back and face her church family.

Satisfied everything was going well, she got up and left to use the bathroom.

Once she returned, everything was arranged. Stone Pier approached her with all of the necessary information. He had done well, and she was pleased.

Minutes before she was set to meet the driver in the lobby, there was a knock at the door.

"Oh, that must be the driver. He's early," Theola said.

Stone Pier looked toward the sound like he dreaded who was on the other side of the door.

Theola had already gathered her things and was prepared to go. She was excited that Ethan was awake even though she still had a lot on her plate.

When Theola pulled the door open and prepared to step out, she stumbled back a bit.

"Where do you think you're going?" Reginald asked.

Theola felt like she had just received a massive blow to her gut.

Chapter 39

"**Y**o, Ray?"

Michelle sighed. She thought they had been caught, but it was Scottie on the other side of the door.

Raymond rolled his eyes. He pulled the door open and looked at Michelle like he was sorry for the intrusion.

"I'll get rid of him real fast," he assured Michelle.

She watched as Raymond pulled the door open. He opened it wide enough to look through it.

"What's up?" he asked Scottie.

"Dawg, your cell is being tossed," Scottie reported in a panicked whisper.

"What?" Raymond yelled. "What the fuck?" He was breathing fire.

"Yeah, man, I've been looking for you."

"Okay . . . okay. Good looking out," Raymond said. He turned to Michelle and sighed. "See the shit is already beginning."

Michelle was worried. She could see the stress in his eyes. He didn't deserve this foolishness. He had so much to deal with already.

"Don't worry about this."

"You don't understand what it's like in here," he admonished. "The shit is just beginning, and I'm trying to tell you, it's gonna go down the toilet even faster."

"All of this over some money?" Michelle questioned.

"Yeah, that's the way it is in here," Raymond said.

"I'll get the money to her. Please, baby, let me help you. I mean, aren't we a team?"

They had already discussed the plan. When Raymond got out, he and Michelle were going to be together. By then, he'd get his out of control baby mama under control, and Michelle's divorce would be final. She'd be a multi-millionaire, and they wouldn't have to worry about sneaking around anymore.

"Listen," Michelle said. "I want you to give me LaUnique's number. I'll get the money to her tomorrow. Baby, I don't want you worrying about this. We can get past this, and especially if they're gonna start harassing you."

"Baby, I'm so lucky to have your fine ass," Raymond assured her. "I'm sorry I didn't get to hit that, but you know we've been in here for a minute."

Michelle knew he was right, but she wanted him to give her a little something. She reached out and stroked his crotch then kissed him.

Raymond wasn't one to be outdone. He grabbed her breasts, squeezed with all his power, and pinned her up against the small wall. Soon, she was breathing hard and heavy.

"Okay, okay," Michelle breathe, "we've gotta go. I don't want to start something we can't finish."

But it was too late. Raymond was already fumbling around in her panties. She knew she didn't have the strength to stop him nor did she want to. She had missed his touch like she would miss air if she couldn't breathe.

"Lemme lick it," Raymond was soon begging.

"No time," Michelle said, although she wanted to let him have his way with her.

"Just lemme taste you, baby, I won't be long. I just wanna go back with your flavor in my mouth. C'mon. It's been way too long," he whined.

Michelle hated when he begged. She was so weak for him, she couldn't offer any resistance whatsoever.

"Well, maybe just for a minute," she gave in.

Raymond worked fast. He pulled down her pants, dropped to his knees and hoisted her up onto his shoulders.

The tiny but powerful earthquakes that rocked her body proved her gamble was well worth the risk. Raymond didn't even bother wiping his face. He rushed out of the small room and left her panting.

Once she pulled herself together, she eased out of the bathroom and headed back toward the class. As she slipped back inside, Pastor Peebles looked as if he hadn't moved since she left.

A few of the inmates looked at her then smiled to themselves when she eased back into her chair. Michelle noticed the strange stares, but she was on cloud nine. As a matter of fact, as she sat there, her body still relished in the memories of all that Raymond had accomplished within a few precious minutes. She had never experienced anyone like him.

And to think her raggedy-ass soon-to-be ex thought *he* was God's gift to women. She wished there was some way to let Damien know just how good she was getting it from her sexy thug.

And his work had instant result. She felt better than she had in days, and despite herself, she simply couldn't stop smiling.

Later that evening, Michelle checked her bank account. She knew she had more than enough money to help Raymond out, but she couldn't wait for Damien to sign the damn papers. That's when she and Raymond would really be on easy street. She made a mental note to call her attorney the next day. They needed to wrap this mess up. She was more than ready to move on with her life.

When her phone rang, it caught her a bit off guard. But she was more than thrilled to realize it was Raymond calling.

"Hi, baby," she cheered.

"Say . . . what's up?"

"Nothing, hey, I can get that money to LaUnique as early as tomorrow," she informed him.

"Baby, are you for real?"

"Yes, of course I am. I mean you're talking about her trying to keep you locked up. Let's hurry up and pay her off. I don't need you stressing about stuff like this. We've got enough going on."

"Damn, your ex is a fool if I've ever heard of one," he chuckled. "I mean, you're a good woman, baby. I just want you to know I will pay you back," he stressed.

"Yes, you will," she emphasized, "but I'm not interested in your money. I've got enough of that." She laughed.

"Oh, that's what's up. Fo' sho." He laughed back. "Say, so what's a brotha gonna have to do?"

"You're gonna work off your debt. What else?" she cooed.

"That's what's up for real," Raymond added. "I like the way you think, ma."

She loved when he fell back into his sexy street swagger. It turned her on more than she could express, and she finally felt alive again.

"So, let's call LaUnique now, on three way, so we can make sure there are no misunderstandings," Michelle offered.

"Hello?" she called out when Raymond failed to respond.

"Uh, you mean, like we call her now—with the two of us on the phone?"

"Yes, I want to make sure I get the information I need so she can get the money. Baby, I don't want her holding anything over you ever again," Michelle stressed.

"Yeah, but uh..."

"Well, it's up to you, but I'd think it's the easiest way to clear up any possible misunderstandings."

"I see where you're going in with this, but look here, LaUnique ain't the type-a chick you can have a cool conversation with," he stammered.

"But how am I supposed to get her the money?" Michelle fretted.

"You know what? Lemme holla at her real quick then I'll get back with you. I just don't want no unnecessary drama to pop off," Raymond said.

Michelle was reluctant. She wanted to be involved in all of the details, especially since she was giving up money, but then she told herself she was just overreacting.

"Okay, so, you'll call her, and then call me back?"

"Give me an hour," he said and quickly hung up.

Chapter 40

Damien couldn't stand still no matter how hard he tried. Every step he took was weighed down by thoughts of all that was wrong with his life. He had tons on his mind. Most of all: What was Jazzlyn doing back at Sweetwater? He didn't like the idea of everyone seeing him with Charlotte. Although he cared about her, and she was cool, he wasn't sure he wanted to jump right back into another relationship.

Then, there was the situation with Michelle. He couldn't believe she really thought she wouldn't have to give him *any* of that money. If it wasn't for him, she wouldn't even be getting that settlement. Damien was aware that his sleeping around, and them thinking he had infected her with HIV probably nearly killed her, but still.

He finally stopped his pace when the doctor walked in and up to his father's bedside.

"So, we're probably going to want to keep him here for a couple more days," the doctor said as he flashed a small pen light into Pastor Goodlove's left eye. "Just to make sure everything is okay."

"Only a few days after he suffered a coma?" Damien asked a bit confused.

The doctor kept working, but spoke as he did. "Well, speaking in laymen's terms, we say a coma. But when a brain-injured patient suddenly talks or seems to click in after months or even years, he or she was almost definitely not in a coma or vegetative state." The doctor hovered over Pastor as he continued. "More likely, Pastor here suffered trauma to his head during the fall, and subsequently, took a modest step up from a so-called minimally conscious state—a higher level of awareness in which patients can sometimes respond consistently, if only with a blink or a raised finger. Now the difference is between that and say a coma suffered as a result of a stroke or heart attack is, the brain isn't deprived of oxygen, so when these patients wake, it can be as if they pick up right where they left off."

Damien and Barry stood by watching the doctor as he worked.

"So does this mean there won't be any long term effects?" Barry wanted to know.

"It's still a mystery to us how these things work. That's why we want to run the tests. But initial results indicate he's fine," the Doctor added, placing some tools into the pocket of his smock.

Ever since the old man woke, both had been thrilled with excitement. But each wondered just when Theola was going to make an appearance.

"So what about his memory?" Damien asked the doctor, hoping to change the subject.

"What about it?" The doctor questioned, still lingering close to the head of Pastor's bed.

"Well, will he remember anything?"

"What do you mean will I remember anything? Stop talking about me like I'm not sitting right here, and where the hell is Theola? And has anyone found Reginald yet?" Pastor Goodlove asked. "Worthless bastard—the worse seed I ever planted."

"Well, I guess the question about his memory has just been answered," Barry tossed in.

"I wish you would stop flashing this light into my eyes," Pastor growled. "When was the last time someone did that to you?"

"I can say it's been since medical school," the doctor replied as he finished checking Pastor's vital signs.

Damien and Barry started laughing.

"Well, *you* may need to hold him for a few more days to figure out if he's okay, but I already know ain't nothing wrong with that old man," Damien joked, looking lovingly at his father.

"Who you calling old man? And of course there's nothing wrong with me. I'm a man of God!" Pastor yelled, sticking out his chest for good measure. He looked around the room at all of the cards, flowers, and balloons. "What's all this?" He frowned, his dark eyes taking everything in.

By now the doctor had moved away from the bed and was reading Pastor's chart.

"People miss you, old man," Damien reported. "Wanted you to see how loved you are."

"What y'all missing me for? I'm right here," Pastor chided.

"So again," the doctor started from his corner in the room. "I say about three more days, and we should be just fine."

"Three days? I'm ready to go now," Pastor insisted in the doctor's direction.

Suddenly, he turned his focused stare to his sons and frowned. "Where is that wife of mine?"

Damien shrugged. "I talked to her earlier to let her know you were up. She says she's on her way."

"On her way from where? Besides, what could be more important than being by your husband's bedside when he's in the hospital?"

Barry wasn't saying a word. He didn't need to get into anyone's business. While he was happy about his father's recovery, he also understood that this meant Amy would be pressing for the wedding even more.

"She should've been holding vigil right here," Pastor pointed to the floor for emphasis, "forcing y'all to pull her away for food and to relieve herself," Pastor added long after his sons thought he was finished.

Damien shrugged, but he didn't add anything else about his phone conversation with Theola. He had problems of his own.

"Well, what's the latest on Reginald?" Pastor Goodlove asked.

Damien was a bit concerned about the way he kept jumping from one topic to the next, but he wasn't about to point it out. He was just glad the old man was back with traces of his old self bursting through.

"I need an update on the finances. What's going on?" Pastor looked around the hospital room. "How long have I been in here anyway?" He started fidgeting with the tubes and wires that seemed connected to his body.

Barry looked at Damien and Damien returned the awkward glance without as much as another word. The truth was, he hadn't heard from his brother. Even when Reginald was around, they were so different it was as if they weren't even related.

Reginald was a complete introvert—borderline weird as far as Damien was concerned. He seemed to live just to be told what to do and how to do it. Even their father had commented that Reginald was a strange bird.

"Somebody needs to get Theola on the phone," Pastor Goodlove said. "Where the hell is she anyway?"

Damien and Barry exchanged knowing glances again. But neither one commented about Theola.

"Sweetwater's been showing out, Pop," Damien exclaimed.

When he saw the twinkle in his father's eyes, it was enough for him to continue. "Yeah, you ain't been in this room for a second alone. We started a special prayer circle. You were being prayed over twenty-four-seven. Then we set up a schedule to make sure that there was always someone at your side."

"Boy, y'all didn't need to do all that." Pastor sounded irritated as he spoke.

"We may not have needed to because the man upstairs was in control all along, but we wanted to do our part, too."

"Uh-huh," Pastor mumbled.

"What the..." It was Barry's words that announced what was happening.

A deafening noise pulled everyone's attention toward the hospital room door. Charlotte and Jazzlyn came crashing through the door scratching and crawling at each other.

They tumbled to the floor. One moment Charlotte was on top, the next it was Jazzlyn. Hair was flying all over the room and Damien stood looking with horror across his face.

"What is going on?" Pastor screamed from his bed.

Damien closed his eyes and shook his head. He didn't need this shit right now. He just didn't.

Chapter 41

As she eased back in her seat and closed her eyes, Theola remembered an interview one of her favorite authors had given about what made his stories so good. The writer said he simply put ordinary people in extraordinary situations. She looked around and wondered if someone could possibly be writing about her own damn life.

Nothing else made sense nor could anything explain what she was going through. The scene that played out with her and Reginald back at the hotel couldn't have been better if it was written by a New York Times bestselling author.

As she leaned back in the bucket leather seat and took a deep breath, she still couldn't believe she had made it onto a plane, flying private back to Houston, but she was. Nearly two hours ago, if she had been told she would in fact make the flight, she would've considered that a work of fiction.

She opened her eyes and squeezed them shut again, and instantly, she was there, back at the hotel. She had just pulled the door open and noticed the cold darkness in her stepson's eyes.

Where do you think you're going? Reginald had asked.

But what was worse was him pushing his way past her and into the room. He looked at Stone Pier then said, "You did the right thing by calling and letting me know what was going on here."

Theola turned to Stone Pier and tossed him a look of utter disgust. She was stunned. But she didn't even bother wasting her words on him.

"I have to go," she cried, hoping Reginald would understand because she didn't have time to go back and forth with him.

"You think you're just gonna run up outta here without talking to me?" he barked.

She hadn't noticed before, but he looked desperate. His hair needed to be cut, he had a five-o-clock shadow that did nothing to help his appearance, and even the bags under his eyes looked like they had bags.

"I have to get back. We can talk about it later. I just need to go," she insisted. "Please let me go."

"What have you come up with? I'm ready to go back home," Reginald yelled, all but ignoring her plea.

"I can't talk about this right now. I need to go. I'll come back, and we can work this out, but I need to get back to Houston now."

"You ain't going nowhere dammit," he spat. "Before you came along, I had a chance at a real relationship with the G-man, but you walked into the picture and everything took a turn."

Theola couldn't fathom all of this. She needed to go because there was no way she'd make the plane if she had to stand there and fight with Reginald.

"You can go," Reginald turned and said to Stone Pier.

He hesitated, acted like he didn't want to leave.

Reginald probably sensed his reluctance because all of a sudden, he pulled out a gun and pointed it in Stone Pier's direction.

"I wasn't *asking* if you wanted to go. I'm telling you it's time for you to go."

Stone Pier grabbed his duffle bag and shuffled out of the room. That's when Theola really started to get scared. She had noticed the desperation in Reginald's eyes the moment she first saw him, but now he had a gun. This changed everything as far as she was concerned.

Alone with him and his gun, she didn't know what she was going to do.

"W-what are you doing with a gun?"

"Don't worry about that," he said, agitated. "I want you to pick up the phone and make a call. I want you to start telling Sweetwater that it was you and not me."

Theola couldn't believe it.

"I think this is something I need to tell them in person," Theola tried. "It would make no sense for me to just start making random calls. Let's just talk about this later."

"No, I wanna hear you, and I wanna hear you now," he pointed the gun at her.

Theola took a deep breath. She closed her eyes and wondered if it was even worth it to try and reason with him. Maybe it was simply her time to go.

But before she had to make up her mind, a loud noise rang out through the hotel. It was a fire alarm. A voice boomed through the loud speaker telling guests they were being evacuated.

It wasn't long before there was loud hard knocks on the door.

"Fire . . . fire! Evacuation," a voice screamed. "Get out!"

Reginald looked panicked and momentarily took his gaze away from Theola. That gave her just enough of time while he was distracted to snatch her purse and make a run for it. She didn't stop until she was downstairs in the lobby.

When the flight attendant's voice boomed over the plane's intercom, it pulled her back to the present.

Flying private meant Theola's trip from Belize to Houston was less than two hours. And luckily, since she landed at the Sugar Land Regional Airport, she was mere minutes from Memorial Herman Sugar Land Hospital, where her husband was recovering.

It was close to ten at night, but still, Theola was on a mission. She strode quickly into the hospital then sped walked, trying to get to the right floor.

When she finally made it up to the floor where her husband's room was located, she thought she had really just stepped into the twilight zone.

Two women were rolling around on the floor of her husband's hospital room. They were fighting like they were auditioning for the WWE.

"Somebody get security up here!" a nurse yelled.

"What the hell?" Theola exclaimed.

Just then, everyone stopped and pulled their gaze up to her.

"Well, it's about damn time. Where've you been?" Pastor Goodlove screamed at his wife.

Theola swallowed hard and dry then she stepped over the two women who were rolling around on the floor.

"Hey, Big Daddy," she cheered.

But the look on Pastor's face said she had a whole lot of explaining to do.

Chapter 42

The next day, Michelle made sure her hair and make-up were tight as she stood waiting outside the prison. She had already paced, glanced at her watch, and wondered what was taking so long. She couldn't go inside until she met with LaUnique. But the girl was already thirty minutes late, and Michelle only had five minutes before she had to check in for her community service. She was determined to get this trick off her man's back.

Just when Michelle was about to give up and check in, a beat up old car pulled into the parking lot with smoke bellowing from its tailpipe like it was truly on its last leg. The only reason it held Michelle's attention was because of the loud popping noise it made as it pulled into the lot. It sounded like a shot being fired off, and that made her jump.

A few seconds later, a door creaked open and out stepped a designer high-heeled stiletto sandal. Wearing a pair of ultra skinny jeans and multi-colored, layered tank top, a woman walked toward Michelle.

She looked like she used to have a nice figure in the past, but allowed herself to get out of hand. As she approached, Michelle could see she had on tons of makeup with fake lashes that looked like legs of a spider. Her hair weave matched the rainbow of colors she wore with her layered tank tops. Michelle thought it was all too much, but she didn't dare say so.

When she got closer, Michelle could see that she was young, but the makeup made her look much older.

"You Michelle?" the woman asked.

That's when Michelle realized she was wearing grey contacts. "Yes, uh, you must be LaUnique. It's nice to…"

"Let's get this over with." LaUnique smacked her gum, cutting Michelle off.

Michelle arched an eyebrow and reached for the bank envelope that contained the cash. She could see why Raymond didn't want to get on her bad side, but what attracted him to her in the first place was definitely a mystery.

Before she could get the envelope out good, LaUnique snatched it from her hands.

"Now, I don't care what you and Raymond are up to, but if he thinks about not paying me for his kids, I'ma make sure his ass stays locked up!" she growled.

Michelle frowned. What more did she want? She got the money but was still throwing threats around.

"You know, it's none of my business," Michelle began trying to sound friendly. "But keeping him locked up isn't gonna get you your money, if you think about it," Michelle offered in the friendliest tone she could muster up.

A wicked smile curled at LaUnique's lips. She eyed Michelle suspiciously then gave a sinister smile. "You know what? You're right," LaUnique said, allowing her eyes to roll down

Michelle's body then back up again. "It really isn't any of your damn business. But thanks for the cash!"

Michelle stood, momentarily stunned, but decided LaUnique wasn't worth the energy it took to get all worked up. As LaUnique took off toward her beat up old car, Michelle headed for the gate.

"Miss Michelle," the gate guard greeted. Michelle wondered how he could be so pleasant every day considering his situation. He guarded the gate, but he was a trustee, which meant he was a trusted inmate, but an inmate nonetheless.

"Good morning," she replied like it hurt her to speak. Michelle wasn't trying to get too friendly with the inmates whether they were trustees or not.

As she bounced down the path and toward the building, she felt really good. She had helped her man out of a tight spot and for that, she was proud. She couldn't wait until she and Raymond were both on the outside. Michelle kept thinking about the irony of her situation. She was devastated when she was sent to the prison, but little did she know, she, of all people, would find real love behind bars.

And she had to admit: Even though it wasn't the ideal situation, there was an amount of mystique connected to their relationship. Every evening, it was a rush wondering, would he call or was he on lockdown for some infraction.

Then, knowing that she was the only woman bringing him pleasure gave her a sense of thrill like she'd never experienced. The irony was something else, but she marveled at the fact that this unlikely relationship with Raymond had brought such excitement to her life.

Today, Pastor Peebles greeted her with a massive smile on his face, and she was so glad to be able to return the favor.

"I don't know what it is," the man said, "But something's different about you. You look like you're feeling much better."

"I do, and I just want to say how sorry I am for the way I've behaved over the last few days. I was just going through some things, but I'm fine now."

"Well, I'm glad to hear it."

It wasn't long before the inmates started filing in. Michelle passed out the items before they even took their seats. Raymond told her that he wouldn't be able to come until the last session since he still had his library duties to take care of.

She wasn't bothered since she knew he wouldn't be there until the last session was nearly over. She couldn't wait to see his face when she finally told him that LaUnique had been paid in full.

Time couldn't move any slower, and Michelle knew it was just lagging because she was anxious to see Raymond.

Across town LaUnique Jones couldn't believe her good fortune. When she found out who her baby's daddy was screwing, her mind went into overdrive. She was sick and tired of being broke, and she figured Michelle Goodlove was the answer to her prayers. It took a minute to get Raymond on board, but now that he was, LaUnique planned to work her jelly and ride this bitch until the wheels fall off. And she planned to make sure she got her share of Michelle's new found wealth.

All she had to do was keep Raymond inline and make sure his simple behind didn't mess everything up.

As she climbed out of the car and walked up to her Northside apartment, her home girl was waiting, wearing a worried look all over her pretty face.

"Whassup? How'd it go?" Jewels Brown asked. She was petite with a lethal body that she used to her full advantage.

"It's all good," LaUnique confirmed with a wide grin.

"W-w-what? Gimme some." Jewels laughed, held her hand up and waited for LaUnique to slap her palm. They celebrated their newfound wealth and the cash cow they decided they would milk completely dry.

Chapter 43

Back at the hospital, following yesterday's fiasco, Damien was almost scared he'd be banned from visiting his father. As he walked off the elevator, his mind went back to the drama that seemed like it came right off of a daytime soap opera. There was too much going on. Damien could hardly keep up. Not only had Theola come prancing in to the hospital room hours late like she was simply making a grand entrance, but she stepped right over the mess that had been bringing Damien grief. It made his head hurt to think back on it now.

"Help me get them up," Damien had said to Barry.

As the two men struggled to pull Charlotte and Jazzlyn apart, Damien was beyond embarrassed. He knew where this was all headed, and he wasn't in the mood, not in front of the old man who'd just barely awakened. He had hoped to prove to his father that he had changed his ways, that he had maintained control while his father was down, and that he was more responsible than he had been in the past.

His father's hospitalization had scared him in ways he couldn't vocalize. The truth was, if anything ever happened to the G-man, Damien didn't know what he would do. He knew his pop wouldn't be around forever, but he needed more time, and he had prayed long and hard that God would deliver, and He had.

But Damien was afraid this scene between Jazzlyn and Charlotte was certain to set him back drastically.

"Please, stop this madness!" Damien yelled at Charlotte. But instead of listening to him, Charlotte turned her venomous words to Jazzlyn.

"I'm so tired of you. I already told you," Charlotte screamed. "I've warned your ass!"

Damien tried to quiet her down. This was not the time or place for this kind of foolishness. He was surprised security hadn't come to break things up.

"Charlotte, you've gotta stop this. Stop it now," He urged.

But Charlotte's rage had completely taken over, and she wasn't seeing or hearing clearly. Her focus was on her nemesis.

"What is going on?" Pastor asked from his bed.

"It's *her*, Pastor," Jazzlyn spat in Charlotte's direction. She'd be dammed if this cow would mess up her plan. Jazzlyn stood huffing and puffing as Barry tried his best to hold her back, but she was stronger than she looked.

"I'm good," she huffed to Barry, struggling to break from his clutches. Her heart raced but she was ready for whatever Charlotte had to offer.

Damien closed his eyes and shook his head. This wasn't supposed to be happening, not now.

Pastor Goodlove looked between his sons and the women who were fighting over Damien. He had questions for his wife, but he could hardly interrogate her with all that was going on.

"Son," he called out to Damien, worry dripping from his voice.

Upon hearing his father, Damien reluctantly released Charlotte and was about to step closer to his father until Charlotte lunged toward Jazzlyn.

Once again, they were at it. Charlotte swung wildly, catching Jazzlyn with a blow to the right side of her head.

"You fat-ass bitch," Jazzlyn cried before clawing toward Charlotte's face. It was like an episode of Jerry Springer on location.

"You dirty skank," Charlotte fired back.

Suddenly Jazzlyn turned to Damien. There was a look of sheer horror across his face when their eyes met. It was as if he was trying to speak to her without using words.

"When are you gonna tell this bitch?" Jazzlyn snarled.

Charlotte's head snapped toward Damien. Her eyes begged him to deny whatever Jazzlyn was implying.

Damien tried to step closer to Jazzlyn. He wanted to somehow communicate to her that she needed to shut the hell up.

"My father, uh, he's barely recovering. This is not the time for this," Damien pleaded.

"What the hell is she talking about?" Charlotte asked, eyeing them both suspiciously. "What is she talking about?" she demanded.

Damien turned to Charlotte, his arms extended as if he was trying to urge her to remain calm. "We need to take this outside. I can't..."

"Oh, this shit stops here and now," Jazzlyn announced, cutting his appeal to Charlotte short. "I'm not going through this with you again, not again, Damien."

"Calm down," he turned, trying to quiet Jazzlyn.

"Forget about her being calm. I want to know what is she talking about?" Charlotte screamed at him the second Jazzlyn finished her tirade.

"Son, what's going on here?" Pastor asked. "I know you're not back to your old ways, are you?"

It suddenly felt like all eyes were on Damien, and he didn't appreciate being the center of attention. He especially didn't like his father knowing he had been backsliding like the practice had gone out of style.

"Pop, can we discuss this later? I don't want to get these two started up again."

"But son, I think we're too late. This thing isn't gonna go away," Pastor said.

"And neither am I." Jazzlyn folded her arms and stood as if she was planning to stick this thing out.

"All I'm asking you guys to do is take this outside. Give my pop and Theola time to talk alone. We don't need everyone all in our business," Damien stressed, growing more nervous by the second.

He snapped back from the memory just as he approached the door to his father's room. As Damien pushed the door open he discovered his father wasn't alone.

"Theola," Damien greeted, and he nodded at Barry who simply nodded back.

In the midst of this, Barry's cell phone rang. He started to ignore it because after all of the fighting, cursing, and screaming, he, too, wanted to know what was going on. But he decided to take the call even though he didn't recognize the number.

"Is this Barry Goodlove?" a no-nonsense voice asked.

"It is," he answered, frowning.

"This is Brenda, Amy's mother." Barry's legs started getting weak. "I'm calling about Amy..." He was blinking uncontrollably. Damien noticed something was wrong. "There's been a horrible accident..."

Barry repeated everything he was being told. That's when the room went quiet. Every eye suddenly turned to him.

"Oh, God!" Damien shrieked.

Damien rushed to his brother's side, and not a moment too soon. Barry collapsed into his arms. As Damien struggled to hold his brother up, his own mind started racing.

"Where is she?" Damien asked his brother calmly.

"Methodist Sugar Land," Barry managed.

Damien turned to his father. "We're gonna go. You need time alone with Theola anyway."

"Yes, go and hurry, son. Call as soon as you know something," Pastor urged, motioning them out with his hands.

Chapter 44

Sure, she had been there when the drama went down between Damien's women. And up until Barry's phone call, she was confident company would always be present, but now alone with her husband, Theola wasn't sure she was ready. She didn't mind the circus that went on inside his room. When the guys decided to leave, she wanted to drop to her knees and beg them all to stay, despite their soap opera-like drama. It gave her a short reprieve from her own depressing life.

When their eyes locked, she felt her heart skip a beat. But it wasn't the kind of excitement she had been experiencing lately. She was afraid of what he was thinking, and what he was about to say.

"So are you at least happy to see me? It's been a while," he said softly.

Taking a deep breath and a step closer to his bed, Theola's eyes wandered around the room.

"Of course I'm happy to see you, Ethan. I was uh, so worried," she said, fiddling with his bed sheets as she stumbled over her words.

But even she knew she didn't sound sincere. It wasn't that she wasn't worried about her husband—she was. But with the trouble she had gotten herself into, it took all of her energy to try and figure out a solution, and she was still at her wits end.

Pastor snatched her hand, forcing her to release a yelp. He had caught her completely off guard. Her eyes grew wide and the next breath was lodged in her throat, threatening to suffocate her.

"What kind of wife is too busy to be at her husband's bedside in the hospital around the clock?" His eyes narrowed. "I was in a coma, for Godsake!"

Theola began to tremble. Everything was an utter and complete mess, and she didn't know what to do. Ethan was right, but what could she do? Tell him the truth? There was just no way.

"I got here as fast as I could," she offered haphazardly. "I mean, you know what traffic is like. I just..."

"Cut the theatrics," he snarled. "I wanna know where the hell you've been, and what you've been doing."

Tears burned in the corners of Theola's eyes. She swallowed hard, and her throat was dry. This was not the time to crumble. She still had to figure out what to do about Reginald. If she came clean about where she was and what she had been doing, wouldn't it let her off the hook? How would she explain Stone Pier? Then would that lead to the service she'd been a regular with? She was stupid to use her credit cards. That would be too easy to trace. Oh, what a mess!

As she stared blankly into her husband's eyes, she searched for signs of mercy. But she was met with coldness, and for the first time, she was scared of what that might mean. Theola didn't even bother struggling. She stood there as her husband tightened the grip he had on her hand. Although she wanted to cry and beg him to let her go, she didn't say a word.

"I've just been uh . . . I was so worried sick. I'm going through quite a bit," she stumbled, searching for just the right words.

Pastor Goodlove pulled her closer to him. His grip moved from her hand to her hips. She didn't know what to do. Just as they were about to kiss, a nurse interrupted.

Theola remembered her being the one who had mouthed off to her, and she wondered what God was trying to tell her.

"Oh, praise the Lord," the nurse cheered loudly. "Pastor, I'm so sorry to interrupt, but I was off and got the word. I just had to come and see for myself. Oooh wee! God sure is good," the woman announced. "Pastor, I know I wasn't the only one, but I got me some serious carpet burns on my knees, 'cause I've been working overtime praying for you."

"And we know, the good Lord is in the business of answering prayers." Pastor laughed. "I'm living proof, and I thank you so much. I'm glad to know that the good Lord found me worthy to finish the work I started."

"Yes, Pastor, yes. And I won't hold you. I can imagine your wife here probably just wants to lock this door and keep you all to herself, so I'ma just ease on back out. Like I said, I was off, but I just had to come and verify the news for myself. God bless you, Pastor," the nurse said as she walked backward out of the room.

Theola released a huge sigh and rolled her eyes in spite of herself. *Did it really take all of that?* she wondered.

"Now that's how a woman shows how much she missed someone. She was off and came up here to see about me for herself. Yet, my own damn wife, it takes hours for her to put me on her agenda. So, let's have it, Theola. Where've you been, and what the hell have you been doing?"

"Ethan, I have so much to tell you, but this isn't the best time. I mean, I have so much I need to do before you get home. I want to make things right for you," she stammered.

"Let's see. There's a full staff at Blueridge, you don't work, and you don't want for a damn thing. Tell me again, where have you been, and what's been keeping you so busy you couldn't come see about your husband who just woke from a coma?"

Theola couldn't think of anything to say. And whatever she would've said, she was sure it wouldn't have been good enough. He was scaring her, the tone of voice he used, the way he fell back into that cold, hard stare he used before the nurse came in. All of it made her feel even worse than before.

When she looked back up and into her husband's eyes, she took another deep breath and began. "Ethan, there's something I have to tell you. But uh . . . I don't know how," she managed.

"There's no way but to say it, Theola," he said.

She couldn't tell if he was softening or not.

"It's not that easy," she admitted.

"I'm waiting," he pressed.

Theola shifted her weight to one leg then another. She took another deep breath and opened her mouth to speak again. But Pastor's hand stopped her before she could start.

"You better make this good," he warned.

"I know where Reginald is hiding," she said.

Chapter 45

Michelle was so vexed she could do something that would definitely have her behind bars as an inmate versus a woman finishing out her community service commitment.

"So you're telling me that I have to give him half of the money?" she barked into the phone. She had been on with her attorney for the past twenty minutes, and nothing he had said was good news to her.

No, the bastard of a soon-to-be ex hadn't signed the papers. No, the divorce cannot be finalized until he does and, no, you cannot give him half of the money you were about to receive in settlement.

"It's not right," she countered.

"It may very well not be, but unless you want this thing to be held up in court until your children's children are grown, I suggest you make him an offer and get this over with. That way you can move on with your life and enjoy your money," the lawyer said with such finality that Michelle couldn't do anything but suck up her anger.

After a few moments of weighing his words, she finally spoke up. "What would the offer need to be,? Uh, I mean for him to accept it? And how'd he find out anyway?"

"Well, I'd say if not half, then close to it. Legally, it's what's owed to him, Michelle," the lawyer said. "And this has been of public record for a while now, so there's no telling how or when he found out. But he does know, and apparently he wants his share."

Michelle wanted to get her facts straight. She was headed to Bible study this evening and was planning to try and appeal to Damien. She didn't know how things were going to turn out, but that was her plan.

 "Okay, well, let me take some time to think about all of what you're saying. Can I call you tomorrow and we decide then what to do?"

"Absolutely," he said. "But let's wrap this thing up this week. You know that way, you and your girls can move on with your lives."

"Okay, well, thanks for the call," she said, although she didn't really feel all that grateful.

By the time she and Raymond met in their secret spot, she was nearly emotionally spent. Ever since she ended the call with her attorney, her mind kept replaying scenarios in which Damien may be willing to allow her to keep all of the money. But she knew that was wishful thinking.

Raymond brought his glistening face up from between her thighs and frowned. "Okay, either I've fallen way off, or you're just not feeling me. What's up, baby?"

"Oh, I'm so sorry. It's good, baby. You know it is, but I've got a lot on my mind," she admitted.

Raymond looked at her cross-eyed. "Whatever is on your mind is more powerful than what I'm tryna do right here, right now?"

"Baby, I found out today that I have to give my soon-to-be ex, three-point-four million dollars," she simply stated.

"Shhhhiiit, maybe I need to be sucking your toes, too," he joked, pulling himself up off the ground. "So, you couldn't get around it, huh?"

Michelle shook her head as she started to adjust her clothes. For once her mind wasn't on the fabulous sex and how Raymond was able to make her feel. She needed to resolve this thing with Damien once and for all.

"Well, I'm sorry baby. I just wanted to make you feel good. I appreciate what you did with LaUnique and all, but I'm sorry you gotta take a hit like that," he said.

"Yeah, but the attorney is right: might as well get it over with versus prolonging this. I mean, three-point-four mil isn't bad no matter how you look at it." She smiled.

"That's your cut?" Raymond asked.

"Yeah, an even split. I just hate giving that dog a single red cent. I'm not being greedy. It's just after all he has put me through, the humiliation, the drama, I just don't think he deserves anything," Michelle stressed.

"Well, that brotha better be glad this is the new me, 'cause back in the day, I'd make sure he wouldn't collect a dime," Raymond mentioned as they both prepared to sneak out into the hallway.

But Michelle's eyebrow shot upward, he had piqued her interest without even trying. "Uh, what's that supposed to mean?" she asked.

"What?" Raymond quipped.

"What do you mean back in the day," she pressed.

"Oh, baby, I'm sorry. I was just kidding. Don't trip. I'm not that man anymore," he assured.

"I know, baby. I know," she kissed his lips, deep and passionate then she reached down and stroked his crotch.

"Hey, I thought you weren't in the mood," Raymond said, enjoying her touch.

"I wasn't until you gave me another option," Michelle sang sweetly.

Now it was his turn to look confused. What other option was she talking about?

"What's up? You want a quickie?" he asked, hand on his belt buckle.

"No. I mean, not right now, but tell me more about your old days, specifically how you would be able to prevent him from taking this money."

Raymond backed up against the wall so he could get a good look at Michelle. He wanted to look into her eyes to see if she was serious.

"What are you saying?" he questioned, removing her hands from his throbbing crotch and pulling them to his chest instead.

"I know the lawyer says it's the right thing to do, but, baby, nobody knows how much that man hurt me. I was such a different woman back then. I believed in him, had faith in our vows and," she took a deep breath and blew it out, "well, let's just say he really shook my faith in men. And to think, he's so heavily involved in the church, for goodness sakes."

"Yeah, but you gotta be careful what you wish for. I mean, he is your kids' father, right?"

"He is, and I don't want you to get the wrong idea about me. But since he and I have been separated, do you know the dog hasn't even tried to see his girls? You think I want that to be their example of what a man should be?" Michelle asked. She felt herself getting more worked up than she wanted. And the last thing she wanted to do was scare Raymond away.

"Yeah, but still..." he said, voice trailing off when she started back up again.

"I was just asking if . . . I don't know," she kissed his lips. "I mean, quite surely you know someone who might want to make a few dollars to help me get rid of this problem of mine," she suggested sweetly.

"Damn, Michelle, you want to knock the brotha off?"

"He's an evil man, Raymond. There's no way he should be getting three-point-four million for making a fool out of me. He should be getting a nice funeral," she exclaimed.

Raymond stood looking at her for a long time. When he spoke he asked one question. "Are you serious about this?"

"Fifty thousand worth," she boasted with a sinister grin. "And a twenty-five thousand dollar bonus once the deed is done."

"Shiiit, you ain't said nothin' but a word for that kinda money!"

Chapter 46

Damien couldn't believe the mess that continued to follow him around like his own personal dark cloud, always hovering over his head.

Here he was consoling his baby brother whose fiancé was just involved in a suspicious hit and run accident, and he had not one, but two drama queens tailing him as they waited in the hospital. Apparently, neither wanted to leave the other alone with him, but for fear of what? He didn't know, but he couldn't think about them right now. His brother needed him.

"Who could've done this?" Barry asked the doctor who stood talking to them in the hallway.

"We don't know. The authorities have been called, and they're investigating. Her father is in there now," the doctor added. "So, it's going to be a few minutes before you can get in to be with her."

Barry was a complete wreck. Damien wished there was something he could do. He didn't like seeing his younger brother hurting like that.

"Let's go take a walk," he tried to say to Barry, more for his sake than his brother's.

"No, I'm not leaving," Barry replied.

He was angry. Sure, Amy had gotten on his very last nerve with all the nagging about the wedding, but never did he want any harm to come to her. This was crazy. And who would've struck her and left her on the side of the road like an animal?

When the room door opened, Barry was prepared to step inside. But the massive imposing figure that seemed to block the entire door frame prevented him from moving. It was Amy's father, Bishop Blackwell. And if looks were lethal, Barry would've been in the right place because he would've been as good as dead.

"This is all your fault," the older man barked.

"W-w-what are you talking about?" Barry frowned.

"We've never had any kind of problems until she decided to marry you. First, that crazy woman stalks my daughter because you were carrying on some sinful affair with her, and now this. If anything permanent happens to my daughter, as God is my witness . . ." Bishop Blackwell snarled.

But Damien stepped between his brother and the threat. "Look, Bishop Blackwell, Barry is hurting just as much as you. We're all hurting here. We don't know why this happened to Amy, but jumping on my brother isn't going to solve a thing."

Damien felt he had to say something, he never expected things to go this far, and he certainly didn't want his brother to take the blame for what happened to Amy.

The sheer disdain with which Bishop Blackwell looked at Damien was enough to make his skin crawl.

"You lowlife, piece of dirt," the older man scowled. "Get out of my way before I crush you like the useless cockroach you are!"

And when Damien didn't move fast enough, the Bishop stormed past him, connecting with his shoulder with such force, it nearly knocked him down to the floor.

Barry rushed to Damien's side. "I don't know what's wrong with him. He's been on my ass since I asked for Amy's hand."

Damien looked at his brother with utter confusion. He asked for her hand in marriage? Did people still do that sort of thing? "Get in there, man," he said, ushering his brother into his fiancé's room.

Charlotte rushed to Damien's side. "Is everything gonna be okay?" Damien shrugged.

Charlotte's phone rang.

"I'll be right back," she said and walked away to take the call.

Damien felt bad for Barry, not just because of what happened to Amy, but because he was planning to marry into a family like that. He wanted to tell the poor bastard to run in the other direction, but he knew better. He knew his baby brother would always do the right thing. And that was why Damien thought he needed to intervene, help save Barry before it was too late, but he never expected this. As a matter of fact, this wasn't what they had discussed—Amy in the hospital? It had gone too far.

As Damien watched Barry walk into Amy's room, he shook the thoughts from his mind and turned to his own brewing turmoil.

"Now, I wanna know what the fuck you're gonna do about this shit here," Jazzlyn hissed, throwing a hand to her hip.

Damien looked confused. "Jazzlyn, don't do this. I'm warning you."

Just then, Charlotte walked back over to them. Damien wasn't sure where she had gone, but he had a feeling she'd reappear at the most inopportune moment, and he was right.

"So, what's going on here?" Charlotte looked between Jazzlyn and Damien. The rage was apparent all over her face.

"Look, this is not the time or the place," Damien began. He didn't know what else to say.

"Well, it looks to me like this is the place because we started at one hospital and ended at another. I want to clear this shit up right now."

"Yeah, let's clear it up," Jazzlyn urged. "Tell your over-weight lover here how I've been doing for you what she obviously can't since I've been back at Sweetwater."

Charlotte's eyes grew wide. She turned to look at Damien and shook her head. "She said you'd do the same thing to me. I guess she was right," she stammered, choking back tears.

"I can explain," Damien turned to her, but it was too late.

"I did everything for you—pleased you every which way you wanted, gave you a threesome, and still you cheated on me?" Charlotte shook her head. He reached out to her, but she snatched herself away from him. "Don't fucking touch me," she spat. She turned to look at Jazzlyn one last time, "You can have him!"

"Charlotte, hold up. Let's talk about this," he called after her. "It was nothing, seriously. Don't do this," he urged.

But Charlotte was halfway down the hall and headed for the bank of elevators. When he turned around, Jazzlyn stood with a victorious smirk across her face.

"You don't need her anyway. You and me, we're two of a kind," she bragged.

Damien shot her the look of death. Why did she have such a big mouth? Why couldn't she keep her trap shut, but more importantly why did he even go back to her ass in the first place?

"There is no us. I wish you would get it through that crazy head of yours. I keep telling you that. I don't want you, plain and simple."

"That's not what you said last night and two nights before that," she reminded.

"No man is gonna turn down easy ass, Jazzlyn. Why can't you get that?"

"Don't sell us short. I was led back here to Sweetwater for a reason. We were meant to be together," she stated.

"It ain't gonna happen," he said as he passed her by and headed in the direction Charlotte went.

Chapter 47

Back in Pastor Goodlove's room, Theola's moment of truth was abruptly interrupted.

"Now we didn't mean to come bursting in on y'all . . . but, Pastor, we had to see you with our own two eyes," Mama Sadie sang. She was seconds away from catching the Holy Ghost all over again.

"I mean, God sure is good," Ms. Geraldine added.

Mama Sadie tossed Theola a menacing frown. They had all but barged into the room baring more cards, flowers, and stuffed animals.

"Everybody is just delighted. We're gonna have a real revival at Bible study tonight," Ms. Geraldine cheered.

"I can't wait to get up outta here," Pastor laughed. "I miss you all more than I care to even think about," he added.

"Oooh, we missed you, too, Pastor, but the good Lord knows best, and he obviously thought you needed the rest. And he sure knew to bring you back in the nick of time, 'cause the saints are acting up!" Mama Sadie said.

Ms. Geraldine nudged Mama Sadie.

"Ooooh!" The older woman yelped.

"Pastor, ain't even out the hospital good. I'm sure Sister Theola here has been updating him on all that's been going on." Ms. Geraldine smiled. She was a handsome woman who had one day hoped to replace the late Mrs. Goodlove before Pastor threw them all for a loop and brought Theola into their church family.

"I'm sure we don't need to be adding to all that she's already told him." Ms. Geraldine gave Theola a knowing glance.

"Now how she gon' tell him something when she ain't hardly ever around." Mama Sadie looked at Theola then turned back to Pastor. "I don't know who's been missing the longest, Pastor—you or that wife of yours," Mama Sadie added.

"Is that so?" Pastor asked, beckoning Theola closer with his eyes.

"Oh, yeah. We lucky if we catch her at service on Sunday evening. Shoot, what am I saying? She was probably long gone by second service, but you probably know all of that already," Mama Sadie said, touching her chest as if that might help control her mouth.

"Missing in action, huh?" Pastor Goodlove added.

"Well, I know a couple of times we tried to take dishes by the house, you know being good natured and all, only to be told she hadn't been seen in days," Mama Sadie added. She was telling it all. And as she did, visions of her croaking and losing the ability to breathe danced before Theola's eyes.

"Well ladies," Theola finally said. "I think Ethan, uh, I mean Pastor could use some rest. Remember he isn't quite out the woods just yet." She smiled sweetly.

"Chile, I dunno what you been told, but my God don't make no mistakes. He didn't wake this man up only to pull him back down. No-sir-ree!" Mama Sadie testified.

Theola wanted to roll her eyes, but she held back, fully aware that her husband's own eyes scrutinized her every move.

Just as she thought this little reunion was wrapping up, in came a few of the deacons.

"We're on our way out. We know y'all probably got lots to talk about. Pastor, we just wanted to see you so we could give a full report to your Sweetwater family, 'cause we sure miss you." Mama Sadie smiled. "You hurry up and get up outta this bed."

Deacons Parker, Jones and Thompson strolled into Pastor's room like rowdy high school boys.

"It sure is good to see you," one of the deacons said.

Theola sighed. She did not feel like sitting around as a parade of church members came through. Thanks to them, she had lost all of the nerve she built up. Now she wasn't sure coming clean was the best thing to do.

As Pastor and the Deacons laughed and talked, she wondered if she should try to sneak out. Quite surely, Ethan didn't expect her to sit by his bedside until he was released, did he?

The Deacons filled Pastor in on a few of the guest pastors who came to preach in his absence. Theola thought it was interesting. Just over a year ago, Deacon Parker was leading the effort to have Pastor removed. Now he stood smiling in his face like he genuinely missed him. *How fake and phony*, she decided, but she didn't dare say a word.

As they were turning to leave, they looked at Theola.

"Sister Theola, we sure have been missing you at Bible study," Deacon Parker sang.

Theola rolled her eyes. Now she was convinced this was part of a bigger conspiracy. Sure, she hadn't been around, but these people didn't like her anyway, so what was it to any of them. If she heard one more comment about the fact that she had been missing in action or gone, she thought she was going to scream. She knew the minute they were alone again, she'd have a lot of explaining to do, and she wasn't looking forward to it.

"Gentlemen," the doctor's voice grabbed everyone's attention. "Oh, and Mrs. Goodlove, I'm going to have to ask you all to leave. We've got a few tests for Pastor."

Theola released a huge sigh of relief. Before the doctor could say another word, she had grabbed her purse and was heading for the door. She needed to get away so she could clear her head and think about what her next step should be. She was no longer sure about coming clean. She had so much to lose.

"Ah, Theola," Pastor called out to her. She stopped and turned to him. "You wanna say bye before you rush up outta here?"

"Oh, I'm so sorry. Uh, I was trying to get over to Bible study. You know it's probably going to be standing room only."

Theola walked over and gave her husband a brisk hug. As she got ready to pull away he grabbed her closer.

"This ain't over," he whispered in her ear.

That's exactly what she was afraid of.

Chapter 48

Michelle arrived at Bible study earlier than usual, and she had been coaching herself on the right thing to say and the right way to say it. She needed to put an end to this squabble with Damien, and she needed to do it as quickly as possible.

She had to give it to her church family because they had gone all out. In addition to playing one of Pastor's old sermons that brought everyone to their feet, there was also a recorded video from him in his hospital bed. Sweetwater members were brought to tears at the sight of their beloved Pastor.

It had been such a long time since she felt at home at Sweetwater, but tonight, things just seemed to be falling right into place.

As service wrapped up, Michelle approached Damien. She was stunned to silence when Jazzlyn of all people came out of nowhere.

"I, ah . . . I wanted to talk to you if you have a minute?" Michelle smiled despite the sight of Jazzlyn. She wanted to ask why she was back at Sweetwater, but she told herself to remain focused.

Damien's eyebrows bunched together. "Ah, sure," he said, sounding quite surprised. "I was heading toward the back. Wanna talk in the G-man's office?"

"That would be nice." Michelle smiled again.

She wasn't sure what Jazzlyn wanted, but since the silly girl didn't say a word to her, she didn't worry about it. Once she followed him into the office, and he closed the door behind them, Michelle took a deep breath.

"You're looking nice," Damien said before he took a seat.

"What? You complimenting me? Didn't think I was your type," Michelle said.

"Not my type? What's that supposed to mean? I married you, didn't I?"

"Let's not go there." Michelle laughed.

"No, seriously. It was never you. It was me. You're still the most beautiful woman I've ever..."

"Save it." Michelle laughed off his compliment. "Seriously."

"Look, I know I'm not one of your favorite people. What I did to you was wrong, and I'm sorry. I don't think I ever got the chance to say that. But anyway, what did you want to discuss?" he asked.

Michelle wasn't expecting him to have kind words for her. His apology held her silent for a bit. She was trying to wrap her mind around his behavior.

"Well, the reason I'm here," she cleared her throat.

What I did to you was wrong, and I'm sorry. She shook the words from her mind and tried to steady her voice. "Um, I wanted to try and reason with you. I wanted to see if you would agree to a settlement in the case. I know it was wrong for me to try and keep the money from you, but honestly, I was just angry. So, I wanted to know how you would feel about doing a three-way split," she said.

Damien's eyebrows inched upward. But Michelle held up her hand.

"By three-way split, I mean you and I and the girls. I want to do more than pay for college. I was thinking we give them each one million dollars broken down at different stages of their lives, but when I think about what's most important, I hope you'll agree that setting up for their future is most important."

"So, I won't have to pay child support anymore?" Damien asked.

His peace offering effort just went out the window with that question. But if that's what it was going to take, she'd agree.

"Yeah, I don't see any reason why you should have to pay to support your children," Michelle said snottily.

"And I'll get at least one million? Ah, one-point-five?" he asked.

"I think that's fair," Michelle quickly said, getting up from her chair. Of course she had no plans on giving him a red cent, but for now, she needed to make a good faith effort.

"Leaving already?" Damien asked, smiling sweetly.

"Uh, yeah. Got an early day tomorrow," she said.

"Oh, that's a shame. I was thinking..."

On the outside, her face held a stoic smile, but on the inside she was screaming at the top of her lungs. She couldn't believe the bastard was trying to sweet talk her.

He got up to walk her to the door. At the door, they shared what Michelle thought was an awkward moment.

"Um, I really thank you for this," Michelle said.

"No, I'm glad we could work it out. I don't like fighting with you. Is there any way I could come over this weekend?"

Michelle didn't react. "You know what. I don't see why that would be a problem. The girls would love to see you."

"Okay, maybe I can take them out to Blueridge. You know — to see the G-man. He's supposed to get released by the end of the week."

On her drive home, Michelle replayed the entire evening in her mind.

What I did to you was wrong and I'm sorry...

She had to think all kinds of thoughts to prevent herself from screaming out as he tried to use his tired-ass charm on her. The time she spent alone with him made her even more resolved to see her plan through. All she could think about was what his last words would be.

Michelle pulled into the driveway and jumped out, eager to catch Raymond's call. The last time they'd talked, he seemed stressed — something to do with that baby mama of his. She didn't want to give it too much thought.

"Hey, baby," she cooed later as they talked.

"You okay? How'd it go?"

"Better than ever," Michelle reported all giddy.

"So, dude just gave in and agreed? Just like that?"

"Well, yes and no. First, he told me how beautiful I am, how I was the best woman he's ever had, and he said he was sorry," Michelle reported. Raymond was uncharacteristically quiet.

"You still there?"

"Yeah, so what's up with y'all now?" Raymond asked sadly.

"What do you mean?"

"I mean, he don' said he's sorry, showering you with compliments, I just mean y'all talking about hooking back up again or what?"

"Raymond? What's that supposed to mean?"

Michelle didn't want to give Raymond the wrong impression, but she did want him to know that if she wanted her loser of an ex back, she could get him.

"I'm just saying: If you and dude decided to hook back up, you just need to let me know 'cause I ain't for no drama," he stressed.

He had his nerve, she thought, but didn't say.

"Baby, I don't understand why you're getting all worked up. I mean, we've got plans, right? And if those plans don't tell you how I feel about him, I don't know what will."

"What you saying?" Raymond asked.

"You know what I'm saying," she assured. "We're still on track to handle the business."

"So look here. Let's hook up tomorrow, and you can holla at me then," Raymond said, suddenly rushing off the phone.

Michelle sat there holding the phone. She was bewildered by Raymond's reaction, but the moment she got to that prison she'd make sure he wasn't trying to back out of their deal.

Raymond wasn't done with the phone when he disconnected from Michelle.

"See, what I tell you?" he asked.

"Damn, I can't believe that shit. She's on one for real. I can't believe she wants that fool dead," the woman exclaimed.

"I tried to tell you," Raymond said.

"Well, whassup? I mean, what are you gonna do?"

Raymond blew out a hard breath. "Seventy-five thousand dollars ain't no drop in the bucket," Raymond said.

"Shiiit, I know quite a few cats who would do it for far less than that."

$\mathbf{D}$amien didn't know what he was thinking when he came on to Michelle. He was just glad she had enough sense to ignore his advances. Lord knows he didn't want to go back to her rigid-ass.

She was boring in bed, never wanted to try anything new, and doled sex out to him like he was a trained puppy. Anytime he pissed her off, he could expect to go to bed with blue balls. He was sorry for the way things went down between them, but he was not sorry to be rid of her. And now that they had reached an agreement, he could sign the papers and get paid.

He told himself he'd worry about Charlotte and Jazzlyn later. Truth be told, he didn't care if neither of them wanted to be bothered with him anymore either. Charlotte was cool, real freaky, just the way he liked his women, but she was very insecure and that was a major turn off.

And Jazzlyn, well, she was only good for exactly what he'd been getting from her since she came back to Sweetwater.

But the major problem with her was that she was still looking for a husband, and he was not about to travel that road again.

He figured once he got his cash, he'd high-tail it out of town for a few days. Maybe he'd go to Vegas, blow a little money, buy some ass, and really have some fun. He deserved it as far as he was concerned.

The knock at the door pulled him from his thoughts. Before he could say come in, Jazzlyn waltzed into the office like she was invited.

"I know you're mad at me," she cooed. "But I just want you to know that I'm the one for you. And I didn't know any other way to make you understand. I mean, don't you feel it? Don't you feel the electricity when we're together?"

As she talked, all Damien could do was sit there and think about everything that was wrong with her and why she would never be more than a piece of ass to him.

"So, see, don't be mad at me," she tried to pout. But with her severe overbite, it just made her face look even more deformed. "Daddy," she cooed, moving closer to him in a seductive manner. Jazzlyn suddenly dropped to her knees and crawled to him on all fours.

She may have been hideous in the face, and she wasn't the most eloquent speaker, but she knew how to be sexy. There was something about a woman crawling that turned Damien on.

He tried to tell himself to resist her. She had caused enough problems for him, but he was already halfway to hard, and he knew he'd soon need relief.

"Oh, daddy, you know I know what you like," she purred.

Damien started squirming in his seat. He wanted to tell her to get up and get out. His brain said that was the right thing to do, but the tingling in his crotch was saying something else.

"I just wanna make you feel good," Jazzlyn said as she rubbed her hands up his legs and started to unbuckle his pants.

Before he could try and talk himself out of what she was about to do, he was nestled deep inside her warm and welcoming mouth. He didn't have to enjoy it, he tried to tell himself.

But if Jazzlyn didn't know anything else, she knew how to give a mean blow-job. Damien was sure Superhead had nothing on her skills.

Giving into the feeling, he threw his head back, closed his eyes and told himself he'd deal with the rest of his problems some other time.

"Jeesus!" Damien cried, clutching the arms of the chair.

Jazzlyn was relentless. She showed no mercy as she devoured him whole. She had him humming and talking in tongues.

"Oh, baby," he went on. "Oh, yes girl!"

"What in God's name is wrong with you?" Mama Sadie's voice rang out.

Damien's eyes flew open. Jazzlyn jumped back from his crotch, and the members of the Ladies Auxiliary got more than an eyeful.

"Good God Almighty," someone yelled.

"Boy, it's like you got some kinda problem or something, and right here in your daddy's office," Mama Sadie admonished.

Damien couldn't pull his pants up fast enough. He couldn't believe he had been caught with his pants around his ankles and Jazzlyn's face buried between his thighs.

"Get! You get, you ol' heathen," the church mothers swatted toward Jazzlyn, who was scrambling to get up from the floor.

"You need to be bathed in the Blood of Jesus Almighty! It makes no sense for someone to be so unholy," one of the old women screamed.

Damien was just disgusted with himself. When was he going to learn? Jazzlyn had already cost him so much, but for whatever reason, she was like a moth to a bright bulb, and despite how much he coached himself, he couldn't stay away from her. He was weak, and this he knew, but he did very little to change his fault or even control himself.

After the old women chased Jazzlyn out of the office, Damien quickly dressed himself. As he was about to sneak out, something thumped him upside his head. When he grabbed the spot and turned to look back toward the office, he saw Ms. Geraldine in the doorway. She had flung her Bible and hit him in the head.

"Shame on you," she screamed.

Instead of complaining, Damien just hurried down the hall and slipped out one of the side entrances. He figured this was a good time to go and check on either his brother, his father, or both.

It didn't take long for him to decide which of the Goodlove men to visit. As he jumped on Highway 59 headed south. His cell phone rang. It was Barry.

"Hey, what's up?" Damien answered.

"Dee, it's Sissy," Barry said.

"What's Sissy?" Damien asked.

"Sissy . . . don't tell me you forgot the woman who vowed to make my life a living hell. Well, apparently she's back, and she may have been behind the wheel."

Damien looked up toward the ceiling sarcastically and shook his head. "So both our stalkers just happen to pop up simultaneously. This has got to be somebody's idea of a really bad joke," Damien huffed sourly.

"Well, I'm not laughing. I, for one, thought Sissy was long gone. Now I know Amy's father is probably sitting up plotting my demise."

"What about Amy? How's she doing?" he asked sincerely.

"Broken ribs, a few fractures in her legs . . . they're doing more tests, saying they want to make sure her lungs are okay," Barry reported.

Now looking at his brother, Damien felt like he was being swallowed whole by guilt. Barry was a broken man. His shoulders slouched, his head hung low, and his eyes looked dark and faraway. Damien felt so bad for his little brother. But mostly, he felt bad about intercepting the call Sissy had made and getting into cahoots with her crazy ass in the first place. He should've known better.

Chapter 50

Theola didn't know if she was coming or going. Her cell phone was ringing like crazy, and no matter how many times she ignored the calls, it seemed like the phone would ring again. Then there was the situation with Ethan. She wanted so badly to call the doctors and tell them this man, the one that they had released a mere three days ago was not the man she had married.

No, her Ethan had been replaced by a man with a mean-streak, one who had put the fear of Jesus in her when she couldn't explain just where she had been spending most of her time.

"Theola!"

She jumped upon hearing him scream her name. This was not going to work. She simply couldn't live like this. If someone had told her a week ago that she would fear her husband, she would've laughed in their face. But here she was scared shitless. And she had good reason to be.

"I know there's been a constant flow of company since I got home, but we got some unfinished business to talk about," Pastor Goodlove said.

"Yes, I know Ethan, but I don't want to get you all excited," Theola stressed.

"So, the staff tells me you haven't been around much since I was down. Where've you been?" he asked, moving close to her and towering over her small frame.

He was already an imposing figure, but add this mean-streak, and Theola didn't know whether she should flinch or try to call for help.

"I do have something to tell you, but I don't want you to be upset with me," she sobbed.

Pastor rolled his eyes and started waving his arms. "I don't feel like listening to any of this bull. You wasn't sitting up crying when I was laid up in that hospital. Now woman, cut the waterworks and get to talking."

The old Ethan would never have talked to her like that. This one seemed more determined than ever to break her, and she was tired of the battle. She wasn't in a fighting mood.

"I just needed some time away. You know how these people feel about me. You know they don't care much about me, much less what happens to me."

"So what's new? It's been like that since you stepped foot in Sweetwater. What's that got to do with you being gone?"

"Well, with all that was going on with you, I just needed to go somewhere to clear my head or at least try to."

"So spill it. Where'd you go?"

"I took a trip to Belize—actually a few trips," Theola confessed softly.

"And who did you take these trips with?" he asked, one eyebrow nearly touching his hairline.

"I went alone," Theola said.

For the next hour and a half, she confessed the entire story to her husband, leaving out the part about just how well she'd gotten to know Stone Pier. Her version of the story centered around how stressed she was, unsure of what would happen with him, and the nasty way she had been treated by the holy rollers at Sweetwater. By the time Theola was done telling the story about how Reginald had set her up, and how she remained in a state of confusion over how best to handle the situation, Pastor Goodlove seemed to have softened a bit.

"So, he told you he wanted to come back home, but he didn't want to face any jail time?"

"Yes, and he thought he could blackmail me into helping him out," Theola said.

She couldn't remember the last time she'd seen Ethan so calm since he'd been released from the hospital.

He took a seat across from her and shook his head. Theola wasn't sure how she should proceed. She knew for sure she wouldn't get off this easy.

"What did you tell him you would do?"

"I didn't get a chance to tell him anything. I got the call that you woke up, and I paid to take a chartered flight out of there. I wanted to be by your side sooner, but I couldn't. There are only two flights leaving every day, and I had just missed the last one."

A silence that seemed to drag on forever hung between them.

"So you said he was trying to blackmail you. If he lured you there in the first place what would he be able to hold over your head?"

Theola sighed. She hadn't thought about that.

"Well, the fact that I was spending all that money to go back and forth. He thought if the church found out, they'd know that it was me who had stolen the money in the first place," she offered. She was speaking so fast, even she didn't believe the words that were coming out of her mouth.

Pastor sat there, nodding slightly as if he was in deep thought.

All of a sudden, his dark eyes turned on her. They narrowed as he sat staring for what seemed like forever.

"Theola is there anything else you want to tell me about this situation?" he asked cautiously.

"Ethan, I was so afraid, I didn't know what to do. I didn't have anyone I could talk to, and no one to confide in. I have been stressing, tossing and turning at night trying to figure a way out."

"I wish you would've said something to someone," he told her.

"I have no one to talk to here. Sweetwater doesn't really care for me, so it's like I'm a loner. That's when I saw the brochure, I was more than a little excited. It actually felt like just what I needed, you know, to deal with the stress."

All of a sudden, Ethan got up and picked up the phone.

Theola could hear bits and pieces of his conversation, but she wasn't trying to be too nosey. She just wanted to know what, if anything, he planned to do to her.

Once he wrapped up his phone call, he turned to Theola and barked, "Go pack."

"Where are we going?"

"To Belize. Go pack. Our flight leaves in two hours."

Wow, was all Theola could think. This couldn't possibly end right for her.

Chapter 51

"**H**ey, baby," Michelle grinned as she answered the phone. She loved the freedom they had with the illegal cell phone. They could talk about anything for as long as they wanted. "You got any news for me?" she asked, anxiously.

"I do, but what's going on with you?"

Michelle hated when he started in with all that small talk when she wanted to get straight to the business. Although Damien had been acting quite cordial with her lately, she still didn't want to hand him a single dime if she didn't have to. And she appreciated his lame apology even though she didn't think it was sincere.

Besides, she knew he was up to his old ways. She had heard the rumors flying around Sweetwater about him screwing Jazzlyn again. And it disgusted Michelle to no end. Every time she thought about all the trouble that tramp had caused, and still, he went back to her, eeewww. Her soon-to-be ex truly was scum.

"So, look. I just wanted to make sure we're on the same page," Raymond was saying. Michelle liked when he talked to her like that. His no nonsense tone was enough to get her juices flowing.

"It's like I said, fifty up front," she said calmly.

"Yeah, and another quarter after, right?"

"Um, another quarter?" Michelle asked. She wasn't sure what he meant by that.

"Twenty-five?" Raymond stressed. "A quarter," he translated.

"Oh." Michelle laughed. "Yes, I'm sorry. I'm with you now." She giggled. She felt silly when she didn't get his slang right away.

"Okay, well, I just wanted to make sure you ain't changed your mind or anything like that," he quipped.

"C'mon, baby. You know me well enough to know once I make up my mind, it's pretty much made up right?" she asked.

"Right, right," Raymond sang. "So dig it," he began. "I'm gonna holla back at you later. I should have some news by tomorrow when I see you."

"Oh, that soon?" Michelle asked, unable to hide the surprise in her voice.

"It's like I told you: That's some serious chedda', and the way times are hard nowadays, it could be done a lot faster than you think," he added.

"Okay, well enough of that, baby. What about you?"

"What about me?" Raymond asked.

"Talk dirty to me," Michelle purred. "I'm so wet right now."

"Uh, yeah. Look at this. I, uh . . . I need to get back with you."

"So, you just gonna rush off the phone and leave me here to play with myself all alone?" she pouted.

"Look, lemme handle this business. We can talk later after I get everything in place."

"But, baby," Michelle whined.

She didn't know what was wrong with him. Raymond usually ended their phone calls with explicit questions about what she was wearing and what all she wanted him to do to her the next day. There were so many nights when she'd have erotic dreams after thinking about their previous conversation. He made her feel like a desirable woman, and she often thought, if he could do all of this while he was on lockdown, imagine what it would be like when he was out on the streets and they were really together.

"Oh, okay," she said, trying not to sound too put out by his rejection. When she hung up the phone, she sat there thinking for a moment.

But the line didn't go completely dead when Michelle hung up. The second she was gone, another female voice said, "Damn, so she serious, huh?"

"I told you she was, man," Raymond confirmed.

"Don't think I missed that little dirty talk that didn't get to happen," she joked.

"Look, man, that ain't your business," Raymond said.

"So what's up with you and her anyways 'cause I ain't for no foolishness," she hissed.

"Don't start that ol' bullshit right now. I gotta keep my head straight," Raymond warned.

"If you wanna pull this shit off right, you gotta keep more than just your head straight. Don't let that straight and narrow bitch get you all twisted. I ain't nobody's fool," she huffed.

"Look, man. I gotta go," he said, sighing.

"Umph, you better call tomorrow."

Raymond hung up without saying goodbye.

The next day, Michelle could hardly wait to get to the prison. She dropped her girls off, pulled up, and parked. She nearly skipped through the gates, even greeting the guard with a smile.

"How are you today, Miss Michelle?" he asked.

"Wonderful," she smiled as she signed her name and skipped to the building where the sessions were held.

It had been a long time since she felt that good, and she wanted to hang on to the feeling. Michelle all but breezed through the first two sessions. She was ready for Raymond in the worse way imaginable.

Once he hit the room minutes after the last session started, they exchanged knowing glances, and she took off to their secret meeting place.

Pastor Peebles barely looked up from his Bible, which helped them sneak out undetected.

The moment they were together behind closed doors, all of the questions she had, took a back seat. First priority, she needed him to put out the fire that burned so deep inside of her.

His lips, his touch, were so electrifying. She closed her eyes and tried to linger in the feeling. Michelle worked like a desperate woman, shoving him onto the toilet seat top. She recklessly pulled his pants and briefs down. Kneeling at his lap, she literally licked her lips as she stared longingly at his unbelievably thick tool. When Michelle's eyes took in the full expansion of his muscled erection, something registered in her eyes and made her mouth water.

She wanted to take that fabulous erection into her hand to feel his skin. She worked him over delicately, like she was handling an explosive that might ignite if not touched with care.

But before Michelle could take him into her mouth, he pulled back, causing her to stumble as she was on her knees. Her heart began to race, and she looked up at him in confusion.

"We need to talk," Raymond said.

Michelle didn't want to talk. She wanted an orgasm, but the look on Raymond's face left her wondering what could be so important that he'd deny both her pleasure and his own.

Chapter 52

There was far too much available ass walking around for Damien to have to beg anyone for forgiveness. That's how he felt, and he'd be damned if he changed his position. Charlotte was cool and all, but if she didn't like what was going on, she could hit the road like many before her had.

"I can't believe you're fucking her again," she'd admonished. Charlotte had the nerve to look at him like he had shit on his face. Days after she decided to walk away from what they had, Damien was at her place to retrieve his things.

Was she seriously looking down her nose at him?

"I don't know what you're talking about," Damien insisted, trying to keep it light and cool.

"A woman ain't gonna go all buck wild like that unless something is going on," Charlotte had said.

Damien shrugged his shoulders. "You don't know Jazzlyn." He pulled out a drawer and grabbed the extra shirts he had in it.

"I know women, and I know what makes us crazy," Charlotte persisted. "Besides, you forget I've been a member of Sweetwater for years. I know her a whole lot more than you think."

Damien rolled his eyes and sighed. Why was he defending his actions to her? Yeah, they had been kicking it for a minute, but he was planning to take off for a little while, and he was leaving his options open. It wasn't like he didn't feel anything for Charlotte. She had mad skills, and she was cool, or at least she was in the beginning. But she was now starting to nag him, just like a wife, and he damn sure wasn't trying to go down that road again.

When Damien walked into her bathroom to get his toothbrush, she followed behind him.

"So are you ready to come clean or what?" she had asked, her head cocked to the side, hands on hips like she was simply waiting him out.

Come clean? Shit, I'm a grown ass man! Damien had wanted to remind her, but he decided she wasn't worth the effort. So, he just stood there, looking like he'd rather be anyplace but there being interrogated by a woman who was not and would not be his wife. Shit, he didn't answer to a woman when he was married. He damn sure was not about to answer to some chick he was banging. Besides, he thought she had told Jazzlyn she was through. Why was she stressing him now?

"Are you gonna be a man about this or what?"

So now this was somehow an indication of whether he was a man? He nearly laughed out loud at that one.

"Look, I don't know what you want me to say," Damien began. Her sad eyes grew cold, and she looked like she was trying to put some kind of hex on him.

"I want you to fess up. That's what I want," she snarled through gritted teeth.

This was becoming way too much for him. This was starting to remind him of those nights he'd get caught sneaking home and into his marital bed at some ungodly hour. Oh, she really had him twisted.

Silence.

Charlotte stared. He stared, but said nothing.

So when Charlotte turned to leave him alone in the bathroom, he simply shrugged his shoulders and continued to gather his things. Soon, he left her place and headed for the hospital.

He was more concerned with his brother's well-being. Amy was still in the hospital, and Barry had refused to leave her side. The guilt Damien felt was immeasurable.

"You should go home, grab a shower and get some sleep," Damien had suggested to Barry.

"I can't leave her," Barry replied.

"You're not leaving her, but you gotta give some of her church family the chance to see her, too," Damien tried to reason.

"No, the Bishop has cut all visitations, and honestly, I'm kinda scared to leave. He might not let me back in."

"That arrogant bastard," Damien snarled. His ringing cell phone pulled his attention away. It was his attorney.

"Hey, Dee, where are you?"

"Sam, my man, what's going on?" He didn't like when his attorney called him sounding all serious and businesslike. He'd be scared if he didn't know any better.

"Are you near the office?"

"No, I'm leaving the hospital. Why? What's up?"

"I need you to get over here as quickly as you can," Sam said.

"Okay, I can't promise a time. You know traffic is a mess over there right now," he warned.

"Yeah, I know, but I really need you to come here as quickly as you can."

Damien figured Michelle wasted no time in getting the news to his attorney. He had hoped to break the news to Sam himself, so he could explain that he agreed to the deal because of his children.

"It's gonna take me at least two hours to make it out there," Damien reported.

What was the big deal, really? He didn't understand why he even had to show up at his lawyer's office just to sign the damn divorce papers. *Sam could be such an ass sometimes,* Damien thought. Maybe he was pissed that Damien had settled for so little.

"I don't know about that," Sam had said.

Did he think sounding seriously stressed was going to make traffic on Highway 59 move any faster, Damien wondered. It didn't matter whether he knew about it or not. There was only so much Damien could do, and he couldn't fly out there.

"Why don't I call you when I'm closer. What's the problem? Just leave the papers with your secretary if you've gotta run out," Damien suggested.

"It's not that, really," Sam said, sounding as if he was now distracted.

Damien wasn't really in the mood. He hated sitting in traffic, so he figured if Sam knew what was good for him, he'd leave the papers and go meet his friends at the nearest watering hole instead of tripping because traffic was a bitch.

"Well, I didn't want to say anything just yet, but there's a young lady here that I want you to meet," Sam finally said.

"You ol' dog you," Damien started laughing.

"No, it's nothing like that. Hey, look that's the other line. I need to take that call, but get here as fast as you can. I'm gonna try and hold her," Sam said.

Before Damien could ask anymore questions, his attorney had hung up. Why would a woman go to his lawyer's office? *Oh, God,* he sure hoped nobody was trying to slap him with a paternity suit. He was always really careful, but he had heard horror stories before. That was just like Sam to get him all worked up and leave his ass hanging.

As Damien pulled on to the South bound side of Highway 59, he thought he'd lose his mind. Traffic was crawling, giving his mind enough time to race with thoughts of who the mystery woman could be and why the hell she was waiting for him at his lawyer's office.

Chapter 53

When visitors from the States came to Belize, people for miles knew they were coming. No one knew for sure if it was someone who worked at the airport that tipped the natives off, but someone always did.

And this time was no different. Before the plane touched down at the old airport, word of Theola's arrival had spread quickly. She was staying in the same hotel because that's what Ethan said they should do. And she thought they were going alone, but two large menacing men she had never seen before accompanied them.

By the time Theola unlocked her room door and stepped inside, she wished there was a way she could vanish into thin air. Stone Pier stood near the balcony as if he was at home. Unfortunately for Theola, he was wearing his customary tight swimming trunks and sandals with the duffle bag close by.

"You're back..." his voice seemed trapped in his throat at the sight of Ethan.

"This is my husband, the Reverend Goodlove," Theola said firmly, hoping Stone Pier would get the hint. She was already embarrassed by him being there, and the fact that he seemed so familiar with her. There was no way she could deny the air of intimacy that hung between them.

Pastor Goodlove was no fool, and the look on his face said he wasn't buying this platonic act they had going for a second, but he was on a mission. He'd deal with his wife later.

"Where is Reginald?" Pastor Goodlove asked Stone Pier.

They didn't waste time exchanging fake pleasantries or anything like that. Pastor Goodlove wanted to get down to business.

"He will be here later," Stone Pier stammered.

Pastor Goodlove looked around the room. Theola could just imagine what kind of thoughts were running through his mind. Suddenly, he turned his attention back to Stone Pier.

"You need to put on some clothes," Pastor Goodlove said.

"Oh, yes, of course," Stone Pier said and immediately started digging into his duffle back.

Theola couldn't remember a time when she'd seen him behave so nervously.

"Uh, this is the young man I told you about," Theola began, hoping to break up the awkwardness. "The one who helped me get out."

"I'm sure he was quite helpful," Pastor stated dryly.

Her eyebrows shot up, but she knew when to be quiet. She didn't want to see any signs of that mean-streak that had a way of popping up.

Pastor Goodlove started to walk around the luxurious suite. His scrutinizing gaze took everything in. Theola stood by like this was judgment day.

Stone Pier stood there trying to appear unimportant.

"So, he'll come here this evening?" Pastor Goodlove asked after he had fully inspected the place.

"Usually, when I come in, he'd show up," she reported.

"Is that so?" Pastor Goodlove glared at her and at Stone Pier. Theola could only imagine all the thoughts running around in his head. She was embarrassed. She felt guilty of everything his mind must've been playing in his head.

"So what do you do here?" he asked toward Stone Pier.

He quickly jumped to attention and began stuttering.

"I'm working with specialty groups."

Pastor Goodlove tossed Theola a you've-gotta-be-kidding glance and listened as Stone Pier basically confirmed that he was part of the welcoming committee for wealthy women who traveled alone. He of course didn't say that, but he didn't need to. Pastor Goodlove got all the information he needed only minutes after stepping into the room.

"Is there a way to call this punk and let him know you're here?" he asked Theola.

Her eyes shifted to Stone Pier. "I don't usually reach out," she confessed.

Pastor Goodlove seemed restless. Theola was uncomfortable and Stone Pier seemed afraid. She didn't know how much longer she could take it. The silence wasn't helping the situation either.

When the telephone in the room started to ring, Stone Pier jumped.

"That is him," he said.

Theola walked over to it and stopped.

"Pick it up," her husband coached.

So she did. "Hello?" Theola's voice was shaky and a shiver ran the length of her body.

"So, I thought I was gonna have to send a search party for you. You stopped answering my calls," Reginald said.

"I was busy," she said.

"I hope you were busy coming up with the plan we agreed on," he said.

When Theola didn't answer, he called out to make sure she was still on the phone.

"I'm here," she said.

"So, I'll be by there later. I'm ready for this shit to be over," she said.

"I'll be here, and we can talk when you get here," Theola said.

The sad thing, Theola thought was, she had no idea what was about to happen. She knew there would be a confrontation between Ethan and Reginald, but she didn't know how out of hand it would get.

Pastor Goodlove ordered room service, consulted with his two companions and did his best to ignore Stone Pier. Theola felt so out of place. For the first time, she realized she and her husband didn't do any kind of leisure traveling. They were so different. It wasn't just the age difference, but they lacked similar interests, conversation and just about every aspect of their lives were separate, except church.

Nearly two hours later, there was a knock at the door. By now, Pastor Goodlove had invited his two friends into their room.

Theola was scared shitless when the two men, both very large and mean-looking jumped into position by the time the second knock sounded.

Pastor Goodlove motioned for her to wait, her heart fluttered, and she looked at him with confusion on her face.

"What?" she mouthed.

He held up his hand again, motioning for her to wait.

When the two guys pulled out guns, she thought for sure she was going to pass out.

"Calm down," Pastor Goodlove whispered. "Just let him in, and we've got the rest.

Theola didn't know what scared her most, the cold look in her husband's eyes or the thought that he was planning to jump his own flesh and blood with two armed men.

The knock came again, this time it was louder. Theola jumped despite herself. Everything happened so quickly, she didn't have time to really react. She swung the door open, and before she knew it, Reginald was being dragged into the room by his collar. His eyes grew wide with fear as a gun was held to his temple.

"You bitch! You double-crossed me," he managed to say.

Chapter 54

Michelle couldn't believe the day had finally come. In less than twenty-four hours, she'd be a multi-millionaire. The minute her community service was done, she planned to throw a huge party. She'd buy her parents a new house, schedule a vacation for her and the girls, and then wait for Raymond to be released.

She was so happy that Damien had agreed to sign the papers. All of the details had been worked out with her attorney and Damien's.

"You are looking better and better each day," Pastor Peebles said, smiling at her in between the first and second session.

And Michelle felt great, too. She decided it was best that she not go on about the money she was expecting so she simply smiled nicely and accepted his compliment.

When the second session wrapped up, the butterflies had started to come alive. She wasn't sure when to expect him, but she knew he'd be there sooner or later.

Michelle went through her duties of passing out pens, paper and Bibles and was about to take her seat in the back when the door swung open. In strolled Raymond.

There was just something about him that turned her on. Maybe it was his sexy swagger, the way he walked into a room like he was barging in to claim what was his.

Raymond took a seat near the back, stretched his long legs and eased back in his chair.

The minute it looked like he was settled, and Pastor Peebles was engrossed in his scripture, Michelle got up and eased out the door. She speed-walked to their secret meeting spot then waited for him to come barging in.

When he finally did, Michelle sprang to her feet and all but jumped into his arms. She showered his face and head with kisses and fought the urge to rip his clothes from his body. Being in his presence seemed to remind her about all that was missing in her life.

"Oh, baby. I'm so glad to see you," she purred.

"What's up?" Raymond asked.

Michelle pulled back a bit gazing at him through cautious eyes. Her heart thumped. She sensed something was wrong.

"Baby, is everything okay?" she asked, guarded.

"Just got a lot on my mind," Raymond mumbled.

"Well, you know we don't have a lot of time," Michelle stressed.

"I know baby," he said. "I missed you," he muttered, but he may as well have said it's raining outside. There was no emotion in his voice.

She reached up and suckled his bottom lip. Then she used her hand to explore his body. It didn't take long for him to get into it. Just as she suspected, he wanted her just as badly.

Soon, Michelle was pinned up against the wall. Raymond unbuttoned her pants, pulled it down freeing one leg, and hoisted her up against the wall.

"Oh, Jesus," she cried.

He manhandled her, and she wrapped her legs around him. They were kissing and caressing each other while he managed to undo his own pants.

Raymond entered her with so much force it nearly took her breath away. But this was exactly what she wanted, what she needed after being forced to spend night after night, lonely and horny.

"Yes, take me," she cried.

"This what you want?" he asked, thrusting his hips to emphasize his words.

"Oh yes, yes," Michelle repeated. She was truly in paradise. The bliss he brought to her was simply unparalleled.

She couldn't wait for him to finish his sentence so they could really do it right.

As they dressed after their hurried lovemaking session, Raymond looked over at her. "So, we still on, right?"

"You keep asking me that. Do you think I'm gonna change my mind?" Michelle wanted to know.

"It's just . . . well, this sort of thing is not something you play with. I mean, you can't go making plans, then have a change of heart. Shit don't work like that," he warned.

Michelle looked at him with bright eyes. She didn't understand what he found so hard to believe. Hadn't she told him about the sheer humiliation she suffered because of Damien?

"Look, baby. You don't have to worry about me changing my mind. I know what I want, and I know I want it done," she said with all seriousness.

"Lemme go out and you follow behind me," he suggested without commenting on what she had said.

Before he turned to leave, she tugged on his arm.

"Are we okay?" she asked.

"Yeah, we straight," he assured her. Then he ducked out and took off in the direction opposite the Bible study classroom.

Michelle waited the appropriate amount of time, then she slowly opened the door, peered up and down the hall in both direction and stepped out once she decided the coast was clear.

Raymond knew what he had to do, and he knew he needed to do it fast. At first he wasn't sure about whether Michelle was serious, but their last meeting told him she was. And he didn't want to get on her bad side.

He couldn't imagine the things Damien had done for her to want him dead. It wasn't enough that she was getting more money than any one person could spend, but she wanted to see that bastard buried six feet under.

When he arrived at his cell block, he greeted a couple of his homeboys. Since word had spread about Raymond and his relationship with Michelle, he was like the big man on the quad.

Raymond wondered if maybe one of them wanted to make some real cash. He quickly shook the thought from his head. What was he thinking?

$\mathbf{D}$amien felt like he had been stuck on Highway 59 for five, long, painstaking hours instead of two. Traffic was moving slower than if he was putting mo in front of jo, and strolling on the freeway. Then his phone rang. He would've ignored it, but he noticed the name on Caller ID.

"What the hell were you thinking?" he barked into the phone.

"You said you wanted me to stop the wedding," the woman said easily.

"Yeah, but I didn't tell you to try and kill her," Damien tried to reason. "I just wanted you to try and I don't know..."

"Typical man." She laughed. "That's why I did what I thought was best versus asking what you thought I should do."

"Well, I guess I should've told you what to do because you've gone too far," Damien stressed.

"Is there going to be a wedding?"

"That's not the point," Damien tried to defend.

"But is there going to be a wedding anytime soon?" she repeated.

"You're not getting my point," Damien tossed in.

"No, you're not getting the point. You said you didn't want your brother to marry her crazy ass. Now you want to try and criticize the way I handled the problem?"

"You know what, Sissy . . . look, I need to go. Um, I'll call you soon. I just need you to leave town. They're already suspecting you," Damien said.

"Oh, I'm not going anywhere. I did my part. Now I expect you to do yours. Talk to your brother. Make him understand that I'm the one for him, not Amy."

"Sissy," Damien tried to interrupt, but she kept talking. She kept reminding him that he had reached out to her. She just wouldn't stop talking, and Damien realized he had made a huge mistake.

When he finally exited First Colony Boulevard and made the left turn to go to his attorney's office, he simply hung up on Sissy and turned off his phone.

He took a deep breath and pulled himself together. He fully expected to be met by the receptionist holding the papers Sam had probably left for him to sign. *Knowing Sam*, Damien thought, he was probably at the nearest strip club, playing Mr. Big Stuff. Once he signed the papers, he figured he'd go meet with Sissy and offer to buy her off.

"Mr. Goodlove," the receptionist said as if she had been waiting on him and him alone. She smiled, stood, and quickly ushered him into Sam's office. "He's been waiting on you"

Upon seeing Damien, Sam, abruptly wrapped up his phone call and pulled his feet from his desk. He reached over to hang up the phone and looked up at his client.

"I don't know what the hell is going on here, but there's somebody I need you to meet," Sam exclaimed.

"Man, what I tell you..." Damien began, hoping he didn't sit in traffic for this kind of bullshit.

He just wanted to sign the papers and get going. Sam had a way of wanting to mix work with pleasure. Signing papers would've turned into drinks at Pappadeaux's, then Sam would've convinced him to take a ride out to one of his favorite gentleman's clubs.

Sam stood and motioned for Damien to follow him.

"You talked to Michelle lately?" Sam asked as they approached the door.

Damien stopped walking.

If this was about to be a protest over the settlement agreement he had already reached with Michelle, he wasn't in the mood. Especially since he had already told her he was going to sign the papers. There was a part of him that did not want to disappoint Michelle anymore. He knew he had already done enough. The many women over the years, the scandal that rocked Sweetwater with Jazzlyn, and finally the whole HIV scare. No, he had done enough to Michelle.

"Sam," Damien began, prepared to launch into the speech he had been going over in his head. He didn't think he needed to explain to his lawyer who worked *for* him why he had reached an agreement with his own wife. He realized that they were soon-to-be divorced, but still, Sam worked *for* him! Plain and simple. "I'm tired of my kids seeing us fight. Michelle and I agreed its best for us to take care of this so we can both move on," Damien said adamantly. "Besides, with the agreement, I won't have to pay child support. The money is going into a trust for the girls."

"But Damien—" Sam tried to interject, but Damien stopped him before he could finish.

"This is not up for discussion. The deal is done, and that's all there is to it, Sam," Damien stressed. When he sighed like it was all he could do to hear what else Sam wanted, Damien closed his eyes. He took a deep breath of his own.

"Damien, what I'm trying to tell you is, this has nothing to do with the agreement you made with Michelle. But I do believe what this young woman has to tell you may impact that agreement."

Damien's eyebrows went up. Sam would stop at nothing to get his point across. He already knew what Sam was up to— bring in a woman who foolishly signed an agreement without her attorney present. Yeah, yeah. Damien got the message.

"Okay, but after I meet with her, we sign the papers, and get them to Michelle so we can finally wrap this mess up?"

"If you still want to sign after meeting with her," Sam shrugged his shoulders easily, "you're the client. I work for you. If you still want to sign, then I'll let you use my favorite pen."

Damien smiled. He motioned for Sam to get the door then he asked, "So who is this woman, and what did you have to promise her for this little testimonial?" Damien chuckled as he walked out the door Sam held open.

They walked side-by-side down the long carpeted corridor that led to the conference room.

"It's not that type of party, pal," Sam said.

"So who is this woman anyway? I mean, what's she got to do with me?"

Sam pulled in a deep breath. Damien wasn't sure what was going on, but it was obvious there'd be no signature until he met with Sam's woman, so he followed his lawyer into the firm's conference room.

Sam pulled the door open. The big screen TV was turned to the Maury Povich show and a large leather chair was facing the TV.

"No, that bitch didn't," a woman's voice screamed at the screen.

Damien shot Sam a cautious look. Sam snickered.

"Eh-hhmmm," Sam cleared his throat.

Nothing.

"Ah, hello," he called out.

But still, nothing.

Suddenly, Sam picked up a remote and turned the TV off. The leather chair spun around with such force it seemed as if it might crash into the large glass table.

"What the hell you doing?" the woman snarled.

Damien's eyes took in all of her. He wasn't sure what held his eyes more, the tons of makeup caked onto her face or the fake lashes that looked like she was dressing up for Halloween. Her hairweave was a bright platinum blond color, and even though Damien knew very little about women's makeup and such, he knew what looked good. And nothing on this woman looked good.

She looked him up and down then turned her attention to Sam. "So, this is him, huh?"

"Yes, Damien, I'd like you to meet—"

She gave him a don't-say-another-word hand then rose from the chair. "No need for introductions just yet," she said, still looking at Damien. "Did you tell him yet?" she asked Sam.

"Tell me what? Damien looked between Sam and the strange-looking woman.

"No, I figured, I'd let you deliver the news," Sam said somberly.

"Coward," the woman snarled in Sam's direction.

"What news?" Damien wanted to know. He was beginning to get frustrated. He didn't know what the hell was going on, and he didn't like being kept in the dark.

"Look, I hate to be the one to break this to you, boo, but your wife put a hit out on you," the woman said easily.

She looked at Sam. "I am still getting paid for this, right?" the woman asked.

Damien stumbled back onto a nearby chair.

Chapter 56

The flight back to Houston was long and uncomfortable. Theola couldn't sleep and her mind wouldn't rest. She sat nervously next to her husband, wondering if a man of the cloth would dare put blood on his hands.

She didn't want to think about it. But her mind had been racing with thoughts of what her husband had done to his son, although she didn't dare ask. He scared her in ways she couldn't describe. And she didn't understand because it wasn't always this way.

"You seem nervous about something," Pastor Goodlove said the moment Theola thought she was about to fall off to sleep.

"No, nothing at all," she lied. She didn't want to hold a conversation with him. She barely wanted to be in his presence.

"So, there's nothing you want to tell me?"

Theola felt like a kid being questioned about a lie. She didn't know if she should come clean or continue to hang on to her lie. What had Reginald told him? Did he tell about Stone

Pier? She was so scared she didn't know what to do. But Theola knew she didn't want to live like this. Lately she'd been thinking about whether her life would be *that* bad if she left Ethan

There was no question he wasn't the man she had fallen in love with. Their sex life had long been over. She stood by his side in the midst of that storm, but when he decided against taking revenge on those who had wronged him, she wasn't happy about that, but decided to let it slide. Back in the day, Reginald and his theft would've been forgiven, but now? Theola wasn't so sure.

When Reginald was dragged into their room in Belize, the two men pulled him through the door, into another room that connected to theirs, and she hadn't seen him since. She had no idea if he was dead or alive, and Ethan wasn't saying.

Theola felt like her husband had turned into a real life Dr. Jekyll and Mr. Hyde. Sometimes he looked at her with such love, she felt guilty about all she had done. Then there were other times when she wondered where her husband had gone. When he looked at her, she saw cold, dark fear, and it chilled her to her core.

"If I wanted to tell you something, I believe you'd know by now." She knew she was getting nasty with him, but she didn't care. She didn't like being afraid of her own damn husband.

Just as he was about to respond, a flight attendant walked by and smiled. "Can I get either of you anything else?"

"No, thanks," Theola said, before her husband could answer.

Over the next few days, Blueridge felt more like Theola's own personal hell on earth than her home. Ethan was on her case about everything. Her days of coming and going as she pleased were now only a memory. She felt trapped, and she wasn't sure what she could do.

They even went to church together. One particular Sunday as they were in the car, he looked over at her like he wanted to say something. The way his face was all twisted up, Theola was sure it wasn't about to be good. Lately, nothing good had been coming out of his mouth in her direction. And she was beginning to get fed up.

Theola sat through several sermons and was thoroughly disgusted by the time their day had wrapped up. Usually, Theola left church after the first or second sermon and found a nice little restaurant to grab herself a cocktail.

She didn't give a damn about drinking on a Sunday. She usually needed that drink to deal with all of the tension she felt after enduring all of the dirty looks, whispers and innuendos she suffered from her brothers and sisters at Sweetwater.

"Let's go," Pastor Goodlove had said in her direction when he finished meeting with the parishioners who needed his ear before the day ended.

Theola had been sitting in the wing of his chamber, bored close to tears. But while she sat there thinking about what she'd do about her marriage to Ethan, she started thinking about her future as well.

Maybe she should leave him and start her own church. Maybe she should start a church where you really are accepted just the way you are. Who cares if you just left the club and woke up in the parking lot, then drove in to hear the Word? At her church, there would be no holy rollers. Those who really felt they were holier than thou would kindly be asked to worship elsewhere.

"I think that's exactly what I'll do," she mumbled under her breath.

Ethan shot her a confused look, but she didn't care. Her mind was already made up. Theola decided, the very next day, she'd go and meet with a divorce lawyer.

"Of course you'll come. That's what I told you. I'm ready to go," Ethan said.

Theola wasn't sure how much more of his attitude she was going to take either. She looked at him, smiled, and started thinking about how when she was in charge, she'd change lots of things.

Once they arrived home at Blueridge, Theola prepared herself for yet another long night. That's all her life was coming down to. She absolutely had to leave this man, especially if she wanted her life back, and she did.

"You're sleeping in my room tonight," Ethan called over his shoulder as they walked into the foyer.

That stopped Theola in her tracks. What was that all about? She wasn't sure if she should fake a headache or take the old man up on his demand. After having been with Hunter and Stone Pier, she knew for sure Ethan could do very little to satisfy her.

"I have a doctor's appointment tomorrow morning," she lied. Ethan looked at her skeptically, but he didn't say anything.

Later that night, Theola lie awake in bed as her husband's snoring irritated her to no end. The more she thought about it, the more she felt like starting her very own church was the best move for her.

She looked over at her husband and fantasized about ringing his neck and whether that would make her life easier.

"Oh, no. I need you alive so you can see just how far I can soar without you," she muttered.

His eyes fluttered a few times and she jumped.

Chapter 57

Michelle took the day off with her probation officer's approval. She wasn't happy about not seeing Raymond, but she needed to meet with her attorney, and it couldn't wait.

The lawyer told her that he had talked with Damien's attorney, and they were expecting the paperwork by the end of the week. Since this was Thursday, Michelle left the office with a smile on her face.

Everything was finally falling into place. Raymond had already secured the man for the job, and once she delivered the down payment as they agreed, even that would move forward.

The only thing she didn't like was her plans to meet with Theola for lunch. It wasn't that she disliked her mother-in-law, but she just felt the timing wasn't right. She was hoping that when she called Theola, she'd be the one to cancel.

"Hey, Theola," Michelle greeted as she hopped on the freeway.

"Girl, I thought you'd stand me up," Theola joked, but Michelle didn't laugh.

"Where do you want to meet?" Michelle asked.

"Let's go to Benny Hanna's," Theola suggested.

"Okay, the one in Sugar Land or the original one on Westheimer?"

"Let's go to Sugar Land. That way we can do some shopping afterward if you feel up to it," Theola suggested.

"Are you at home?" Michelle asked, thinking she should say something to her father-in-law.

"Oh, no, I'm actually coming from my lawyer's office," Theola slipped and said.

"Your lawyer?" Michelle questioned.

"Did I say that? I meant a doctor's appointment," she quickly corrected.

Michelle really couldn't care less. She just wanted to meet her for lunch, walk to the Coach store in the nearby First Colony Mall, then return home to wait for Raymond's phone call.

One of the main reasons she even took Theola up on the lunch offer was because she didn't want to give the impression that she would pull away from the family once the ink dried on the divorce papers. She didn't need to give Sweetwater anything else to talk about. She figured once the truth about her relationship with Raymond leaked, that alone would be enough.

When the sleek, black car pulled outside the restaurant, Michelle was excited. She wanted to hurry up and get lunch with Theola over with, so that time could fly a bit faster.

"Hey, giiirrrrl," Theola sang as she entered the restaurant.

"Hey yourself!"

"You look good. I'm so sorry we've been hitting and missing lately, but chile, I've had a lot going on," Theola said.

"Don't worry about it. I'll charge it to your head, not your heart. Girl, I understand."

"Well, let's go 'cause I'm starved," Theola said.

As they sat at the table, watching the chef go through his routine, Michelle decided this was the perfect place to meet after all. They were able to talk a bit, but not too much, and that was just right for Michelle.

Over dinner, Theola was still able to go on and on about how Ethan had changed since waking from the coma. She described how he had become abusive and how he could hardly find a nice word to say to her.

Michelle listened to all of this and thought, like father like son, but then reminded herself that soon, Damien wouldn't be her problem anymore.

After they ate and had a couple of cocktails, they made their way to the mall.

"You gotta be somewhere?" Theola asked with a frown on her face.

"No, why do you ask?"

"Oh, you keep looking at your watch," Theola said and looked at Michelle's watch as if to prove her point.

"Nasty habit. You know with my community service," Michelle shrugged innocently. "Always dying for time to fly."

"Oooh, girl, I feel so bad for you. But then I thought about it, and I was like wait, so she's sitting up there surrounded by a bunch of men who ain't been with or seen a woman in years? I'll bet there are all kinds locked away in that prison, hard bodies..."

"Uh, it's not all that wonderful," Michelle interrupted.

They both started laughing. But her comments made Michelle wonder if people really would look down their noses at her for dating Raymond.

As they walked around the mall, Theola continued to complain about Ethan and how he really was too old for her. Michelle wasn't sure what to say. She wanted to come up with some kind of excuse to end this little girlfriend's outing before she gagged.

Did this woman know any boundaries? Michelle wondered. When Theola's cell phone rang, Michelle hoped it would be the emergency she'd been praying for.

"I told you after the appointment I was spending the day with Michelle. Yes, your daughter-in-law," Theola said into the phone with an attitude.

When she got off the phone, she turned to Michelle and started in with a slew of new complaints about her husband. Michelle was bored sick. Before she knew it, it was five-thirty.

"Oh no! I don't want to get stuck in traffic," Michelle cried. "I'd better run. I've had such a good time. We should really do this more often," she sang.

Theola stood looking confused, but Michelle didn't wait around for her to protest. She simply started walking toward Macy's, the store they entered the mall, and soon, Theola ran to catch up.

"Where has the time gone?" Theola said as she walked, struggling to keep up with Michelle.

Later, it felt like the phone rang the moment Michelle walked into the house. It was Raymond.

"Hi, baby," Michelle greeted him.

"Whassup?"

She smiled so hard, her face started to hurt. "I missed you today," she purred. Her parents and her children were all asleep, so the house was nice and quiet, just the way she liked it when they talked.

"We doing this or what?" Raymond asked.

"Yeah, I got the down payment and everything," Michelle reported.

"Okay, you here tomorrow, right?"

"Of course. I wouldn't miss seeing you two days in a row," she said.

"Cool. Bring it in the trunk of your car."

"So, what are you doing?" Michelle asked, feeling like now that business was out of the way, they could have a little phone sex.

"I'll see you tomorrow then," Raymond said.

Before Michelle could say another word, the dial tone was already ringing in her ear.

Chapter 58

Damien feared every stranger he saw. Was this the man coming to try and kill him? Would this man give it a shot? He didn't know what to do. Sure, they had called the police, but *they* said they weren't ready to pick Michelle up just yet.

Instead, they said they needed to check the story out first. Damien was livid. How much more evidence did they need? After what she had done with the poison, and now this? To hell with waiting, he wanted her behind bars!

"Sam, what's the latest?" Damien wanted to know. He paced in Barry's apartment. Barry had all but moved into Amy's apartment since she was released from the hospital. They still hadn't caught Sissy. Not that Damien was looking forward to that day. He feared she'd finger him, and his life would really spin out of control.

"Is that officer still outside?"

Damien peeked out the window and confirmed the police cruiser was still posted outside. But still, he didn't feel safe.

He couldn't wrap his mind around the fact that Michelle hated him that much, but it was obvious she did.

"Just hang in there for a few more days, buddy. We'll get this taken care of," Sam assured.

Damien didn't want to believe it when that hoochie looked him dead in the face and told him all about the plan. The girl claimed she was on the phone when Michelle finalized the deal, had heard it with her very own ears.

At first Damien thought she was just trying to come up on a quick hustle, but she seemed to know far too many details about Michelle.

"She's fucking my baby daddy," the girl had said, eyeing Damien like she was ready to exact some revenge of her own. There was nothing appealing about her to Damien.

Damien looked at his lawyer who shook his head. "What do you mean she's fucking your baby daddy?" he asked.

That's when the girl told them the entire story. She told them how Michelle and Raymond were an item after hooking up in Bible study. Then, how she bragged to Raymond about all the money she was coming into. She even disclosed the plans they had made to be together once Raymond was released.

Damien felt like a fool. How could Michelle risk having some ex-con around her two small daughters. How could he have trusted her? After all, she was a woman scorned. What was he thinking, giving her the benefit of the doubt? And to imagine, he had agreed to give up millions for her, and the bitch wanted him dead!

He felt trapped, like a prisoner inside his brother's apartment, and he didn't like the feeling. As if the impending hit wasn't enough, Jazzlyn had been calling every hour on the hour. He was considering taking out a restraining order against her. Obviously, he couldn't be too careful.

Damien was so sick and tired of the women in his life. He couldn't understand why they were so crazy, all of the women in his life. The phone rang, breaking his thoughts. He jumped for it because he knew it was no one but Barry.

"Hey, bro," Barry said, the minute Damien answered. Despite his own female troubles Damien felt good, knowing his brother was sounding much better.

"How's Amy?" Damien asked, mostly out of guilt, but wanting to see if his brother suspected anything.

"Better. She's got a ways to go, but she's improving. Her father has the place stacked with private nurses and such. You know how he is," Barry growled quietly.

"Man, I feel sorry for you. That's one family I wouldn't want any association with."

"Yeah, man, well, good thing I'm marrying her and not her family, huh?"

Damien just laughed that off. "Well, I was just checking in on you. I'm about to call our old man. You talked to him lately?" Barry asked.

"No, he and Theola just came back from vacation about a week ago," Damien said.

"Vacation? Where'd they go?"

"Belize, I think," Damien said.

"Well, that's cool," Barry chuckled. "I better get going. I'll check with you later. Oh, and stay out of trouble," Barry warned jokingly.

The next call that came in to Damien was the detective in charge of his case.

"Mr. Goodlove," the officer greeted.

"Yes, what's up?"

"I just wanted to let you know, your wife has been taken into custody. We will inform the officer standing guard, but I also have to warn you that the press has been notified, so you may get some requests for interviews. You don't have to feel obligated to talk to the media. Just let me know how you wish to proceed."

Damien didn't know what to say. He swallowed the extra-large, dry lump in his throat and blinked a few times.

"Mr. Goodlove, are you there? Are you okay?"

"Uh, yes. I'm here. It's just . . . well, it's taking a moment, that's all."

"That's understandable. Let me let you go."

Just then, his other line rang. Damien clicked the line. It was Charlotte. He rolled his eyes but answered and quickly said, "Uh, hey what's up?"

"We need to talk," Charlotte said somberly. Damien didn't like her tone. "Can you come over?"

"No. Not right now. What's up?"

"I need to talk to you, and I wanna do it in person," Charlotte sulked.

Damien wasn't in the mood. He had a lot going on. He wasn't sure what she wanted, and he really wasn't all that curious. He had enough to deal with.

"So, when can we get together?" Charlotte asked.

"Not sure. Why can't you tell me what you want over the phone?"

"Damien, I'm pregnant," Charlotte blurted out.

The line was silent, and then the doorbell rang. He stood frozen for a moment but he didn't say anything.

"Did you hear me? Damien, I said I'm pregnant," Charlotte repeated.

"Uh, I need to uh, get the door. Someone's at the door," he stammered.

On weak and unreliable legs, Damien made his way to the door. Without asking who was there, he pulled it open to find Jazzlyn standing there with her face glowing.

"Damien, I have wonderful news. We're pregnant," she cheered.

He stood there for a long time staring at her. He couldn't believe this was happening.

"Aren't you gonna say something?" Jazzlyn asked.

That's when Damien heard the dial tone from his phone and felt the bile that swirled in the pit of his belly.

***

Theola contemplated her very next move. She walked around the hotel room at the Four Seasons in Downtown Houston, and her mind was constantly plotting.

What would she do? How quickly should she make her move? Will she be able to get what she deserves?

Her cell phone had been ringing, but she needed time to think. She needed time to figure out whether she should answer or try to avoid his calls like her attorney had suggested.

Because the phone wouldn't stop ringing. Theola finally gave in. She pressed the green button, but before she could answer, her husband's baritone voice rang loudly in her ear.

"You need to get back here before this thing gets out of control," he warned.

"What happened to Reginald?" Theola screamed.

"That's none of your concern. Your place is here at Blueridge," he said sternly.

Theola could picture the look on his face, the scary frown that had probably taken over his dark features.

"What did you do to your own son, your own flesh and blood? And I'm done, I've had enough. Since you woke up, it's like you've lost your ever-loving mind! I can't take it anymore. You'll hear from my attorney, Ethan!"

There was silence.

Theola's heart was beating so fast and hard, she heard it thumping loudly in her ears.

"Ain't no need for no attorneys," he calmly replied.

"You really got me mixed up," Theola insisted.

"Look, I'm heading to the hospital to visit Sister Brown. By the time I get back, you better be here," Pastor said with authority and abruptly ended the call.

Theola was tired. He had changed so much since waking from his coma or sleep, or whatever it was, and she was ready to move on.

Their argument began when she started asking questions about what he had done to Reginald when Pastor found out he had blown through all of the stolen money. But Pastor wouldn't answer. He kept saying it was none of her business. Theola couldn't shake the bad feeling she had about what may have happened to Reginald, and whatever it was, it scared her to her core.

She had already contacted one of the top divorce attorneys in Houston, and in their consultation, she had warned Theola to gear up for a fight.

Now all she had to do was try to find a way to stay away from Ethan and the rest of Sweetwater until he was served with the papers.

***

On the other side of town, Michelle was topless, her pants clinging to one leg, and she was riding Raymond with such intensity, she didn't hear the footsteps outside their secret love nest. But the steps were quickly shuffling in her direction.

"Oh God!" she cried, her eyes squeezed tightly as she rode sheer ecstasy to the fullest.

"Yeah," Raymond huffed, clutching her tightly. He was in the zone, too.

Suddenly there was a loud, crashing noise. The door collapsed on top of them. Michelle's heart slammed up against her ribcage and felt like it was about to burst right out of her chest. Her eyes grew into wide saucers as the scene before her finally registered in her head.

"Oh, shit!" Raymond managed as he moved quickly, trying to get to his feet. When he did, he inadvertently shoved Michelle to the floor.

After tumbling down, she scrambled to grab her clothes and cover herself.

"Michelle Goodlove," one of the officers said with his gun pointing directly at her. "You are under arrest for solicitation of murder and illegal contact with an inmate. You have the right to remain silent."

She was stunned speechless as she listened and watched the other officers begin to slap handcuffs onto Raymond's wrists. The officers started to read him his Miranda rights, too.

Michelle stood as if she couldn't move. She was literally frozen.

So when the officers reached for her with handcuffs extended, she resisted a bit and tumbled back to the floor.

"No, no," she cried. Impulse caused her to start kicking and screaming. "Get your hands off of me!"

But that only made the officers angrier. Soon there was a tussle. Michelle swung wildly as she tried in vain to explain. Raymond dropped to his knees, laced his fingers behind his head and didn't put up a fight.

"Raymond, baby don't say a word!" Michelle screamed. "This is just a misunderstanding! I didn't do anything wrong."

Having learned what to do after her first arrest, Michelle immediately clammed up. She stopped talking except to scream, "I wanna talk to my lawyer!"

On the ride over to the police station, Michelle's brain was working in overdrive. She'd find a way out of this—she just had to.

As she thought about her game plan, she marveled at how quickly she had arrived. It seemed like only seconds ago she was in the bathroom, loving Raymond. Now, they were turning the corner and heading toward the station.

When the patrol car pulled up at the police station, she was pissed to see the media crowded at the entrance.

The officers pulled into a parking spot and pulled her out of the car. She couldn't believe they weren't even trying to shield her from the camera's lenses.

"Mrs. Goodlove, did you try to kill your husband again?" one reporter shouted.

"Is it true? Did you try to hire a hit man?" another screamed. "Is the inmate your lover?"

"Why'd you do it?" another one asked.

Michelle couldn't believe all of the questions. She could barely walk straight because for every step she took, the reporters were hot on her trail.

But inside the police station was where she finally threatened to break down. The sight of her mother and father in the lobby made her instantly choke up. She felt sick. The bile was beginning to rise.

"What are you guys doing here?" she managed.

Her mother's eyes were swollen. Michelle could tell she'd been crying. Thank God her kids were in school.

"Your lawyer called us after he saw it on the news. He's parking," her father said.

Michelle's heart shattered into a million pieces. She was shuffled into a small room and handcuffed to a table. Images of her parents standing there kept flashing through her mind. How could this have happened? Once again, her obsession with getting revenge against Damien had backfired.

But now, she was more determined than ever. As she heard the knock on the door, she looked up. Suddenly, it dawned on her—could Raymond have betrayed her? She hoped not because she'd hate to have to add his name to her list.

"Scott," she said to her lawyer as he walked into the room. "I want the best defense money could buy," Michelle said, sitting up straighter and bracing herself for the uphill battle ahead.

Reader's Guide

1. How did Pastor Goodlove's illness impact his congregation?

2. Was Michelle's punishment fair for poisoning Damien?

3. What could have Sweetwater's members done to help Theola while Pastor was out?

4. Are there members in your church like Kim and Tammy?

5. How surprised were you that Damien fell so hard for Charlotte?

6. Would you take a tropical vacation alone like Theola? Why?

7. How was Raymond able to manipulate Michelle so easily?

8. What would you do if your spouse changes after waking from a coma?

9. Has Theola made the best decision in the end?

10. Is there any hope for Damien?

11. Should Barry marry Amy?

12. What do you think should happen to Michelle given the ending?

P.L. Wilson
a.k.a.
Pat Tucker

An author by many other names…by day, Pat Tucker Wilson works as a radio news director in Houston, TX. By night, she is a talented writer with a knack for telling page-turning stories. A former television news reporter, she draws on her background to craft stories readers will love. She also co-hosts the literary talk show, From Cover to Cover.

She is the author of six novels and has participated in three novellas and a short story in Zane's New York Times Bestselling Anthology, *Caramel Flava.* She is married with two children.

Books by Pat: *Daddy By Default, Proceed With Caution, Led Astray, Infidelity, The Hook Up, Summer Breeze* (Novella), *Around the Way Girls 3* (Novella), *Caramel Flava* (anthology).

Under PL Wilson, *Holy Hustler.*

Under Rikki Dixon, *Try Me*

Email Pat at sylkkep@yahoo.com or visit her at www.authorpattucker.com

LaVergne, TN USA
10 December 2010
208278LV00008B/38/P